Shocked BY CHAMPAGNE

Bohemia Bartenders Mysteries
Book Six

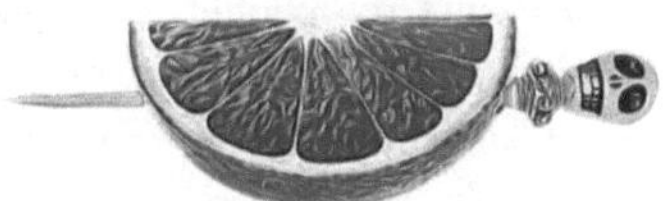

LUCY LAKESTONE

Velvet Petal Press
Florida

Cover design: Sky Diary Productions

First edition

Paperback ISBN: 978-1-943134-44-1

Velvet Petal Press, P.O. Box 922, Cocoa, Florida 32923

Learn more about the author at LucyLakestone.com

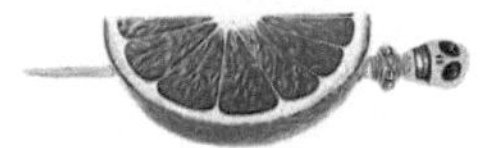

FATALLY FIZZY ...

The holidays in Bohemia sparkle with fun under the palm trees, even if mixologist Pepper Revelle and her Bohemia Bartenders friends are working their glasses off. With all the cocktailians in town, the season promises to be festive—at least until a murky death in the swamp puts one of their friends under suspicion.

Rumor has it the victim was on the verge of a fantastic discovery, but Pepper and her would-be boyfriend Neil find nothing but questions surrounding it. What was she looking for among the alligators? And was it a motive for murder?

While Pepper and Neil search for answers and try to date among the disasters, Pepper's dog Astra snubs distiller Mark's impudent pup, and her ex Mr. Mixy gets into more trouble than he's worth. When Pepper gets too close to the truth, will she be blasted like a cork from a bottle of bubbly?

Shocked by Champagne is the sixth book in the Bohemia Bartenders Mysteries, funny whodunits with a dash of romance set in a convivial collective of cocktail lovers, eccentrics and mixologists. These quasi-cozy culinary comedies contain a hint of heat, a splash of cursing and shots of laughter, served over hand-carved ice.

*For Holly, sparkling friend and fellow word geek.
There will never be enough rum to thank you.*

Chapter One

When you are owned by a sweet little dog as I am, you know that when you're alone in the shower, half asleep, shampooing under a cascade of hot water in the most vulnerable moment of the day, that dog is going to bark to let you know a serial killer is coming for you with a knife.

Of course, the reality is, nine times out of ten, Astra barks for no discernible reason. And the tenth time out of ten usually signifies a package has been left at the doorstep that contains a bomb that is going to obliterate the entire town of Bohemia Beach. Or, more likely, it's another cocktail book, because as a mixologist, I order a lot of them.

And so it was that when I was in the shower and heard Astra bark, I rolled my eyes.

But then, on second thought, I got a little nervous.

I'd come away from the Bohemia Bartenders' Kentucky gig two months ago with a lingering worry. My newfound nemesis —guitar-strumming con man Beau Reed—was on the loose and had made it clear he wasn't going to forget me, and not in a good way. I hadn't heard from him since his veiled threat after my narrow escape. Had he finally arrived to get even?

And besides, as a classic-movie nut, I'd seen *Psycho.* I mean, could you see that and ever look at a shower in the same way again?

So I rinsed hastily, squeezed out my hair, stepped out of the tub/shower in my retro (that is to say, unremodeled) old bathroom, and took the extra precaution of wrapping myself in a towel. Another thing I'd learned from movies was that many young women considered a towel an adequate defense against would-be murderers.

Was I still young? I had a pretty big birthday coming up. This year would be my last as a twentysomething, and that made me kind of sad. I co-owned a great bar in Bohemia and generally loved my life, but my *love* life?

At least I had Astra, the Cavapoo I shared with Aunt Celestine, who lived in the duplex that adjoined mine. The dog had stopped barking. But now I heard her on the other side of the bathroom door.

Growling.

Was she protecting me?

Maybe I needed more than a towel. My phone was in the other room, so I couldn't call anyone. But I wasn't going to wait here all day. Chances were, that new cocktail book was sitting on the front stoop and her fuss was all for nothing.

Astra's growls grew more insistent, and then I heard a "Shhh."

Crapnoodles. Somebody was out there.

My heart beat faster as I scanned the small room, assessing my weapons. I had a few chemicals under the sink, and the bottles were nearly full, given I didn't love cleaning. But the risk of blowback made me shy away from bleach. And suppose it was just my aunt?

Though Astra wouldn't growl like that at my aunt. And Aunt Celestine wouldn't say "Shhh" unless a surprise party waited on the other side of the door. My birthday was over a week away, on New Year's Day, and we had other big plans this morning.

It wouldn't be Neil, either. Though we were Officially Dating now, he was determined to take it slow, and he hadn't yet shared my bed. Who knew a nerdy mixologist would be such an expert at torture?

I wished he were here. He'd know what to do, though it might take him three days to mount a counterassault. It was taking him a lot longer to mount me.

I shook my head to get myself back in the game. I needed a weapon. I feared I wouldn't get the shower curtain rod through the doorway. The soaps and shampoos weren't much use. The countertop sported a big whelk shell I'd found on the beach, but I'd have to get pretty close to stab the intruder in the eye with it. Plus, *ew*. The top of the toilet tank was heavy —too heavy. I'd probably drop it on my toe.

My gaze fell on the toilet plunger. That would do for a brief distraction. Whack the intruder in the head and get out the door. And take Astra with me.

I was overthinking this. I had to act fast. Take them by surprise.

I tucked my towel more securely around the girls and made sure I was covered. I couldn't have body parts flopping around while I was swinging my weapon. Though said parts might also prove distracting, if I do say so myself.

I grasped the shaft of the plunger in my right hand, set my left on the doorknob, and counted to myself like one of the rocket launch countdowns here on Florida's Space Coast: *Three, two, one...*

"Hiyaaaa!" I screamed as I yanked the door back and lunged forward. Or should I say plunged? I came out swinging as a tall male figure who'd been sitting on the bed stood in front of me, a dark shadow blocking my escape. The stinky rubber of the plunger caught him squarely on one ear.

"Oowwww!" he shouted. "Pepper?"

Still riding the wave of adrenaline, roaring as Astra barked, I swung in the opposite direction and whacked him on the skull before I realized it was my loathsome ex-boyfriend Mr. Mixy. The plunger bounced off his head like a Super Ball.

"Why'd you do that?" he exclaimed, staggering back.

I pulled up short, panting. "What the hell are you doing here?"

And my towel, overexerted in the attack, slid off.

I screamed again, dropped the plunger, grabbed the towel and rushed into my closet, slamming the door behind me.

"Heeeeyyy," Mr. Mixy called, sounding a lot less upset.

I uttered a few choice curse words to the darkness in the closet—the light switch was on the outside—and felt around until I found my satiny green robe, the one that matched my lichen-colored eyes. You know, the symbiotic fungi-algae life form? Long story. Anyway, the robe was long enough and opaque enough to cover me a lot better than the failed towel. Mr. Mixy hadn't seen me naked in years, not since my gawky early adulthood, and it made me furious that he'd had the chance again.

Especially when I now heard another voice, a deeper one.

"Pepper, are you OK?"

I opened the closet to find Mr. Mixy, a stupid grin peeking out from his gigantic black beard, facing Neil. In my bedroom.

"Uh." Neil looked back and forth between us. "I thought I heard you screaming."

"Pepper does like to scream," Mr. Mixy said in a smarmy tone that made me want to smack him.

Astra had stopped barking and ran up to Neil, putting her

paws on his legs. Neil, who had a much trimmer beard than Mr. Mixy and nice, thick, dark brown hair with hints of red, reached down and picked her up and scratched behind her ears. He'd learned that giving Astra a little love was an essential ingredient in our dating relationship.

Finding my ex in my bedroom was not.

"I *was* screaming. I came out of the bathroom and found this idiot here," I tried to explain.

"Hey, that's not nice. Though you sure look nice, Pepper." Mr. Mixy, wearing jeans and a colorful plaid shirt and a red hipster scarf, waggled his thick eyebrows.

"Oh, shut up." I looked pleadingly at Neil. Surely he didn't think I'd entertain this oaf voluntarily.

Neil, wearing tan cargo pants and a black T-shirt advertising his bar, The Junction Box, gave Mr. Mixy what some might consider a stern look.

Mr. Mixy looked a little scared. "Uh, maybe I'll wait in the living room," he said, rubbing the ear I'd hit first.

As he left, I kept my eyes on Neil's. And then I saw the sparkle of amusement.

"Don't you dare," I said as he burst into laughter.

"You had me for a second," he said, gently dropping Astra on the bed and sauntering over to me. "I couldn't believe my eyes."

"Neither could I." Mr. Mixy probably couldn't believe his eyes either, but I didn't mention the Towel Incident. "I have no idea what he's doing here."

"Mark invited him on the airboat. Maybe Mixy thought he could get a ride with you."

I raised an eyebrow. "He's never getting a ride with me again."

Neil chuckled. "I suppose since I'm driving you and your aunt, he could come too."

"Why are you so nice?"

"Don't you like nice?" he murmured.

"Sometimes I like naughty."

Neil didn't take the bait, exactly, but he put his hands on my shoulders and slid them down to the ends of my silky sleeves. "I like this on you." His voice sounded husky, and he leaned in for a kiss.

Mr. Moron forgotten, I slipped my arms around Neil's waist and tilted my head to make the most of it as he dug his fingers into my wet hair. Oh, yeah. I'd love to wake up to this every day.

Just when I thought we might be late for our appointment—

"Pepper!" came Mr. Mixy's whine from across the house. "Do you have any Cap'n Crunch?"

Neil froze, then broke the kiss with a rueful sigh. "So you didn't ask him to breakfast?"

"No! I didn't even know he was in town."

"Apparently he's been invited to appear as a celebrity at the New Year's Eve party we're working."

"You're kidding." Developer Raquel Tocks had hired the Bohemia Bartenders to make cocktails for a charity 'do on the big night. Though we were skeptical of working for her, given our previous encounters, the cause —raising money for the zoo—was a good one, and Neil liked the paycheck, so he'd agreed. It must have been a pretty good paycheck considering we'd already be working our glasses off over the holidays at our respective bars in Bohemia. "He's not going to make cocktails with us, is he?"

Neil snorted and released me. "Of course not. She told me he'd do live streaming for his fans."

I rolled my eyes. Mr. Mixy, known to the DMV as Stephan Sully, had started as a lowly barback at the same bar I'd worked at in Bohemia, back when I had poor judgment and boundless naivete. He cheated on me, I told him to go to hell, and he moved to L.A., where he became a social media darling. Then he somehow connived himself into a TV show. He was also writing a memoir/cocktail book, and I had a very real fear I might appear in it despite the threats I'd made if he dared include anything personal about me.

"If you didn't invite him, how'd he get in here?" Neil asked. "Do we need to look at your security again?"

Neil had insisted I get a security system for the house after my nemesis almost killed me—and Aunt Celestine had agreed in a flash—so both sides of the duplex had alarmed doors and windows now. She owned the place, and I rented my side from her at a *very* sweet price. I owed her a lot.

But I hadn't been all that awake when I'd let Astra out this morning. "Um, I think that's my fault. I let Astra do her business in the backyard and forgot to lock the doors when she came back in."

"Pepper." There was worried Neil again. But at least I knew he cared.

"I guess I should get ready." I tried to lighten the mood with a flirtatious smile. "You could stay while I get dressed."

His glower eased, and he returned my smile and shook his head. "I think I'll go make coffee."

I quirked my mouth. "I don't know if I should drink any. You know me and small boats."

"It's an airboat. Totally different," he reassured me. "It'll be just like flying."

"Yeah, right. Flying over the heads of hungry alligators." I pulled my robe open just enough to tease him without actually revealing anything, and his eyes widened. I grinned. "We could stay home."

"No, we can't." Why did Mr. Responsible have to be so hot? He swallowed, his eyes straying to all the things he couldn't see, and I gave myself a mental fist-pump of victory. "See you in a minute."

And then he was gone, and I was faced with dressing for a bumpy boat ride with my crush, my ex, and several thousand mosquitoes.

Chapter Two

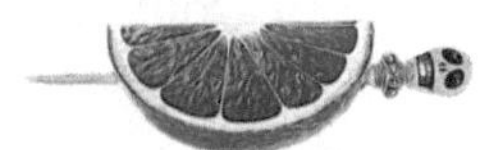

"Where's your houseguest?" I asked Aunt Celestine as we piled into Neil's black SUV.

"Diana had a message from that colleague of hers who's doing research in the swamp," said my aunt. She'd stuffed her silver-streaked red curly hair under a cute white bucket hat and wore a loose blue-and-white tie-dyed tunic over navy capris. "Diana decided to run out there early this morning to see her. We're going to pick her up along the way."

"You mean out in the swamp?" I asked as Neil turned onto the soaring causeway bridge that took us over the lagoon to downtown Bohemia. "How are we going to find her?"

"The airboat captain will know where to go," she said. "Apparently the property is pretty well known."

Once a NASA engineer and now an author of science-based books about natural healing, Aunt Celestine was playing host to botanist Diana Silva after they struck up a friendship on some plant nerd forum online. Diana traveled the world finding interesting botanicals for our friend and distiller Mark Fairman's gin.

Aunt Celestine had given me a quizzical look when Mr. Mixy emerged from the house with Neil and me. I could tell from her grumpy expression she was even less thrilled the big-bearded one now sat next to her in the back seat. She knew our history. I'd left Astra behind, not wanting to tempt alligators with such a tasty morsel.

"Hey, can we go through a drive-through or something?" Mr. Mixy asked after a few minutes of wending through downtown and hitting the western frontier of strip malls and fast-food joints. He didn't have a car; he'd arrived at my place by rideshare.

"No," I told him. Neil just chuckled.

A banana and coffee had been enough breakfast for me. I didn't want to overload my belly in case I had my usual reaction to small-boat rides, even though Neil kept telling me this would be different. And my aunt really wanted me to come along, especially since I rarely had quality time to hang out with her.

West of I-95, then a bit north and across a bridge over sparkling wetlands, Neil pulled into a gravel parking lot. Next to us was a cluster of wooden buildings under a tall sign that advertised Whirlwind Airboat Tours and Fish Camp. A huge, 3-D fake alligator mounted atop the sign grinned at us.

"Do you think there are a lot of alligators?" I asked, annoyed at the squeak in my voice.

Neil just laughed, and Aunt Celestine leaned forward and patted my shoulder. "Not in the boat."

"I thought you grew up in Louisiana? You should be used to this," Mr. Mixy said after we'd gotten out and I stowed my fat messenger bag in the back of the car. I exchanged my nerdy cat's-eye glasses for sunglasses, put my hair in a ponytail, then slipped my phone in my jeans pocket as Neil locked the SUV. Following his lead, I'd worn a white T-shirt from my own bar, Nola. I'd added fleur-de-lis earrings and the leather gator-tooth bracelet with beads that a voodoo priestess in New Orleans had given me as a necklace once upon a time. I figured I might need the luck.

"I grew up in New Orleans," I told Mr. Mixy. "I saw no need to go out to the swamp." And I'd left in my teens after my parents sent me off to Florida to live with Aunt Celestine after Hurricane Katrina.

"It'll be fun," Neil said, putting an arm around me as we walked toward the boat ramp near the restaurant. A familiar redheaded figure stood there, waving and grinning: Mark Fairman, the hunky London distiller who was spending the holidays at his luxe condo in Bohemia Beach and who had, on occasion, flirted hard with me.

Was Mark the reason Neil was acting territorial? Worked for me!

"Hot Pepper! Neil! And Mixy. Hullo." Oh, yeah. Mark's slightly gruff English accent was still as hot as ever. And so were his black-T-shirt-clad torso and his muscular legs, though they were as pale as a pearl peeking out from his green cargo shorts. December felt cool to us Floridians, but to a Londoner, today's mid-seventies probably felt tropical.

"Hi! Mark, you remember my aunt, Celestine?" I said.

"Oh, yes. We met at the film festival, didn't we?" Mark reached out and shook her hand, arresting her gaze with his hypnotic golden eyes and a cheeky smile.

Her eyelashes fluttered, and her response was like warm butter. "Nice to see you again."

No kidding. Mark was a rogue, but he was a good egg.

I was just going to ask him if *his* house guest would join us when a man with light brown hair—close to my caramel color—and similarly gray-green eyes emerged from the restaurant, a big smile on his face. "Pepper!"

"You made it!" I gave Neil a quick squeeze and ran over to

meet Royce, my newfound half brother, who owned a whiskey distillery and cooperage in Kentucky bourbon country. We exchanged a big hug. "When did you get in?"

"Last night. Mark picked me up at the airport."

"You know you could've stayed with me."

"He has plenty of room, and we have some business to discuss." Royce provided barrels for the aging of some of Mark's spirits. "And you and I will spend plenty of time together—I hope? You're not working the whole time, are you?"

"I have a lot to do, but this is the week Jorge takes off from his job at the Space Center, so he'll be my backup. Plus our staff is really top-notch right now." Jorge Listo, my business partner, co-owned our bar and had become quite a skilled mixologist himself.

"Excellent."

"Royce, I'd like you to meet Celestine. She's my aunt. And —your aunt."

Royce beamed at her. "Pepper's told you all about me, then?"

She clasped his hand with both of hers and squeezed. "She has, and I'm so pleased to meet you. And just to reassure you, I haven't discussed you with my sister. I'm sure you'll want to tell her in person who you are."

There was both welcome and warning in my aunt's words, but I knew she said them with love.

"Absolutely," Royce said. "I'll be making a trip to New Orleans soon to have a chat with her and my parents."

"I'm glad to hear it. Welcome to the family."

The modest dock and its boat ramp offered access to a calm, irregular waterway fringed with mangroves, grasses, palm trees and other tropical foliage. Plants grew out of the water and clung to skinny islands between which more water winked. The wide stretch of river extended north under the bridge we'd crossed and south into what looked like a bigger body of water.

Roaming around the airboat at the ramp was a tan, stocky fellow in his thirties with wavy, dark brown hair and a slightly unkempt beard, clad in a brown fishing outfit. His flat-bottomed vessel had two thinly cushioned benches in front and a high seat in the back, behind which loomed a massive caged fan. Er, propeller. The boat's sides weren't nearly tall enough to keep me from falling out. I gulped.

"Where's Alastair? Working?" Neil asked with a trace of irony.

"It's the holidays. Of course he's working!" said Mark, who was the secret investor behind The Dandy Tipple, the London bar run by Neil's snooty frenemy Alastair.

"Really?" I asked in disbelief.

Mark laughed. "Of course not. He came over on the jet with me and Diana. He's at the beach, no doubt getting a sunburn. Though I told him he also has to keep Victoria company."

"You actually brought her?" I clapped my hands. Mark's sweet Cavalier King Charles spaniel had been my loaner dog in London.

"Indeed, and she needs to meet your Astra," Mark said.

I agreed, though I was a little nervous about the prospect. Astra had sniffed my suitcase for fifteen minutes after I came back from London, then proceeded to ignore me for a whole afternoon, at least until I served dinner. With chicken. I wasn't above a little bribe.

"Oleanna is supposed to be here," I said. "She's staying at the hotel where Melody works." Oleanna Lee was a movie star we'd befriended during the Bohemia Beach Film Festival. "Who else is in town? Did Cray make it?"

"Not only that, but he's staying with Gramps," Neil said of the old New Orleans rum collector who frequented our cocktailian events. Gramps—Reginald Rockaway—was Neil's mischievous treasure-hunter grandfather.

"Those two should get along great," I said.

"And we'll meet up with everyone else later," Neil told Mark.

"At my bar tonight," I added. It was Monday, so Nola was closed for regular business, and the rest of the Bohemia Bartenders—Melody, Barclay and Luke—were off from their bars, too. Well, Luke worked for Neil, but Neil had given them both the night off. It was a perfect night for a party, just two days before Christmas and all the craziness that went with it.

"Great," Mr. Mixy said. "I need to get some of the atmosphere for my book."

Mr. Mixy wasn't even supposed to be here, but I couldn't very well uninvite him. I shot him a dark look. I didn't know what atmosphere he was talking about. The bar had changed completely. When Mr. Mixy, then simply Stephan, and I worked at the bar, we were lowly employees of the previous owner. That was before Jorge and I bought and transformed it.

The airboat captain, apparently satisfied with his inspection, hopped down to the dock and strolled our way.

"Good morning, good morning! I'm your captain, Otter Vance. Just call me Captain Vance. Is this everybody?" His slightly nasal voice cut through our chatter.

"Except for the one we're picking up later," Mark said.

"Hmm. We usually don't take more than six guests."

"She's quite slender, and I tip extremely well."

"Great!" Captain Vance didn't even blink. "Everyone

empty? There's no place to pee unless you want to piss off an alligator. Or piss on one." He laughed, and we exchanged glances.

Captain Vance didn't need to tell me twice. After most of us made a quick trip to the bathrooms in the restaurant, we were ready to go. He stood on the dock and directed us in.

"Just slide on in there. Wherever you want." He pointed at Mr. Mixy, who'd settled into the chair on top. "Not up there. That's my seat."

The big-bearded one took in my scathing look and shrugged. "He said anywhere!"

I scooted in next to Neil in the front row, and Royce sat on my other side, heading off Mr. Mixy. Stephan ended up next to Mark, with Aunt Celestine on Mark's other side.

A cozy little crew. I felt somewhat protected with two guys I trusted on either side of me. Not that they were armed to fend off alligators or anything else. Captain Vance was, though. He had a handgun on his hip.

"Life jackets are in the compartment up here," he said. "Anyone want one? The water out here is pretty shallow, but you never know." Was it my imagination, or did he enjoy freaking us out?

None of us took him up on the life jackets, but we did take the plastic earmuff hearing protectors he offered. "This here's a six hundred horsepower engine running an aircraft propeller," he said as he handed them out. "The only people who turn down the hearing protection are husbands sick of being able to hear their wives. Or vice versa," he amended as Aunt Celestine gave him her death stare. He just laughed.

As Otter Vance settled into the perch above us, he slipped his gun into a closed box at his side. Then he revved up the engine, first at a low idle.

My earmuffs squeezed my head like a tequila hangover, but they were effective. I took mine off again so I could hear what he and Mark were talking about.

"These are the coordinates," Mark was saying as he handed Captain Vance a slip of paper. "The Swamp Shack at the old Boyle place? I was told you'd know it."

"Indeed I do. That's where our other passenger resides?"

"She's visiting a fellow botanist out there."

"Oh, yeah. Alice and her mysterious doings. I'll get you there," Captain Vance said. "You all might like that. That's where Phantom hangs out."

"Who's Phantom?" Royce asked.

"Big boy alligator."

I tried to sound curious, not scared. "How big?"

"Oh, probably thirteen feet long." Otter Vance clearly enjoyed this part.

"Is he vicious?" I asked.

Captain Vance seemed to take pity on me. "If you don't bug a gator, he won't bug you, as a rule, unless he thinks you're food. People who feed 'em sandwiches or walk their dogs by their retention ponds are asking for it. Of course, he's a prehistoric animal, and if provoked, he'll tear you apart if he has to. After he grabs you and does the death roll to make sure you're drowned and dead."

Greeeaat. Do not provoke the gator. Check.

"Are they endangered?" Mark asked.

"Oh, no. They once were," said Otter Vance. "But now there's plenty of 'em and serious penalties if you molest the wildlife."

Royce looked back at Otter. "Why is he called Phantom?"

"Half his face is all scarred up from fighting for his territory. You know, like in *The Phantom of the Opera?*"

"You like musicals?" I didn't think Otter was the type.

"Well, I prefer Sondheim," Captain Vance said with a grin as he eased the rumbling airboat, still at a low idle, away from the dock.

We rotated slowly. At the back of the restaurant, a party deck and bar became visible, already crowded with drinkers. "A little early for me," I said into Neil's ear.

"Probably fishermen," he replied. "They've been awake way longer than we have."

"Even you?" I teased.

"Maybe *slightly* longer than me." He smiled. I'd come to the conclusion Neil didn't sleep much but never seemed the worse for wear.

The boat headed for the passage under the bridge, and the prop sped up. As Captain Vance cleared the bridge, he cranked the engine, and we accelerated. I put the head clamp, I mean earmuffs, back on. A squawking great blue heron flew across our bow, incensed at the noise. My tummy did a shimmy but held firm. So far, so good.

The cool wind blasted me in the face. Thank Dionysus I remembered my sunglasses. I looked around. We all had sunglasses on except Mr. Mixy, who wrapped his scarf around his mouth and squinted into the sunlight as he filmed himself with his phone.

What followed was a good half hour of high-speed skimming the water, with a couple of slowdowns so our guide could point out gators swimming or sunning themselves on a muddy bank or a beautiful pink roseate spoonbill flying overhead. And I didn't even get sick!

Random sights caught my eye: a tiny house on stilts Captain Vance said was a weather shelter. Weird-looking logs he said were railroad ties where the train ran decades ago.

And the waterway was getting narrower. Or should I say the network of waterways? They were all braided together. Now we cruised among cypress trees, some dripping with Spanish moss. I pulled out my phone and took a random photo of their eerie reflection in the water. It was noticeably darker here, and I shivered.

"We're getting closer to the Boyle place," Otter called as we slowed down and the noise lowered.

"So somebody lives out here in the swamp?" I asked, taking off my earmuffs.

"A lot of people do, and it's really a marsh here. But the Boyle place has a fair amount of dry land. Your botanist friend Alice told me over a beer one night that old Bill Boyle leased a chunk of the marsh to her to do some research. She's staying in the Swamp Shack."

"Not the marsh shack?" Mr. Mixy asked through his scarf muffler.

Otter gave him the side-eye.

I imagined Diana's friend Alice and Otter Vance having a beer. Hmm. Did all the swamp people hang out together? I supposed there wasn't much else to do out here if you weren't fishing.

Even with the airboat slowing, it still rumbled, but I swore I could hear another engine. Just then, another boat came around the bend, white with a small awning topped with blue lights. The side bore official-looking logos and lettering: *Fish and Wildlife Commission State Law Enforcement.*

Captain Vance actually turned the engine off as the boat approached us. "Ernie! I mean, Officer Alder," he called out.

The game warden angled closer and idled next to the airboat, and I got a better look at him in his tan FWC cap, uniform, life vest and gun holster. He was fiftysomething, I guessed, though his creased face was sun-worn to the point of brown leather. In spite of his tired appearance, his startling blue eyes were bright and penetrating.

"Otter. How you doing?" Ernie asked.

"Fine, fine. Good to be seen and not viewed." Our captain chuckled at his own joke.

Ernie's eyes narrowed. "Not your usual tour route, is it?"

"We're heading out to the Boyle place. Supposed to pick up a passenger."

Ernie's gaze got sharper, if that were possible, but he maintained his even tone. Still, I got another chill when he asked, "Seen anyone else out here?"

"Not for a while, and nowhere near here. Just some anglers a ways back."

Ernie scratched his chin, which was covered with gray scruff that showed up almost white against his deep tan. "I'm on my way out to the Boyle place now. I'm not going to tell you not to come, because there's a chance you might know something that can help me."

Otter Vance's voice lost some of its enthusiasm. "Trouble?"

"You could say that. We got a call about a dead woman."

Chapter Three

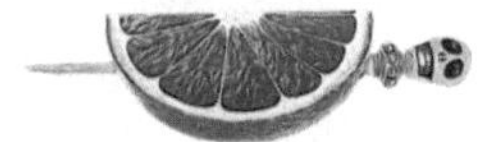

We *got a call about a dead woman.*

The game warden's words seem to suck all the air out of the swamp.

There was a dead woman at the Boyle place? Who? My mind flitted to the worst.

So did Mark's, apparently. "My God. Diana," he said from behind me. "Let's go. Quickly." He pulled out his phone as Captain Vance cranked up the airboat and followed Ernie Alder's FWC boat. We picked up speed, skimming back and forth between the trees to the bone-shaking roar of the propeller.

I left my earmuffs off so I could try to have a conversation. "Did she text you?" I shouted to Mark, feeling sick to my stomach for the first time this morning.

"No. Nothing." Mark looked grim. He tapped the phone's screen, then held it to his ear. After several moments, he spoke. Loudly. "Diana, please call me. It's Mark," he added. "It's urgent."

I wondered if she would hear any of the message over the noise of the boat.

"I'm amazed it went through," Neil said, barely loud enough to be heard.

"We're actually not that far from civilization," Captain

Vance shouted. "You can get to the old Boyle house by land. Getting to the shack requires a boat."

This screaming was getting old. What a terrible way to have a conversation about something terrible. I put the earmuffs back on. By mutual agreement, we continued in silence. Neil's fingers threaded through mine, and I squeezed his hand, willing the news not to be true.

A few minutes later, Ernie Alder's FWC boat slowed ahead of us. Captain Vance followed suit.

We'd entered a wide clearing, the sun shining through, framed by a profusion of green plants. A patch of blue sky and scattered clouds reflected in the water. Ahead of us, a structure adjoined a small island bristling with several cypress and oak trees and lots more tropical scrub.

I say "adjoined" because the rustic old wood-walled house rested high on stout round stilts planted in the water. As ramshackle as the shack appeared, a square of solar panels was attached to one side of the peaked roof.

A couple of crossbeams bolted into trees enhanced the structure. It reminded me of a treehouse. I couldn't see all of it, but one side had a screened porch that looked like a late add-on. The shack had few windows.

Our glide around the house revealed a long, skinny dock that led to a wooden staircase, which climbed up to a small landing and the decrepit door.

Where the dock connected with the land, a wooden bench on top of a small platform appeared to double as a storage box. Behind the shack, where the back edge hovered over the shore of the island, there was a pile of stuff under a blue tarp.

A bright green two-person kayak and a small boat with a motor were tied to the dock, and on the dock sat a woman, a well-worn canvas backpack next to her.

She stood. She wore khakis and had short, brown hair. Could it be—

"Diana!" Mark exclaimed. "Thank God."

It *was* Diana. I let out a huge breath. I'd last seen her in Kentucky, when she attended the festival weekend at Royce's, but I didn't want to leap to conclusions. Now that we were closer, it was clear her usual brisk energy had deflated, and she wiped under her eyes.

Crying. If Diana was crying, it was bad.

Of course it's bad, Pepper, if a woman is dead. Was it Alice, whom we hadn't even met?

Captain Vance stopped the airboat well short of the dock.

"What are you doing? Get over there!" Mark ordered.

"Chill, my man. Not till Ernie says it's OK."

I saw what our captain meant. Ernie had held up a hand in the "stop" gesture, warning us to stay back. His boat sidled up to the dock, and he tethered it to a post and climbed out. He had a hand on his gun as he stepped slowly toward Diana. I couldn't hear what they were saying, but it was clear she was explaining. She must have made the call. She finally gestured back to the other side of the shack—to the island or beyond—and Ernie nodded.

He turned and gave us the come-hither sign, and Captain Vance eased up to the other side of the rickety-looking dock. I hoped it could handle all these boats tied to it.

"You can get out," Ernie told us, "but stay here till I have a look."

"I'm coming with you," Mark declared. "I'm—Diana's boss."

Sort of, I supposed, since she was on retainer. But it wasn't like he was *the boss of her*, to use the expression. Or her lawyer. Still, I had to admire his protective instincts.

"You will wait here," Ernie said in a matter-of-fact voice that forestalled all objections as we climbed out of the boat. He patted the gun at his hip.

"It's all right, Mark," Diana said, though her usually brisk, vibrant alto voice with its English accent seemed close to cracking.

He nodded at her, but he fumed as Ernie and Diana walked out beyond the shack and into the trees.

"Was he going to shoot me?" Mark muttered as we clustered on the dock.

"He's a wildlife officer," I said, treading carefully on the uneven, weather-beaten boards, grateful to be off the water. "Just being prepared. Even if there's not a mad killer out here, there's Phantom." I looked around for the alligator.

"Not to mention trigger-happy poachers and worse," Captain Vance said. "I, for one, am glad Ernie is armed."

"What do you mean, 'and worse'?" I asked.

Otter Vance just shrugged, but the corner of his mouth twitched. He was teasing me. Seriously?

I eased up next to Neil, who'd taken a few steps away. "We could check out the shack," I whispered.

"What?" He seemed startled. "No."

"Why not? Clearly, it's not a crime scene or Ernie would have gone up the stairs."

"You don't know that. You have no idea what happened. Something could have happened in there."

"We can find out."

Neil pulled me farther away from the group, to the base of the stairs. "It looks like Diana is in enough trouble," he murmured. "What if she's involved? I don't want you getting embroiled in this."

"What if she is involved but didn't do anything wrong? She needs our help. And we need to know as much as possible."

"Hey, guys." Mr. Mixy had come up behind us. "I'm going to go into the shack and see if there's a bathroom."

"No," Neil and I both said together.

"It might be a crime scene," I said. "You can't go—um—"

"Leaving your bodily fluids in there," Neil cut in.

I looked at him. "Ew."

"Sorry. Not the best way to put it. Physical evidence. You can't leave physical evidence. Look, it's a swamp. You can pee behind a tree."

"There's an outhouse right this way!" came Captain Vance's voice at that moment, from several feet away on the island. "Just add a scoop of the sawdust stuff when you're done." Royce, Celestine and Mark followed him to where a mini shack sat amid the cypress with a glass window set high in the door. I hadn't even seen it, it blended in so well, but it looked newer than the Swamp Shack.

"Fine," Mr. Mixy said. But he turned to Neil before he went. "You're weird, man."

I couldn't help a guffaw as Mr. Mixy went off to stand in line in front of the outhouse.

"What? I was trying to keep him out of the house," Neil said.

"Maybe we shouldn't have watched *Dr. Strangelove* the other night." The running "precious bodily fluids" joke had us giggling. It was the only date we'd had that didn't end in disaster: a fun evening with popcorn, Mai Tais and classic movies in Neil's apartment above his bar—before he sent me home.

Neil seemed annoyed. "Very funny."

"It was at the time." I glanced around. "Quick. While they're busy." And I trotted up the stairs.

I heard Neil cursing behind me, but he followed me to the landing.

I smiled at him in approval.

"There could be an axe murderer in there," he explained. That was Neil. Always gallant.

I quirked my mouth, then looked down. I had a moment's vertigo when I saw the water moving beneath me, ripples of light and shadow through the wooden slats. We had to be ten feet above the water. Then I turned the corroded old metal doorknob, pushed the door open and stepped inside.

The living space was sparse, with a couple of threadbare soft chairs and a beat-up wooden coffee table in the middle.

To my left, windows and a rough wooden door opened into the porch, where plywood tables along the screen-covered windows supported trays of young green plants. A table just inside the main room held a microscope and a weird-looking wooden box with straps around it.

Ahead of me, a ladder went up to a loft that housed a cot rumpled with unmade bedding. Under the loft at left, a lamp and laptop computer sat on a wooden desk. A couple of shelves above the desk held several books, mostly about plants, though there were tomes on Florida history, a couple of spy novels, and a few blank spines.

To the right of this office space, a skinny door flush with the edge of the loft probably hid a closet. To its right, a tiny kitchen space with a linoleum floor was tucked under the loft as well. It held what appeared to be a small gas stove, a half-size fridge, and a water cooler with a big bottle of drinking water. An old Formica and chrome table had three bentwood chairs. Literally an odd number. A simple round metal light fixture hung from the ceiling, holding a single bulb. The solar must provide just enough power for the light and the fridge, I thought, and maybe the computer.

A large plastic washtub sat on the edge of this space, a coiled hose hanging over the edge, a shower head on the end. Neil wandered over and had a look. "I think this is a recharge-able shower hose. It has a USB cord."

"That's her shower?" Wow. Alice was dedicated to whatever she was doing if she was roughing it like this.

"Pretty neat, actually," Neil said. "Heat up a gallon of water on the stove, dump it in the tub, take a quick rinse, soap, another rinse and you're good to go. And I bet that outhouse is a composter."

"I'd rather have indoor plumbing, thanks."

Then my eyes shifted to the closest window, and what I saw made my stomach drop.

"Whoa no," I whispered.

Chapter Four

"What is it?" Neil came to stand next to me as I stared down through the trees at the figures on the other side of the tiny island.

Diana and Ernie, the game warden, stood at the edge of the water. Near them lay a figure, half in the water, a fair-haired woman who wasn't moving at all. It had to be Alice. Suddenly all these reminders of her life, the clever and dedicated way she must have lived, seemed empty and sad.

It looked like small tools rested on the shore next to her. Maybe she'd been digging up plants. There was other gear I didn't recognize, something boxy, maybe electronic.

Diana faced away from the body, as if she couldn't bear to look at her. Ernie appeared to be talking on the phone.

"They'll bring reinforcements soon," Neil said.

"You're right." In other words, we should get out of here. "I can't see anything obvious that's gone wrong here. It all seems orderly, if primitive."

"She may have simply drowned."

"What is that?" I pointed to something white in the distance. "Is that the house?"

"The Boyle house? It must be."

If I focused, I could see a two-story structure a ways out,

but I couldn't make out details. My impression was that it was an older house, maybe even late nineteenth century, like the ones in the historic area of downtown Bohemia along the river. There was plenty of water between this little island and the house, so a boat was necessary to get here unless you really liked swimming with alligators.

Diana and Ernie had started to walk back toward us, and in the distance, I heard sirens.

"Maybe we can get some details out of Ernie." I moved toward the door, and Neil followed.

We got to the bottom of the steps to find Mr. Mixy loitering there. Mark paced nearby while Royce and Aunt Celestine sat on the bench chatting quietly and Captain Vance, to my shock, fished off the dock.

"Find any bodily fluids?" Mr. Mixy asked.

"Yuck. Go away!" I said.

This time, Neil chuckled. Mr. Mixy smirked and wandered off.

"It's even worse when he says it," I told Neil.

"Let's not go there."

"OK. Be cool. Here they come." We strolled down the dock toward the boat, and the others took our cue and converged there.

Royce hugged me and whispered in my ear, "What did you find out?"

Thus was my reputation. We ended the hug, and I shrugged. "Nothing of use, I don't think."

Captain Vance reeled in his empty line, and we all turned in anticipation as Ernie and Diana arrived.

"What happened?" Mr. Mixy asked. At least he didn't mind blundering in, and for once, he wasn't filming himself.

"Alice Dalworth is dead," the game warden said in his flat way. "Probably an accident, but the Bohemia Police are sending a team. They have a boat trailered nearby."

"What kind of accident?" Captain Vance asked.

Ernie hesitated, then he said, "I'd guess electrocution. Monkey-fishing accident, maybe. All the gear was there."

"You can fish for monkeys?" Mr. Mixy asked.

Captain Vance snorted a laugh.

"There are no monkeys here," Aunt Celestine said dryly. "Silver Springs, that's another matter."

"You're right, ma'am," Ernie said. "Monkey-fishing is what they used to call electrofishing gear, when they used to have to crank it like a hurdy-gurdy. Popular with poachers. Scientists use more updated versions now with generators for fish counts. The backpack versions use an electrified pole to stun the fish, and then they put them back. Unfortunately for Ms. Dalworth, the gear can be dangerous if used improperly. It can cause heart attacks or worse. Even if it didn't kill her, she might have been stunned and then drowned. The ME will have to tell us that."

"An electric charge shocks the fish and brings them to the surface," Captain Vance explained to our puzzled and horrified expressions. "Not very sporting, but it's an easy way to catch fish."

"Maybe she wanted to have a fish fry," Mr. Mixy said. I think we *all* gave him a dirty look.

"Alice is a scientist. But she is—was a botanist," Diana said. "She didn't study fish. It doesn't make sense."

Ernie regarded her coolly. Almost as if Diana was a suspect. Did he think this was more than an accident?

Aunt Celestine stepped up and slipped an arm around

Diana's narrow shoulders. The botanist usually seemed so hearty and energetic. At the moment, she seemed as fragile as a ghost orchid.

We had to wait about twenty tense minutes before the sound of another engine heralded the arrival of a new boat from the direction of the old house, this one with Bohemia Police markings.

Ernie turned to the crew aboard—two uniformed officers and a familiar face, Detective Cleo Kleene. She caught my eye and raised an eyebrow. She hadn't been too happy with me amid the tomfoolery during the Bohemia Beach Film Festival. She wore one of her sleek pantsuits, an elegant gray that looked great against her deep brown skin, and she still wore her dark brown, curly hair buzzed short.

"Come around to the other side of the island," Ernie told her. "I'll meet you over there and fill you in."

Detective Keene nodded. "We have a forensics team on the way. I'll have Officer Brown pick them up after he drops us off. I also want them to check out an old Ford we found at the Boyle place, plates registered to the deceased."

The barrel-chested Officer Brown turned their boat to navigate around the curvy piece of land, and they chugged off.

"And how did you get here?" Ernie asked Diana.

"I leased this motorboat for the week." She gestured toward the small boat tied to the dock. "I'm researching the plants here and thought it would be most convenient."

"Where are you keeping it?"

"Whirlwind Fish Camp."

Ernie looked skeptical. "Then why were these folks picking you up?"

"We hoped to have a fun tour on the water before they brought me back here. I was initially supposed to visit Alice this afternoon, but she emailed me last night and said she'd like to talk to me first thing. It sounded urgent, so I rearranged my plans, thinking I'd have an hour with her before the airboat came. I thought she might even come along."

"We normally only allow six passengers," Captain Vance said idly. Mark gave him a dark look.

"What was so urgent?" I asked, and Ernie aimed his blue-laser eyes at me before turning back to Diana.

"I don't know. She didn't say."

"How well did you know her?" Ernie asked.

"Fairly well in our youth. We were friends at university, though not terribly close. As professional colleagues, we met up at a couple of conferences."

"She was English?"

"Yes, of course. Though she had an interest in the Americas, endangered plants and animals and vanishing habitats. We'd struck up an email conversation about the wetlands of Florida, and she'd invited me to come see what she was working on when I visited. I think she had some sort of grant. I don't know why she wanted to see me first thing this morning."

Ernie was silent for a moment. Then he said, "Detective Keene and I will need to talk with you later at the downtown police station. Let's say four o'clock. Do you need us to take you there?"

Crap. Diana *was* a suspect.

"I'll take her," Mark said.

"See that you do." Ernie turned back to Diana. "Where are you staying?"

"With me." Celestine gave Ernie the address, and he wrote it in a little notebook.

"Leave your boat here for now," the wildlife officer said.

"We'll take it along with your friend's car and let you know when you can have it back."

Diana didn't argue, and he walked off without a word, back to the crime scene.

Or did he think her boat was part of the crime scene?

I shivered.

"We should go," Captain Vance said.

"My thoughts exactly," said Mr. Mixy. "I'm hungry."

"I've got some gator jerky aboard to share. It's usually part of the tour."

"Awesome." Mr. Mixy rubbed his hands together and climbed aboard.

Gator jerky? That seemed like waving a red cape in front of a, well, gator. Especially out here in the domain of the dinosaurs. Then again, I had a gator tooth on my bracelet. I hoped it didn't provoke Phantom.

Mr. Mixy took a piece of jerky from the captain and gnawed like Astra with a stolen cocktail garnish.

The rest of us boarded the airboat, including Diana with her backpack. She sat between Mark and Celestine in the second row, squeezing Mr. Mixy over to one end of the bench, and the captain started the engine at a low *thrum, thrum, ruuummmm* ...

"Look, there he is!" Captain Vance called out, pointing at a floating log in the middle of the water.

"He?" I asked.

"Phantom!" Otter Vance seemed pleased he'd delivered the goods to the tourists.

Then I noticed the log had yellow eyes with slits for pupils and a half-mottled nose that stuck out in front of his long, spiky, body. He was *huge*.

"He's coming this way." I leaned into Neil and away from the general direction of the gator's approach.

Royce chuckled at my maneuver. "He looks like a wily old buzzard."

"He's a survivor," Captain Vance said. "Though it looks like he's been in another scrape." A hint of blood glinted amid the alligator's scars.

Mr. Mixy threw him a piece of jerky, prompting several of us to say "No!" We'd heard the speech earlier about the perils of feeding these beasts.

The gator glided by it, ignoring it, and little fish popped up, trying to nibble the dried meat.

Phantom, inexorable, swept past Royce's and Mr. Mixy's side of the vessel, creating a small wake that competed with the airboat's. Then he submerged.

"Lifeless eyes, like a doll's eyes," Royce said with his usual dry humor.

In spite of our group's mood, I smiled at the quote from *Jaws*. "You're going to need a bigger boat."

"You aren't supposed to feed them," Captain Vance warned.

I feared the oblivious Mr. Mixy would throw the animal another piece of gator jerky. Plus, wasn't that cannibalism? I was pretty sure Phantom knew it, too, and was plotting revenge.

"Are you OK?" Mark asked Diana.

"I will be. I just need to think."

Captain Vance handed out small bottles of water, then turned to his controls, cranking the engine to full throttle. We picked up speed, zipping out of the clearing, weaving through the cypress trees, cruising back to the chain of channels and lakes where we'd started our fateful trip.

I needed to think, too.

Especially about ... What did *Diana* need to think about?

Chapter Five

Captain Vance didn't say much on the way back to Whirlwind Airboat Tours and Fish Camp, but he rallied after several minutes and made an effort to slow down for a couple of tourist stops anyway. Maybe he wanted to take our minds off what we'd just seen.

As we paused to watch a couple of small gators on a muddy bank, sunning themselves while keeping a wary eye on a great blue heron standing on one leg nearby, Mr. Mixy shouted, "Cows!"

We all looked to where he was pointing. Yep. Cows, grazing on the riverbank.

"Don't the alligators eat them?" asked Mark, determinedly cheerful. "They look like a fine steak, if you ask me."

"Oh, no, they leave 'em alone," Captain Vance said.

"But why are there cows in the swamp? And the, uh, marsh?" Royce asked.

"There's a lot of cattle land around here, and as you go up the Saint Johns, there's a mix of private and public land, especially by Lake Poinsett. It's hard to build out here, but development is creeping out anyway. What a lot of people don't understand is this marsh is like a big sponge for all the water when a hurricane rolls through. Without this, you'd see a lot more flooding in places like Bohemia. The marsh filters out pollutants, too."

"Reckless development is putting thousands of species in danger of extinction as well, including plants," Diana said. I was a bit surprised to hear her speak, given her pensive mood, but she seemed to have regained her cool and looked around with interest. "We lose dozens of species around the world every day, and Florida has kept apace. And we can't just snap our fingers and bring them back. Speciation takes five thousand years or more."

OK, so maybe she wasn't cheering us up, but at least she seemed to take an interest in what was happening around us again.

"It's mighty sad," Otter Vance agreed. "Even those of us who hunt and fish, especially us, want to preserve as much of these wetlands as possible."

Aunt Celestine liked to tell me most of Florida would be underwater in the not too distant future anyway, but we were right there with everyone else, living in a duplex on a barrier island, about as fragile a spit of land as you could imagine. Florida was one big low-lying wetland. Our backyard, which she stuffed with native tropical plants and an herb garden around the pool, wasn't all that different from the lush greenery out here.

My philosophy was to do the right thing *and* live for the moment while drinking the best cocktails possible. If Hurricane Katrina and subsequent events had taught me anything, you never knew what was going to happen next, and there were no guarantees. I mean, look at poor Alice.

"In fact," Captain Vance said as he began cranking the motor up again, "I've heard the Boyle place has been sold to a developer. But they haven't moved on it yet, and Alice was still there on a lease of some kind. So maybe it will stay wetlands after all."

Fat chance, I thought. But his words got me thinking. If a developer owned the land, why was Alice out there? And why would she be counting fish with that electro-thingy device? Something didn't add up.

I tightened my earmuffs as the airboat screamed back to full speed, then pulled out my phone. We had a decent signal again after almost fifteen minutes of dead zone. I sent a text.

I looked up to see Neil watching me with a quizzical expression. So I sent him a text too. "I asked Millie to find out which developer owns the Boyle property."

He shifted to pull his buzzing phone out of his pocket, read it and frowned. Then he gave me a look that didn't require a text to translate: *You should not get involved.*

I shrugged and smiled. *I'm not getting involved. I'm just curious, that's all.*

He bent over his phone, tapping, and a moment later a picture arrived by text. It showed a cat.

"Ha ha," I said. *Curiosity killed the cat.* I texted him back: "Not a nice thing to wish on anyone."

"Not a wish," he sent me back. "A caution. And the wildlife officer seemed to think it was an accident."

Another text buzzed in on top of his. Confused, I realized it came from Millie, our Girl Friday scheduler and organizer who ran an event planning business. She was also a terrific researcher. And darn quick when she put her mind to things.

"It's in the property records," she wrote back. "Property purchased by Tocks Development Corp. six months ago."

My head snapped up with a gasp. Raquel Tocks! I still suspected she had a hand in the nefarious goings-on at Cocktailia in New Orleans last spring, but she was also a powerful figure in Bohemia who made herself look good by sponsoring events like the Bohemia Beach Film Festival.

I looked over at Neil, whose eyebrows perched high in a question. I showed him my phone.

His eyebrows lowered, and he texted me back. "And guess who our meeting is with this afternoon."

I typed back, "I was sure Raquel would dump us on one of her underlings."

Neil chuckled. "Chief sponsor and chair of the event," he typed to me. "I think she likes control."

Well, then. It looked like I'd get to ask Ms. Tocks personally what she knew about the Boyle place and poor Alice Dalworth.

I tried to pretend Neil wasn't watching me with worry and turned to Royce. "You doing OK?" I shouted at him.

He looked baffled. I was pretty sure he didn't hear a word I said, but he got the gist and gave me a thumbs-up.

It was a huge relief to get back to the dock given what had happened, not to mention the bone-rattling ride, the jet-engine noise, the grit—possibly bug parts—in my teeth, my dehydrated eyeballs behind my sunglasses, and the feeling that in spite of my SPF50 sunscreen, my skin had crisped like a thin slice of potato in hot oil.

Mark quietly tipped Captain Vance, who looked very pleased indeed and handed out business cards to anyone who wanted one. I grabbed one. It had his contact info on one side and a photo of an alligator on the other.

"Hey!" I said, my voice sounding loud in the delightful quiet at the dock, even with my ringing ears. "Isn't that Phantom?"

Otter Vance nodded. "I'm very proud of that photo."

"Does he know you're using his likeness in advertising?"

Mark asked. "I hope you're paying him a fee commensurate to his stature as the king of the swamp." Then he gave Diana a subtle glance to see if his joke had had any effect at all.

She gave him the side-eye—but also a small smile.

I breathed a little sigh of relief. But she wouldn't get over this morning instantly, and besides, she had to talk to the police this afternoon.

I eased closer to Captain Vance as the others stretched and chatted and some ran to the restrooms in the restaurant. "May I ask you a question?"

"Sure, shoot," he said as he grabbed his cooler with the jerky and waters, his gun and a small trash bag.

"Why is the game warden going to talk to Diana this afternoon with the Bohemia Police?"

"Game wardens—Florida wildlife officers—are police officers too. They'll work with the local force if it makes sense for a case. This is an unusual death that will require an autopsy. Maybe Ernie thinks there's more to what happened than just an accident, but of course, he wasn't going to tell us all that. He holds his cards close to the vest."

"Thanks," I said, as if it didn't matter, but my already quivering belly did a slow roll.

He smiled and nodded and walked off, leaving me with a very bad feeling.

I returned to the group. We all naturally clustered around Diana.

"Shouldn't we get lunch?" Mr. Mixy said.

"The restaurant is pretty good here, if you like fried stuff," Neil said.

"Fried gator?" Mr. Mixy asked, his hazel eyes lighting up.

"Pretty sure," Neil said.

"Great! I'll see you in there." And Mixy marched off to the restaurant again.

Neil looked at me. "I guess we're eating lunch here."

"He's tempting fate," I said, "eating all that gator with Phantom lurking around."

Royce chuckled, then stopped. It was like we didn't know what to say or do with Alice's death hanging over us. Jokes seemed in poor taste.

But Diana looked around at all of us—me, Neil, Royce, Mark and Celestine—and spoke. "It's all right," she said. "You don't have to walk on eggshells. Alice and I hadn't been close for a long time, but this morning was a shock. I'm sure the police won't be much trouble, as I've done nothing wrong." She looked at me pointedly with a gaze that I imagined said *I need your help,* then at Celestine and Mark. "Except for, perhaps, this one tiny thing."

A thrill went down my spine.

"What is it?" Mark whispered as we all took a step closer.

Diana pulled her backpack off her shoulder. She unzipped it, looked around to be sure no one was watching, then reached in and pulled out an envelope.

"I took this from Alice's cabin."

The envelope was about the size of a normal greeting card, plain white. On the front of it, a few words were written in blue ballpoint pen but in an elegant script: *Diana. For Your Eyes Only.*

So of course I needed to see it as soon as possible.

"Put it away for now," Celestine said gently. "We don't want to flash this around here. Too many strangers who might know a certain wildlife officer."

My aunt was right.

"We'll dump Mr. Mixy and have a look after lunch, all right?" Mark murmured. "Before I take you to the police."

Diana slipped the envelope into her backpack, and we headed into the restaurant. But as I nibbled on fried catfish bites and we talked about what we'd seen on our tour, I couldn't think of anything but what was in that envelope. A final message from Alice?

And would her last words tell us why she died?

Chapter Six

Neil drove Aunt Celestine, Diana and me back to Bohemia Beach, where we took Mr. Mixy, full of fried alligator, to his hotel. Which, I was sorry to note, was the same hotel where Melody worked at the bar and Oleanna was staying—meaning there was a fair chance we'd run into him again here.

Mr. Mixy seemed anxious to hang around, but I cut him off.

"It's my day off, and I'm going to take a nap," I told him as Neil idled under the hotel's porte cochere.

"Oh, all right." He reluctantly exited the car. "I'll see you at the party."

Sigh. I didn't even want him in the same time zone.

When Neil pulled into my driveway, I climbed out of his big SUV, grabbed my bag, exchanged my sunglasses for my clear nerdy ones and headed for the mailbox. Aunt Celestine and I had two mailboxes side by side, so as not to confuse the U.S. Postal Service, but we always checked each other's.

I handed Aunt Celestine her gardening catalogs and a missive about one of her many lucrative investment funds. And I stuck my small brown box into my big messenger bag to open later. It was probably just another dog toy. I'd ordered a bunch for Astra's Christmas stocking, even if she had more toys than I had cocktail glasses.

For now, I was a lot more curious about Diana's letter. But we couldn't talk about it until Mark showed up.

"Where's Mark? He left at least five minutes before we did," I remarked. When he'd left the fish camp, the rest of us were waiting in line for the restaurant's restroom, a consequence of over-hydrating after the long airboat ride.

"Maybe he's hitting the thrift shops," Neil joked.

Mark and Royce showed up a minute later, pulling into Aunt Celestine's driveway. The first occupant to exit his car was a familiar furry one who'd been sitting on Royce's lap.

"Victoria!" I shouted in delight, and the Cavalier King Charles spaniel ran over to me, her long ears streaming behind her. Her tail wagged so hard, her butt wiggled. I crouched, scooped the dog up and gave her love. Then I heard Astra barking from inside the house. I could swear dogs were psychic.

I watched Mark climb out of his sparkling cherry-red Miata. It was always a pleasure to watch Mark do anything, but I hadn't noticed the car at the fish camp.

"Is that yours?" I asked him as he disembarked.

"He can't stop buying cars," came Diana's mild rebuke. "He has at least two here already, polluting the atmosphere. I still hate myself for flying over on his private jet."

"Not fair. The Jag's electric," Mark said.

Diana rolled her eyes. "This new one's not."

"Decent mileage, though." Mark grinned.

I looked the Miata over with a bit of envy. My Angry Orange, a small Honda Fit hatchback stuffed into the garage, was a lot less glamorous. "You have to admit it's pretty hot."

"I thought so, too," said Royce, who also had a thing for

cars. As did our fellow bartender Barclay. Too bad we wouldn't see him till later.

"No Alastair?" Neil asked of his frenemy.

"He's passed out on the couch. I'll make sure he rallies before the party." Mark's expression sobered, and he turned toward Diana. "You don't mind that there's a party, do you?"

"I do not. It will take my mind off things." She stood a little straighter, her voice taking on that self-assured tone I recognized. "But I still want to find out what happened to Alice."

We pondered that for a moment before Aunt Celestine said, "Why don't you come through my place and into the backyard? It's a nice little oasis, and I'll bring out some dessert."

"And Pepper and I can make drinks," Neil added.

"I could do with a gin and tonic," Diana admitted.

"G&Ts all around?" Mark asked. At everyone's assent, I handed Victoria to Mark, and Neil and I went into my place while the rest headed for the backyard through my aunt's house.

Astra greeted me at my door with excited barks, and I reached down and played with her while she spun in circles and jumped.

I disabled the alarm, set down my bag and crouched in front of her, giving her a good petting. "You were a very good watchdog this morning, and now we have a special visitor for you," I told her, trying to make Victoria's arrival sound like a plus. "And remember, good dogs get treats."

The combination of my loving tone and "good dogs get treats," which I sometimes said when she wasn't being so good, confused her. The excitement stopped for a second, and then she barked more insistently. She wanted to know what I was talking about.

"OK, let's see how this goes." I led her to the sliding doors in the back of the house and let her out into the fenced poolside yard, where our friends were exploring the lush tropical foliage and my aunt's herb garden in raised beds and pots.

Astra's bark hit a hysterical level, almost a howl. *There's another dog back here!*

The dogs had similar caramel-and-white coloring, but Astra was curlier and plumper. She rushed up to Victoria, and they did some cautious sniffing. I was sure Astra's glance at me said, "So *this* is who you cheated on me with!" Then she growled at Victoria.

"Hey!" I called, reaching in to put a hand on Astra's back. "Be a good girl. Remember, good dogs get treats."

Astra made a small noise I might call a grumble, then sat and pretended not to care. Meanwhile, Victoria's tail wagged furiously at the talk of treats.

"All right, you both get treats. I'll be right back."

Neil stood in the doorway, watching with amusement. "Are they friends yet?"

"I don't think so." I led him inside. "Maybe treats will help."

While I had a cute vintage art deco bar in my living area, it didn't have easy access to ice, so we made the G&Ts in the modest kitchen.

"Good thing I have Mark's Frilly Fairy on hand." I measured the gin into ice-filled vintage highball glasses, their sides decorated with gold leaves.

"But no Lightning Bug Premium Tonic Water. He may never forgive you," Neil joked as he cut slices from the stash of fresh limes I kept in my fridge.

"I don't think I can even get his tonic water here yet. Do you think he'll be able to tell?" I asked, topping off the glasses with another good brand.

"Probably," Neil said in a grudging tone as he dropped in the lime slices. "He knows his stuff."

I placed the drinks on another vintage item, a gold-colored pressed-tin tray with indentations for glasses, each circle decorated with oranges. I loved souvenir kitsch. The circle at the middle of the tray showed the state of Florida and was a perfect spot for a couple of dog treats.

I hooked Neil up with a pitcher of ice water and a stack of cups, and we headed outside and set everything up on the rectangular cast-aluminum table under the covered part of the patio. The air out here was fresh and just warm enough, the palm trees rustling in the sunlight. December was glorious in Florida.

Aunt Celestine had brought out a tray of her famous buttery lemon-rosemary shortbread cookies. The top of each pale, leaf-shaped cutout was pressed with darts of fresh rosemary from her garden.

"Ooo, biscuits. Yes, please." Mark took a cookie and put the whole thing in his mouth. The others chuckled, pulling up patio chairs so we could all hear one another. They grabbed glistening cocktails and cookies as they settled in, and the dogs eagerly scarfed down their treats.

Victoria came to me when she was done, so of course I had to put her in my lap. Astra gave me a dirty look and went to Royce, whom she'd grown fond of in Kentucky. He looked at me with a snicker and picked her up.

No one said anything except for some "mmms" over the cookies. Until Diana, after a deep sip of her cocktail, said,

"That's not Mark's tonic, is it? But I recognize the gin." She should, since she helped him develop its blend of botanicals.

Neil and I laughed. "Accurate," Neil said.

"I thought it tasted *almost* perfect," Mark added.

Diana gave him an amused glance, then looked around at us, sensing our anticipation. "All right. I suppose we should look at the letter." She set her glass on the table, wiped her hands on a napkin and dug into the backpack at her feet until she found the envelope. She wasted no time in sliding her finger under the flap and tearing it open. Then she slid out what appeared to be a ...

"Is that a thank-you card?" I asked.

"It does say 'Thank You.'" Diana sounded as puzzled as I felt. "I don't know what for." The words, in calligraphy, were surrounded by a lovely drawing of leaves in a wreath. "I think she drew this. She's published some very fine drawings and paintings of plants." A look of sadness passed over her face for a moment, and then she opened the card. After a minute, she lifted her eyes to us. "This is rather odd."

"Perhaps you should read it to us," Mark suggested.

Thanks, Mark. I didn't want to seem too eager.

"All right. Here it is." And Diana read the note.

My dear Diana,

I can't thank you enough for your interest in my work. I fear I will not be doing it for much longer. The winds are changing, as are the seasons. Beware the Ides of March, as they say. It's getting a bit too hot for me. And after a few setbacks, I find I don't want to prove

the adage that bad things come in threes. Sometimes life is a puzzle, but the prize is worth it.
I hope my work will live on.

I feared we might not get to see each other,
and so I have written you this note. How I
miss our salad days together. But the key is to
concentrate on what's next, not what is left behind,
and I wished to express a dear wish that you
will move ahead. And that's what letters are for.

With respect and affection,
Alice

"Seems a little ominous," Aunt Celestine said. "Or at least indicative that she planned to stop her project?"

"I agree," Diana said. "'I hope my work will live on' gives me a chill. Did she think she was in danger?"

"It's also sort of weird." Royce, his brow creased, stroked Astra's head. "Odd, like you said. Like she's talking around something."

"How well did you know her?" I asked, thinking of the reference to "salad days."

"It's as I told the police. We were friends in school but not best mates. We knew each other professionally and met at conferences—two, I think. We talked about old times, had a few laughs over cocktails. We occasionally exchanged emails. I knew she was doing research here, and so when I decided to visit Celestine, I naturally asked Alice if she wished to meet. I thought she might have some ideas for unusual botanicals here that would work in gin or another spirit, if not for Mark, then someone else."

"Hey!" Mark said, but he smiled. Diana did consult for other distillers on occasion.

"She wants you to move ahead," Neil said.

"It suggests she feels she might be left behind," Royce added.

"There are several things in this note that suggest that she is ending things here," I noted. "But she doesn't come out and say what's going on. She says it's too hot for her and that bad things come in threes. What else happened to her out in the swamp?"

None of us had an answer.

"Are you going to give the letter to the police?" Mark asked.

"I'm not inclined to do so yet," Diana said. "Though I suppose it will look bad if I produce it later."

"Then again, it would look bad if you produced it now after you swiped it from the shack," I said.

Diana angled her brown eyes at me. "An excellent point, Pepper. I think I shall keep it to myself unless circumstances demand I give it up."

"That seems reasonable," Celestine said, and we all nodded, bound in our minor conspiracy.

"I intend to find out exactly what the police know," Diana said.

"You do know they want to question *you*, don't you?" Mark pointed out.

"And I have nothing to hide. Well, almost nothing." She slipped the card back into its envelope. "I think someone should hang on to this for me until the interview is over."

Mark plucked the letter from her hand. "My pleasure."

"Given the situation, I think you might want a lawyer to go

along with you," Neil said. "If it's OK with you, I'll call my father. Someone in his firm can represent you."

"Won't that make me look guilty?" Diana asked.

"I think it will make you look intelligent. Of course, you *are* intelligent," Mark said to her raised eyebrow. "But you know what I mean."

Diana thought for a moment. "If you think it's wise, that would be all right, I suppose."

Neil nodded and stepped away to make a phone call to his dad.

The conversation eased into more pleasant topics after he returned. Diana seemed to have recovered from the morning's shock and looked comfortable in her habitual khaki outfit, with a healthy glow and no makeup.

She told us what led her to her PhD and unusual career. "My father is a conservation biologist in England, though he's a native of Brazil. His chief passion remains preserving the Amazonian rainforest. He took me on local searches for rare plants as I was growing up. I still remember finding my first spiked rampion. Such a thrill! Then we traveled to Brazil on family trips a few times when I was a teenager. They ignited my passion for botanical adventures."

Ah. Now I understood why Diana's English accent had a little something extra.

"What about your mother?" Celestine asked.

"She's a UK native and an English professor at the same university where my father works," Diana replied. "My mother held down the fort while my father traveled during much of my youth. The separation was extremely stressful for her. She took up cocktail-making as a hobby, so I learned a bit about making drinks properly."

"Which led you to botanicals?" I asked.

"Yes, indirectly. They remind me of the pleasant aspects of those times with my mother, though I realize now she led quite a lonely life. Not for me. I don't see much point in a relationship where you're apart most of the time, and I rather like being on my own. I prefer the company of plants."

"Not very cozy, though, are they?" Mark asked.

"They are when they're incorporated into a very fine gin." Diana smiled and finished her glass. "That's probably enough for me. I don't want to go babbling all my dark secrets to the Bohemia Police and Ranger Ernie."

I answered her smile. "Do you have dark secrets?"

"You know my only one. Probably." She gave us a sly look, and we laughed. It was good to see Diana make a joke.

"And *we* have to go talk to Raquel Tocks," Neil reminded me.

Oh, yeah. The owner of the old Boyle place and its nearby Swamp Shack, where Alice met her end.

Neil must have spotted my keen expression. "We're talking about the New Year's Eve gig. That's it."

"Oh, really?" I took a sip of my G&T and stroked Victoria's long, soft ears. "I guess we'll see where the conversation takes us."

Chapter Seven

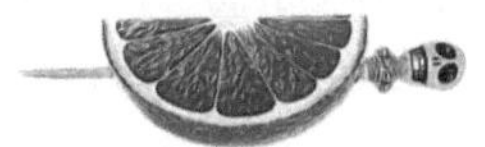

While Mark took Diana to see the police, Aunt Celestine volunteered to watch Victoria, in hopes she might bond with Astra. She also invited Royce to stay for the rest of the afternoon so she could get to know her new nephew—if a fortysomething nephew could be new. Having a half brother sure was new to me. I had yet to talk to my super-religious mother about her secret baby, and he hadn't spoken to his father in New Orleans yet, either. It was complicated.

I changed into a slightly more professional vest-and-blouse combo to go with my jeans, and Neil ducked into my guest bathroom to change into nice trousers, a dress shirt, suspenders and a bow tie. Of course.

Also, yummy.

Neil, never thrilled to see me behind the wheel—or maybe he just didn't love my tiny car—drove us back across the bridge to Bohemia and Tocks Development Corp. in his SUV.

The Tocks building was about a mile from downtown on a large, green lot. The office building had four stories, each with a slightly different feel. It was mostly white, but the walls on the lower floor and other accents were painted what I'd call Miami pink. Rows of generous windows lined each story.

A corner of the building was actually a slightly bumped-out semicircle, and it was on this rounded corner where the front door was located. We had to walk through manicured land-scaping to get to it and paused to watch a great egret, a little blue heron, several white ibis and a handful of ducks enjoying the large, meandering retention pond.

"This looks like a golf course," Neil said, carrying a leather satchel not quite as fat as my canvas bag.

"I was thinking a moat. The pond goes almost all the way around the building."

"Maybe she needs to be able to defend the castle."

"Given what we know about her, I wouldn't be surprised."

We'd first encountered Raquel Tocks in New Orleans, where she was a Cocktailia sponsor and also suspiciously involved in the mystery we unraveled there. Millie did some research and learned that Raquel's father, from whom she inherited the business, had mob contacts and served time for fraud and conspiracy in a fake mortgage scheme.

Raquel's operation appeared cleaner on the surface, but her company was dogged by fines for environmental issues and lawsuits for sketchy deals. She also had, shall we say, interesting associates. A couple of goons with records followed her around. One of them had given me a lot of trouble in New Orleans. Her lawyer was less than reputable as well. Was it too much to think she might be involved in Alice's death?

"We're just here to finalize details for the New Year's Eve party," Neil said, as if he could read my thoughts.

"You don't have to keep reminding me. I know what you're here for."

He gave me a look that said he knew I was double-talking him with the "you're," but I kissed him on the cheek to ease his mind before leading the way inside.

The airy, bright lobby had an elegant coffee station, like the kind you see in some hotel foyers, along with scattered sofas, chairs and a couple of tables for impromptu meetings. A beautifully made-up woman helmed the reception desk at the back of this space, in front of a huge mural of photographs—a collage of houses and buildings, presumably the company's work.

We gave her our names and appointment, and after a quick moment on the phone, she directed us to the fourth-floor executive suite. The elevator felt like the rest of the building, clean and new and efficient. At the top floor, we followed the signs to the right, where glass walls and a heavy glass door led us to another receptionist. A few minutes later, she'd led us through a rat's maze of elegant dark wood and colorful carpeting to yet another office foyer of rich brown wood and modern rugs, ruled by another secretary. Raquel had enough assistants to fly a moon mission.

"I'm Lissa Schumacher," she informed us, not bothering to get up as her colleague left. She didn't look as put-together as the woman downstairs and not as old, either—younger than me, and I was in my late twenties. About to be very late twenties.

Lissa's long, dark hair had escaped its coiffure, and I was pretty sure she wasn't going for the "messy bun" look. It seemed more like a squirrel had tried to nest in her head. Her flowery dress looked OK, but her lipstick had partly worn off—probably thanks to the half-eaten sub next to her computer—and she bit her lip as she focused on the task before her.

She dabbed at the bottom of a high-heeled shoe with red paint from a glass jar, eliminating scuffs and dings from the scarlet leather. She struggled to find a place to put the slender wet brush and the shoe on her messy deskscape, finally settling the shoe upside-down on an empty glass Perrier bottle and balancing the paintbrush precariously on her computer mouse. She picked up the chunky desk phone.

"Bohemia Bartenders are here for you, ma'am." She paused. "Yes. No problem." Another pause. "I'll make sure he's there." She hung up and tapped the cell phone sitting on her desk for a full minute.

Neil raised an eyebrow.

"I'll take you back in five minutes," Lissa said, grabbing the shoe again. She noticed my stare. "Ms. Tocks insists that the soles of her Louboutins remain impeccable."

"I see." I did not see. The more fashionable among us loved fancy heels the height of the Empire State Building—like Melody and my friends Penelope and Sloane, who could afford them—but they killed me. And since I usually worked on my feet, I had no ambitions to obtain such treasures, except for cheap finds for very brief occasions. I guessed touching up the bottoms of the shoes allowed the peasants upon whom Raquel stomped to experience perfection in their abasement.

Or maybe I was imagining her as the villain in the historical mystery series I was binge-reading.

I sat and watched Lissa, fascinated, while Neil wandered to the window to look at the moat.

"Any dragons?" I asked him.

"No, but there are a lot of Teslas. And Mercedes."

"Hmm."

"That's what Ms. Tocks drives," Lissa volunteered. "A white Mercedes convertible. I just washed it this morning. It's beautiful."

"You're her—assistant?" I ventured.

"*Executive* assistant," Lissa said, resting the shoe again on the Perrier, reaching to the floor and picking up another one. "It's a foot in the door."

Or a shoe, I thought.

Just then, the alarm sounded on her cell phone. "Time to take you in." She set the imperfect, unpainted shoe on the desk, stood and led us through a sleek wooden door into a spacious office with two straight walls and one rounded one, like a fat slice of pie. We stood in the curved top corner of Raquel Tocks's building.

Along one straight wall, cabinets and a bar flanked the door we came in; another door was set between sparsely decorated shelves on the other. A couch and a couple of comfy chairs were positioned in front of the right angle. The curved wall opposite was almost all glass.

Strategically placed in front of the rounded windows was a huge circular glass desk—really two semicircles that gave the impression that our client, sitting in the middle, piloted a UFO. She worked on a wafer-thin laptop next to a device with a tablet-size screen I guessed functioned as her phone.

Raquel Tocks typed for another moment, then looked up and gestured for us to sit in the two simple mid-century-style chairs that faced her. They were square, soft and slightly reclined, putting us lower than her level, certainly on purpose.

In possibly her late thirties, but ageless in the polished way of the exquisitely maintained, she had short, slickly styled blond hair that clung to her delicate skull, big earrings, heavy eye makeup, pale pink lipstick and almost silver-blue eyes. Her creamy silk pantsuit flowed over her slender frame like water.

A bulky, pasty guy with a big black mustache in a black suit stood next to her. He looked us over, nodded at Raquel's side-long glance and went out the side door.

Goon One. Where's Goon Two?

"Where's Enzo?" Raquel called to Lissa.

"On his way."

"Tell him to come in when he gets here."

"Yes, ma'am." And Lissa disappeared, leaving us to sit and face our enemy. I mean, client.

Maybe Enzo was Goon Two.

"It's nice to see you again, Ms. Tocks," Neil said.

"Just call me Raquel, Neil." Her eyes warmed as she looked him over. Then she glanced at me. "And don't I know you?"

She damn well knew me. "Pepper Revelle."

"That's right. I'm glad you agreed to mix up our drinks for New Year's Eve. If you'll just wait a moment." She tapped the screen, and Lissa's voice came out of the speaker.

"Ma'am?"

"Enzo?"

"Sending him through now."

"Bring a chair."

The office door opened, and a handsome man in his forties came through, with light brown hair threaded with silver, just long enough to run a hand through. He had the slightest scruff on his chin and hazel eyes that sparkled with enough colors to please Monet. He wore a tan sport jacket over a white shirt and brown pants. He didn't look like a goon. He looked very, *very* nice.

Lissa staggered in behind him, puffing as she hauled a heavy chair from the reception area.

"May I present Enzo Desjardins?" Raquel said, pronouncing it *day-jhar-den*. "This is Neil Rockaway and Pepper Revelle of the Bohemia Bartenders. Enzo will be supplying champagne for the event."

We stood to shake hands with him, Neil first, then me.

"Enchantée," Enzo said, then drew my hand up for a kiss.

"Oh. Hi." Did my voice just flutter? My hand felt extra warm as I withdrew it.

Neil gave me the side-eye, then looked at Enzo. "You're not related to the Desjardins champagne house?"

Enzo's smile broadened. "Indeed I am. I *am* the champagne house." His voice, with a touch of roughness, had a pleasing French accent.

"Then we're lucky. You make excellent champagne." Neil nodded and sat, and so did I. He was such a smarty-pants.

With a thump, Lissa plopped the big chair next to Raquel's desk so it faced us, then left the room, puffing.

Enzo acted like she'd never been there at all and sat in the chair. Raquel leaned back. "Menu?"

"Forwarded as requested," Neil said. "But I have a copy if you'd like to see it."

A glint entered Raquel's eye, and she touched her phone screen again.

"Ma'am?" came Lissa, still a little out of breath.

"Neil sent a menu. Do you have it?"

"Oh, yes, ma'am. I'm sorry. Just a moment."

Raquel smiled and looked back and forth from Neil to me to Neil, where she lingered. I didn't like that smile. It brought to mind Royce's distillery cat in hunting mode.

Lissa hustled in a few moments later and handed copies of the menu to Raquel and Enzo.

"None for our guests?" Raquel asked.

Lissa's face got almost as red as the bottom of the shoes she'd been painting. "Oh—I—"

"No need." Neil pulled a tablet computer out of his satchel and tapped it a couple of times.

"Very well." Raquel gave Lissa a steely look, and her assistant almost ran out of the room.

"What did you think?" Neil asked.

"I see you have five cocktails planned, four of them with champagne and other liquors, plus a whiskey drink. But only one champagne cocktail contains vodka."

I tried to keep a straight face. Vodka had its place for the unambitious, but you didn't hire craft cocktail experts to focus on vodka drinks.

Neil didn't blink. "I wanted to spend a little more time on the featured vodka punch." He pulled a prettily printed recipe card from his bag and handed it to Raquel.

She looked it over and nodded. "Poinsettia Punch? This is acceptable. And what about this whiskey drink? Why doesn't it have champagne?"

I explained the recipe, as it was one of mine, and Enzo spoke before she could dismiss me. "It sounds wonderful. We can't have champagne in everything. We need something for the whiskey drinkers. It is America, is it not?"

His charm made me dizzy.

"If Enzo's fine with it, I suppose I am," Raquel said. "He'll work with you to make sure you have what you require. He needs something to do while he's living off my dime."

Enzo chuckled, but I wasn't sure it was a joke. "I'm happy to help while I'm in town discussing business," he said. "Not much business gets done over the holidays."

"Just a lot of drinking," I pointed out.

Enzo smiled. "Mostly I am sightseeing."

"I have a list of what we need," Neil, immune to the banter, said to Enzo. "Can you give me your email?"

"*C'est bien.*" He handed Neil a business card.

I saw an opportunity. "Where are you sightseeing?" I asked Enzo. "Have you tried an airboat ride? They're really fun. And fast."

"No. A boat that floats on air?"

I giggled. "Almost. It skims the water thanks to a very loud jet engine."

"Propeller," Neil corrected me, giving me a *Don't you dare* glare.

"Whatever. We got to cruise past the old Boyle place this morning. I understand you own that, Raquel?"

Her eyebrows lifted, and she sat up a little straighter as she considered me. "Are you interested in real estate, Pepper?"

"Not—I mean, a little bit. As a business owner." I felt like such a fraud. "I just thought it was interesting you had a renter out there."

Raquel leaned back again but rocked slightly in her chair. "She came with the contract," Raquel said dryly.

"It's such a shame, what happened to her."

Raquel's face turned a whiter shade of pale, but it was Enzo who came out of his slouch and spoke. "Something happened?"

"It's so sad. Alice Dalworth was found dead this morning."

Both Enzo and Raquel now stared at me with total focus. "Dead?" she asked, her tone still dry. "How unfortunate."

"Yes. Very unfortunate." I could feel Neil's eyes scorching my scalp as I continued and Enzo's gaze drifted away. "I just thought it was interesting that you had a renter on a property like that."

Raquel lifted an eyebrow and pressed her phone screen. "Fiji water," she barked. She cleared her throat.

Then she looked at me. "It was an unusual arrangement, to be sure. To purchase the property, I had to agree to honor the long-term lease Bill Boyle had set up with Dr. Dalworth. He said she was doing important research. I play a long game, and I'm used to waiting for what I want. I was in no hurry to develop that land, but I was anxious to get ahold of it." A note of sarcasm crept into her voice. "The dry parts, at least, are quite valuable."

Funny. Captain Vance would've said the wet parts were what was valuable.

Lissa burst through the door carrying a tray full of bottles of Fiji water. No local water for Raquel. Raquel was the only one who took a bottle, and Lissa hustled back out to her lair with the still-loaded tray, awkwardly closing the door behind her. Raquel took a long drink, put down the bottle, and smiled at Neil like a gator who'd swallowed a cat.

"Well, I think we should be going," he said. Now I couldn't agree more. "If we need anything, we'll talk to Enzo. Thanks again for thinking of us."

Raquel nodded. "You're the best. I've seen you in action." In fact, Raquel had seen us lose a cocktail contest for which she was a judge, but she was right. We *were* the best. "You know, if I can answer any questions personally, please call me," she purred to Neil. "Here's my cell number."

She scribbled on a business card and handed it to him with a flutter of her heavily mascaraed eyelashes, and I almost choked.

"I'll walk you out." Enzo stood, and we followed him out the door, which he closed behind us. I waved at Lissa, who was busy painting the bottom of the other shoe.

"Wait a second!" she called out, setting down the paintbrush and ruffling through a drawer while holding the shoe in her other hand. "Here. My card. Call me if you need anything. Ms. Tocks prefers not to be contacted directly."

Unless it's Neil calling her, apparently.

I tried not to worry as Enzo accompanied us all the way down in the elevator and outside. "It gets a little, how do you say, stuffy in there," he said. "But it is lovely out here."

"Beautiful," I agreed.

Enzo looked at me. "Why don't we set up a meeting to talk about what you need for the event?"

"I'll send you the list," Neil said.

Enzo's eyes held mine. "Oh, but I find personal meetings so much more effective."

I smiled at him. "You could come by my party tonight."

For a second, Neil looked like he was about to pop his cork, then he nodded at Enzo. "We can talk then."

"Ah, but tonight I'm already committed to a party," he said. "I'm meeting someone at Nola, the bar in Bohemia."

"That's my bar! That's my party!" I grinned at him. "Who are you meeting?"

"Well, I don't know if I should say."

"The only people coming are our friends, so I know everyone who will be there."

"Ah, then you know Oleanna Lee?" Huh. Enzo knew our movie-star friend.

"We sure do," I said. "We met her at the film festival here. How do you know her?"

"I'm talking to her about a marketing campaign for my champagne. But shhhh." Enzo put a finger to his lips. "It's a secret. All right?"

"Sure," I said, and Enzo smiled.

Neil, resigned to my impulses, added, "Great. We'll see you tonight."

"Wonderful." Enzo took Neil's card, sketched a little bow to me and went back into the building.

"I like how you pulled that vodka drink out of your hat back there," I told Neil.

"I'm aware of her tastes. I try to be prepared." He glanced

at me as we walked back to the car. "You really had to ask her about the swamp?"

"Wasn't her reaction weird? You'd think she'd be more shocked about Alice." My mind was already working overtime. "And that info about the lease was really interesting. She couldn't develop the land with Alice still there. It's awfully convenient that she isn't anymore. I mean, it's horrible, but for Raquel, it's *really* convenient."

Neil unlocked the doors, and we climbed in. "I don't think you can judge anything from her reaction. She's not the warm and fuzzy type."

"Oh my God! Lissa is like her personal slave. She probably knows where all the bodies are buried, so to speak." I turned to Neil. "It looked like Raquel wanted to take a bite out of you, too."

Neil looked over at me, his dark-blue-rimmed gray eyes smoky. "I'm reserving that privilege for someone else."

Yeooow! Did it just get hot in here?

He was such a tease. Two could play at that game. "I'm glad Enzo is coming to the party. That accent!" I looked over at Neil to get his reaction, but I could tell he was trying not to smile. He had me figured out. I might get distracted by a hot dude with a French accent, but Neil was my catnip, and he knew it.

"I wonder what he knows about Raquel," he said.

"And what he's doing in town with her." If Alice was murdered, Raquel was a prime suspect with a lot to gain, and Enzo might have inside information. "I'm going to find out."

Chapter Eight

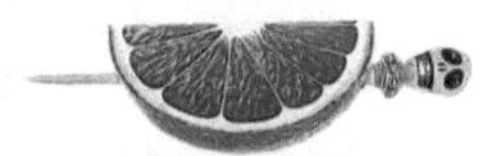

"I miss all the good stuff!" Melody exclaimed after I told her what had happened earlier in the day.

"I'm not sure I'd call it good stuff," I said in a lower tone of voice as I pushed an Air Mail in a Collins glass across the bar to her. Served over ice with a curlicue of lime peel, the classic dark amber cocktail featured champagne but also had rum, lime juice and honey. Neil planned to serve it on New Year's Eve.

I answered all of Melody's questions as I spun up drinks behind the bar at Nola, the bar-restaurant I owned with my business partner, Jorge Listo. In his late thirties with dark, wavy hair and brown eyes, he shot me one of his friendly smiles from down the bar. He loved this break from his engineer life. He had the week off from his job at the Space Center and was helping me serve drinks tonight.

Decorated in dark wood, gilt trim, damask wallpaper and lush details, with art and masks I'd picked up in New Orleans, our NOLA-themed joint wasn't packed. Still, the main dining room was full of our chatting, laughing friends enjoying a self-serve punch, our handcrafted cocktails, and platters of delicious munchies from the kitchen. A mix of New Orleans jazz, rock and the occasional retro Christmas tune played on the sound system. A glistening Christmas tree sporting lots of purple and gold in a corner gave the room a festive air.

Melody, my blue-eyed blond best friend and fellow Bohemia Bartender, wore a fabulous short dress covered in reflective green fringe. The deep V-neck was sexy, given her perfect figure, but she sort of looked like a disco piñata.

I'd also worn green to bring out my eyes, a sleeveless satin number with a retro sweetheart neckline and a full skirt that wrapped around from high to low for an uneven hemline. It puffed out thanks to the red crinoline peeking from beneath. A sheer black shrug matched my black nerd glasses and gator-tooth bracelet, and vintage red costume jewelry and red lipstick topped off my holiday look. Plus, I wore funky sparkly red sneakers, since I was working.

"So," Melody asked me, "how's the dating experiment going?"

"That's a good way to put it. Sometimes I think it's exploding in my face. We hardly ever get together because we both work such crazy hours. Once we tried to go to a concert, and Neil got a flat tire. Another time we had tickets to a Chamberlain Theater matinee and the power went out."

"Oh, I remember that day. All of downtown was out. Great for making out, though." Melody lifted an eyebrow.

"If they hadn't kicked us out, maybe. Our next chance was that movie night at his place, which was really fun, but it ended with him kicking *me* out, so I don't know if making out was even on the table."

"You had a fight?"

"No. He just told me he was tired and I should go home. We had a solid good-night kiss, though." I got tingly just thinking of it.

"Hmm," she said. "Haven't you tried to jump his bones?"

I sniffed and took a sip of the Sazerac I was nursing behind the bar. "I have some pride. I've thrown myself at him enough. But he's trying my patience. He's just so *nice* about it."

"That's Neil." Melody looked around—Neil still hadn't arrived—then back at me. "What are you getting him for Christmas?"

"What?" Panic seized me. I'd been so busy, I hadn't even thought about what I was getting him for Christmas. *Oh my God.* It was Christmas Eve *eve!* Even if I wanted to, I had no time to produce something amazeballs, did I? "Am I supposed to get him something? I mean, I guess we're dating. Sort of. Whoa no. I have no idea!"

"And you want to make sure you get him something that's on the level he's getting you," she said, "to avoid extreme awkwardness. I mean, normally in a relationship, you could just show up in a red satin negligee and a Santa hat and any normal guy would be thrilled."

"But Neil isn't normal," we both said at the same time, then laughed.

"I mean, he's not abnormal," I added. "Just weirdly traditional. Or maybe he's playing mind games with me."

Melody took another long sip and sighed. "I think he's courting you. It's kind of sweet."

I didn't have time to think about her notion before the door opened again. "Hey, look who it is!" I called out to Barclay and Luke.

The guys each wore holiday aloha shirts. Barclay's green and red floral pattern complemented his light brown skin and pale green eyes. Luke's shirt was bright red with embroidered green palm fronds and a couple of funny parrots on one side, with a Santa poking up from the pocket on the other. It didn't match his brown eyes, but they twinkled anyway. While

Barclay had short, black curly hair, Luke's was longish, light brown and streaked with blond.

They both had tattoos running up their arms, as did Melody. Barclay's included a dragon and Korean characters; Luke's featured tropical foliage and parrots; and Melody's, flowers and musical notes. The only one I had was hidden from view on my lower back, a cocktail-shaker-turned-rocket flying to the stars. The jury was out on whether Neil had any hidden away, but in spite of his teasing hints, my bet was on a big *no*.

"I had to wait till it calmed down so I could leave the club to the staff," Barclay said. "It's Monday, but it's the holidays, so people want to party." He managed a nightclub in downtown Bohemia, not far from my bar.

"And Neil is working us to death," Luke said to our laughter. "He's still there."

"At the Junction Box? He'd better get over here," I said.

"We're closing early tonight, so he'll be here soon," Luke replied. "Crazy week. I mean, even I have to work the bar New Year's Eve."

The Junction Box had its own party New Year's Eve, so instead of joining us for Raquel Tocks's ballroom gig, Luke, as a good employee of Neil's, would be in charge of things at his bar.

Melody's hotel bar was closed that night—probably wise—and I had no idea how Barclay had gotten out of working his regular job on New Year's Eve.

He lit up just then because Gina walked in. A slender, pretty computer geek who also worked at the Space Center, she was Jorge's youngest sister and shared his long nose and dark eyes that crinkled at the corners. She was also Barclay's sweetheart.

I hooked them all up with cocktails and filled them in on our strange day, leaving out the detail about the letter. I didn't want anyone to overhear and accidentally get Diana in trouble.

"You're like a death magnet, Pepper." Luke sipped his gin-champagne punch and eyed me.

"Ouch. Not true!" I protested. "We just happened to be in the wrong place at the right time. Or whatever you want to call it."

"Poor Diana," Melody said. "Is she coming tonight?"

"Mark took her to the police interview. They're supposed to be here." I was a little worried about them, too.

Barclay caught my tone. "Don't worry. I'm sure she didn't get arrested."

"I should hope not." But his words eased my fears. He knew more than average about law enforcement since his dad was a police detective in South Florida.

They scattered to mingle as the next half hour brought a swirl of arrivals and hellos and sips with our friends: Our planner and organizer Millie and her sand-sculpting boyfriend, Bennett. Dash Reynolds of Bohemia Distillery. Alastair Markham, Neil's frenemy mixologist from London, who sniffed at me and demanded a French 75. Our friends Dick and Dale from Cocoa Beach, who'd gotten married during the Hookahakaha weekend. Mr. Mixy, who asked for a vodka tonic and went on the prowl. Alex and Sloane and the whole clique of friends who knew one another from the local art and theater scene, including our costume designer friend Penelope and her boyfriend, Jace Edison, a ridiculously hot film and stage actor who caused a collective swoon when he walked in.

Then Oleanna Lee arrived, and those two movie stars had an intense chat, no doubt talking shop.

Royce and Aunt Celestine showed up with Astra and

Victoria. I'd let the dogs come since it was a private party, but as Victoria charmed everyone, Astra stayed standoffish. I'd never seen her this jealous before. And Cray and Gramps Rockaway rolled in, already giddy, confessing to pre-gaming with some very fine rum.

But I didn't know how much tension I harbored till Neil arrived, still in his bow tie. No, wait—a new bow tie. This one sported holly leaves and berries against a black background. He came up to me, leaned across the bar and gave me a peck on the cheek.

"Hi." I smiled at him as a flush of heat shot through me.

He smiled back. "Sorry I'm late. Trying to get things set up for the week."

"I haven't seen Enzo yet."

"He texted me. He'll be here. Said he was having a late business dinner with Raquel."

"Gee, that sounds like fun."

Neil chuckled at my wry tone. "Need help back there?"

"I think we've got it." Just then, the front door—where I'd hung a sign that said "Closed for private event"—opened to reveal Mark and Diana. I let out a sigh of relief. "Finally."

"I was wondering how the interview went." Neil turned to greet them, shaking Mark's hand and giving Diana a brief side-hug. Diana, I was surprised to see, had changed out of her traditional adventure girl outfit. Sure, she still wore khaki pants, but over a silky white blouse she wore a soft-looking shawl in sage green, and her simple diamond stud earrings sparkled.

"I'm so glad to see you. You were so late, I worried," I told both of them. Celestine and Royce drifted over to get the scoop.

"I took Diana out to dinner at a lovely Italian place called Marco's," Mark said. "Good name."

"And good food," Diana agreed. "He bullied me into it, but I do love a good pesto dish."

"I thought she needed a quiet moment to unwind, though I wouldn't say no to a drink now," Mark added. "Something with rum?"

"And champagne?" I asked. "How about an Air Mail?"

"Excellent," he said, and Diana added, "I'll take one, too."

I looked them over as I made the drinks. Mark was his usual jolly self, and Diana seemed calm if distracted. With Royce and Celestine, our entire airboat crew was here except Mr. Mixy, who was trying to chat up Oleanna Lee and Melody over by the Christmas tree.

"How did it go today?" Aunt Celestine asked.

"Awful," Diana said. "Irritating. They wouldn't tell me anything."

"At least you're not in jail," Mark said. "Not that you should be, but you know."

Diana nodded at Neil. "I'm grateful your father came to represent me."

Neil looked surprised. "He came himself?"

"He said it was the least he could do for a friend of yours." Diana smiled. "It was all handled cordially, given the ghastly circumstances. They seem to know him well and respect him."

"And they don't think you did it?" I asked, then bit my lip.

Mark snorted, and Neil gave me one of his "really?" looks, but then he was distracted by me biting my lip. So I gave him a coquettish glance. Satisfyingly ruffled, he turned back to Diana.

"I don't think I'm a suspect," she said, "but Detective Keene and Officer Ernie were quite tough on me. I explained exactly what happened when I found Alice. They wanted to know if I'd seen anyone else around."

"Had you?" Neil asked.

"No, though I thought I might've heard another boat on my way there, perhaps even in the distance after I stopped. But that's not unusual. All sorts of boats were out on the river, and mine was loud enough to drown out half of them."

"Do they think she was murdered?" Aunt Celestine asked.

Diana shook her head. "I don't believe so. I think they're more or less in agreement she died of misadventure, but Ernie seemed concerned when I told them I didn't think Alice was doing fish counts. Or fishing, for that matter. It's not clear why she would have electrofishing equipment."

"Maybe someone just left it there and she didn't know what it was and, you know," Royce suggested.

"Zap," said Mr. Mixy, who'd snuck up behind our group as we were talking.

Diana shuddered as I tried to drill holes in Mr. Mixy's head with my eyes.

I changed the subject. "That's a beautiful shawl you're wearing," I told Diana.

Her expression softened. "Thank you. I purchased it in Peru on one of my expeditions. Alpaca."

Aunt Celestine patted her shoulder and pronounced it softer than Astra, and the door to the bar opened again, revealing Enzo Desjardins in a sleek, dark blue suit, no tie, dashing and handsome in the continental way.

"Oh, my," my aunt said.

"*And* he's French," I added.

"Tell me more." Celestine took a sip of her drink, and she and Diana scrutinized Enzo as he looked around uncertainly until his gaze alighted on Neil and me.

"We have business to discuss," Neil said as Enzo smiled and headed our way.

Geez, what a buzzkill. Why rush into business? Aunt Celestine was interested, and maybe Enzo was available. My aunt almost never expressed an interest in men. She never seemed to want to put herself through the hoops required to date.

But Aunt Celestine just shot me an amused glance, shrugged and led Diana and the others down to Jorge's end of the bar. Enzo came up to Neil and me.

"Mr. Rockaway," Enzo greeted him. "Ms. Revelle."

"Mr. Desjardins," I said, trying to pretend I knew French when I pronounced his name. "Can we just go with Enzo, Neil and Pepper?"

A corner of his mouth lifted. "Of course. I see Ms. Lee—Oleanna over there, but perhaps we can talk about the party first? Is there anything special you need?"

"Just a moment," Neil said. He walked away.

"Okaaaay." I quirked my mouth at Enzo, who chuckled. "What can I make you?"

"You specialize in whiskey drinks here?"

"How about a Whiskey Spritz with whiskey and champagne? And apricot brandy and a special aperitif I think you might like."

"Marvelous." He watched me work.

"Tell me about your champagne."

Enzo gave me a mischievous look. "I hear it's very good."

"You *know* it's very good. I've tasted it. It's wonderful." I stirred ice into the Japanese whiskey and the aperitif in a delicate round glass. "I mean, tell me about your operation."

He nodded. "It's not large. Not that long ago, it existed mainly to supply the big houses with grapes. But I inherited it from my parents at quite a young age and decided to focus on bottling the fruit myself, to make something unique and better than what is often considered the best by the world at large."

Better than the best? Enzo didn't lack for ego. "What makes it different?"

"I only use perfectly ripe fruit, for one. Many growers and bottlers pick their fruit far too early. Of course there's a risk of waiting too long or poor weather claiming the crop, but my results speak for themselves. My grapes are gently cultivated, not drenched in pesticides. The terroir helps. The grapes grow on the south sides of hills, for the most part, and the qualities of the land are not blended away in great vats with grapes from so many growers."

"Fascinating." I'd added apricot brandy, then topped the drink with champagne—not Enzo's, but a good one nonetheless. "I'd love to visit Champagne one day."

"That can be arranged." His eyes twinkled as he accepted the cocktail from me, garnished with raspberries and a strawberry. He took a sip. "Lovely. And I am pleased to see you using true champagne and not your sparkling wines."

"Of course." I was glad I hadn't pulled out one of my favorite California sparklers. Officially, champagne came from the Champagne region of France, but it had become a term that most people, including me, used as shorthand for any kind of sparkling wine.

Neil came back, accompanied by a cute couple. "Pepper, do you know Landon and Kayla?"

"Of course. How are you guys? Having fun?"

"Oh, yeah," said Kayla, who wore a green velvet dress and her long, light-brown hair up in a twist. "This punch is killer."

Hopefully not *killer*, given my day.

Landon, broad-shouldered with short, dark hair, a beautiful

smile and a skinny tie, had an arm draped around Kayla's shoulders. "It's great. You want to talk about the party?"

Kayla owned historic Milkweed Mansion, once known as Bohemia's most famous haunted house. Landon specialized in restoring old houses, and they'd worked together to turn it into a popular venue for weddings and parties, including Raquel Tocks's New Year's Eve charity event for the zoo.

I let Neil do the official Bohemia Bartenders rundown with Enzo, Kayla and Landon while I helped Jorge fill our thirsty friends' orders, then drifted back down the bar when Kayla and Landon walked away and Oleanna Lee came over.

"Oleanna! It's so nice to see you again," I told her. "Need a drink?"

The leggy Chinese-American star from Hawaii, in a simple, stunning black sheath dress, lifted her champagne glass half-filled with the gin-champagne punch. "I'm delirious. This is Mark's gin, isn't it?"

"It is." I'd kind of hoped Oleanna and Mark would hit it off after Mark's round of flirtation with me, but I hadn't seen sparks fly yet. Maybe the holidays would do it. "What are you up to?"

"Developing a new project. Producing and directing a little indie movie, actually. Not much call for fortysomething actresses, but I just so happen to star in it. It's a labor of love."

"There will always be a need for elegance like yours," Enzo purred.

She looked at him with delight. "You're Enzo, aren't you?"

Enchantée." He touched his glass to hers, and his hazel eyes crinkled at the corners. "A pleasure to finally meet you in person."

"We have a lot to discuss." Oleanna's sultry tone suggested

she was talking about more than the endorsement deal Enzo had mentioned earlier.

"I hope so," he said. They sipped their drinks and eyed each other. A few drops sloshed out of Enzo's glass as he stared her down. Was he nervous? I supposed movie stars made a lot of people nervous.

"There's a nice cozy spot by the Christmas tree." Oleanna gestured to the corner, and they drifted off, basking in each other's glow.

Neil watched them go. "Hmph. And what were you two chatting about?"

"You were standing right there. Her new movie," I said, pretending not to know what he meant.

"Not Oleanna. Enzo."

I cocked my head at him. "Grapes."

Neil just stared at me for a second, and then he laughed. "Touché."

"Want a drink?"

"Please."

I made Neil a Vieux Carré, one of his favorites, as Diana and Mark came back over to us.

Mark had better up his game if he wanted a shot at Oleanna against the suave Frenchman, but he was his usual happy-go-lucky self. "Pepper, Diana wants a word," he said in a low voice.

"I don't need your introduction," she told him, then turned to me. "I want to go back to the shack, and I want you to go with me."

"You what? Why me?" Especially when I hated boats.

"Because you're scrappy and curious, and I think you'd be an asset," she said. "I've been thinking about Alice. She never really told me what she's working on, and that strange letter seemed to indicate it was important to her. I think we should go back and look."

"Surely the cops have grabbed her stuff by now," I said. "There was a lot on her desk."

"So you saw inside?" Diana gave me a knowing look.

"I—um—"

"We both did," Neil said. "And you obviously did, too, if you found the letter. Why do you want to go back?"

"Perhaps the police didn't take everything," she said. "Or anything, if they didn't think it was a crime scene. I want to see if I can find her notes. Even if her death was just a tragic mishap, I'd like to help save her work if I can. She was a friend."

Well, I could hardly turn down a request from a friend, for a friend. "How would we get there?"

Mark smiled. "I've already pinged Otter Vance. He said he'd take us for an exorbitant fee."

"Of course," I said.

"At least Mark will be spending his money on something worthwhile," Diana snarked. "Neil, will you come?"

I could see the gears turning in his head. "I have a lot of work to do. But we have limited hours tomorrow, since it's Christmas Eve. I can make it happen."

Great! Or not? If Neil was with me, I couldn't shop for a Christmas present for him. Then again, what was I going to buy? A shellacked gator head from the fish camp gift shop?

"Is anyone else going?" I asked.

"I think we should keep this little operation stealthy and tidy," Mark said, "so as not to have everyone we know cooling their heels in the nick."

Diana laughed. And I chuckled till Mark spoke again.

"We need to be at the boat ramp at 8 a.m.," he said.

"I'll drive us over there," Neil volunteered. "Pepper, I'll pick you and Diana up first, at 7:15, then Mark."

I groaned. Were sleep deprivation and a bumpy boat ride any way to spend the morning after a party?

I needed another Sazerac.

Chapter Nine

I didn't see this time of day very often, but the morning air was fresh and birds sang as we stood by the dock at Whirlwind Airboat Tours. Stupid chipper birds.

It was dawn—dawn!—when Neil picked up Diana and me from Bohemia Beach. The sky glowed in pastels over the ocean, as I saw when we picked up Mark at his condo, but come on. Were people really meant to be up this early? Especially after two or three Sazeracs? And maybe a glass of champagne punch?

Diana wasn't chatty, to my relief, but she was at full energy. A morning person, clearly. She'd had a go-cup of tea in the car, while I drank coffee. And Mark, ever cheerful, must have the constitution of an ox after the beverages he'd consumed last night.

He wore cargo shorts, a T-shirt, and a floppy hat—a wise choice given his ginger complexion. He had a fancy camera slung over his shoulder.

"You into photography?" I asked him as we stood there watching Otter Vance prep the airboat.

Mark held up the camera and regarded it with indifference. "Not particularly, but Diana suggested we might want to document what we see today. I was told this was the best, so that's what I bought."

Of course. Following that logic, my bar would be full of impossible-to-afford liquors. In fact, Jorge, who kept a close eye on the books, had told me I needed to sell more of my collectible quaffs before I stocked any more. I respected his direction, but part of the pleasure of owning a bar was proximity to beautiful, delicious, rare elixirs. I liked seeing them on the shelves. And there was always a tourist who asked for "the best whiskey/gin/rum you've got" and paid accordingly.

"I've been thinking about Raquel Tocks buying the Boyle property," I said. "She would have only one reason to do that, and that's to develop it. It's what she does."

"And now she can," Neil pointed out.

"Exactly." I shifted my cross-body bag on my shoulder. "She has every reason to be glad Alice is no longer on the property."

"And you're suggesting she might have helped her along, shall we say?" Mark asked.

"I'm just saying we should keep it in mind."

"A development there would destroy sensitive habitat for any number of plants and animals," said Diana, who'd donned her usual adventure khakis and carried her seasoned backpack. "I'd imagine there are practical challenges as well, given how wet it is."

"It must be dry enough on the part of the property where the house was built," Neil speculated.

"What all is out there besides water lilies?" I asked, knowing Diana had explored for a couple of days on her own before her appointment to see Alice.

Her face lit up. "Wonderful plants! I especially enjoy the carnivorous ones—pitcher plants, butterwort, sundews. Of course, there are interesting non-natives too, like what you might call nutmeg plant or Barbados nut—you can break a leaf stem and blow bubbles from it! It has medicinal properties but is considered invasive." She was on a roll, and her energy was contagious. "Did you know Florida has more than a hundred native orchids? Hawaii has just two. Some of your plants are quite rare and grow in microclimates that can't be found anywhere else. Of course, that means they're threatened as well." She glanced at Mark. "I'm not sure yet if any of them are suitable for botanicals for your gin, but if so, we'd have to find a sustainable way to source them, if not here, then elsewhere in Florida."

"All right," Otter Vance called from the boat. "Everybody empty? I'm all set."

We looked at each other. We'd all availed ourselves of the restroom at the restaurant, which was serving breakfast.

"We're good," Mark said. "Let's go."

We didn't try to talk over the roaring engine as we bounced and skimmed along the St. Johns and connected waterways. My tummy tolerated the ride fairly well. Maybe because I'd had a couple of my aunt's cookies with my coffee this morning to neutralize the acid. We didn't dillydally, though there was plenty to see, from elegant wading birds to a smattering of alligators sunning themselves on muddy banks. We weren't in tourist mode today. Captain Vance took us right to the Swamp Shack.

Still, we had a good twenty-five minutes of twists and turns before we entered the clearing amid the cypress and oak trees and saw the shack, peaceful on its stilts. Reflections from the water shimmered over its weathered wood surface.

Captain Vance slowed the boat and approached the dock at a crawl.

"I don't want to cross any police lines," he called out over the idling motor. "But I don't see any tape."

"They don't think it's a crime scene," Diana said.

"Yet," I added, and the others looked at me.

Diana's rental boat was gone—the police must have taken it away—but the two-seater green kayak was still there. "That must have been Alice's," Diana said. "She'd said something in the email about us going out paddling."

"I don't like this," Captain Vance said. "We might not want to linger."

I surely wasn't the only one who pictured Officer Ernie showing up in his game warden boat. He hadn't told us to stay away, but our very presence here might be considered suspicious.

"Why don't you wander off and come back in half an hour?" Neil asked. "Drop a line somewhere."

Otter Vance's worry lines relaxed as the rest of us nodded. "Good idea," he said. "Ping my phone if you need me sooner."

He let us off at the dock, then spun the boat out of the clearing and disappeared into the trees.

"Good thinking," Mark told Neil.

"Our presence will be less obvious without that big boat hanging around," Neil said. Ooo, I loved it when Neil gave in to his devious instincts. He kept them on a short leash.

"What will happen to all of Alice's stuff?" I asked as we walked down the long dock toward the steps to the shack's door.

"I honestly don't know," Diana said. "I would hope her landlord would attempt to deliver it to her next of kin, presumably in Britain, but I don't really know if she has any. Her parents are dead, and she was an only child, unmarried. Would some distant cousin want bits and pieces of her life here?"

"In other words, we shouldn't feel bad about rescuing her work," Mark said, bolstering our purpose.

We climbed the steps and crammed onto the landing at the shack's front door. The boards protested with a creak.

"Um ..." I looked down through the slats at the water. Was Phantom down there?

"No worries. Solid as a rock," Mark said. He pulled a handkerchief from his pocket, wrapped it around his hand and tried to turn the doorknob. "Uh-oh."

"It wasn't locked before!" I said.

"The police must have locked it. Or someone else." Neil sounded grim. "I guess that's it."

"Oh, come on." Mark examined the distressed wood of the door. "The Big Bad Wolf could blow this down."

"We could see if it takes credit cards." I was sure I'd seen this trick on *Law & Order*.

"I don't know if that works in real life." Diana sounded weary.

"Depends on the lock," Neil said. "Go ahead, Pepper. Try a thin card."

Hmm. Neil's criminal knowledge went deeper than I'd realized.

I found my wallet in the depths of my bag—that stupid box I'd gotten in the mail was still in there; I needed to do something about that—and pulled out a card. "Will a Cheesy Does It loyalty card work?"

"You have a Cheesy Does It loyalty card?" Neil asked.

"Hey, every tenth purchase, you get a free block of sharp cheddar."

Mark chortled. "You really should be English, Hot Pepper."

I just gestured to my curves, wrapped in jeans and a black V-neck tee. "Everything you see I owe to cheese."

Mark's eyes followed my motion, and he grinned.

"Get on with it, won't you?" Diana prompted.

"Sorry." I bent down—I didn't have to go far, considering my height—and eased the card into the narrow crevice between the door and the doorframe. The fact that the frame had been worn there from years of use only helped me, giving me a bit more wiggle room to slide the card forward and press against the strike plate—and, hopefully, the latch.

It gave with a gentle pop. I turned the knob and pushed. "We're in!"

"All well and good, but be careful, all right?" Mark wiped the doorknob with the handkerchief, then followed me in. "Don't touch anything you don't have to."

"We'll gather any notes she has, take a quick look around and get out," Diana promised. She gestured to the table by the door to the screened porch, where that strapped wooden box still sat next to the microscope. "Too bad I can't take her microscope and plant press, but that might look odd if anyone asked."

Still, we all took a moment and stood at the center of the room. Three of us had been here before. My sense was that little had changed, but it felt disrupted, rearranged. Though the furniture was still there and the plants still sat in their trays out on the screened porch.

"I expect the police have had a go," Diana said.

"The laptop is gone," I pointed out. "Isn't that where she'd keep her scientific notes?"

"Possibly," Diana said. "But probably not all of them. I prefer paper notebooks in the field. They're hard to erase, people don't want to steal them, and they never need charging up."

"Are any of those notebooks?" Neil took a step toward the desk and pointed to the two loaded bookshelves we'd seen on our first visit.

Diana and I joined him while Mark walked around the space, checking out the odd little kitchen and the shower tub and taking photos. I watched as he opened the narrow closet between the desk space and the kitchen to find it stuffed with cleaning supplies, a pile of small plastic boxes and a few clothes, shoes and jackets—nothing remarkable. I turned my attention back to the books.

"This looks promising." Diana ran a finger along a few slim volumes that had colored bindings with patterns but no writing on the spines. She pulled out one with a red binding, whose cover sported yellow drawings of flowers. "If it was the police who took her laptop, they must not have considered these important."

"If they even noticed these," I said.

She opened the book and flipped through the pages, which had lines on left-hand pages and grids on the right. "Wouldn't have mattered. It's blank."

She put it back and pulled out the next, with a blue binding, covered with artistic renderings of mathematical calculations and constellations. This one had writing on the pages.

"Looks like accounting," I said as she flipped through. "Expenses."

"And grocery lists." Diana sounded amused. And a little bit sad.

Milk. Tea. Pasta. Bananas. Simple foods for a simple life.

"Try the next one," I suggested.

She put the blue book back and retrieved the one with the green binding. The cover was printed with sketches of plants and faux botanical notations in white and dark green. "These are lovely. I should buy some," Diana remarked, then opened it. "Golly."

She flipped through it. There was a great deal of writing in this one, along with charming sketches of plants. But it just didn't compute.

"Is that English?" I asked.

Neil peered over our shoulders. "I don't think it's anything."

The writing just didn't make sense. There were words, but they didn't spell anything that I could make out.

I looked at Neil to see if he was thinking what I was thinking.

"I wonder if it could be some kind of code," Diana said.

So she was thinking it, too.

At the sound of a motor, we all froze.

"Is it Otter?" Neil asked.

"Mark?" Diana called.

He was already moving to a window that looked out through the screened porch. "Motorboat. Not the airboat."

"Be cool," Neil said. "They might just be passing by."

Diana stuffed the notebook in her bag, and we all lined up at the porch windows.

The small boat was not just passing by. It pulled up next to the dock. The motor cut off, and a wiry, balding little man with skin like tanned leather, wearing long shorts, a white shirt halfway open down his chest, a gold chain and thick leather sandals, hopped out and tied off the boat.

He looked around furtively.

Then he made his way down the dock toward us.

Chapter Ten

"Crapnoodles," I hissed.

By instinct, we scattered to the few windows around the place, each of us trying to see where the interloper was headed.

I ended up at the window that looked out on the stairs and beyond. Sure enough, the man headed into the trees. "Outhouse," I whispered as he opened the skinny door and headed inside.

"Everybody has to go sometime," Mark said, and the three of them crowded up behind me, waiting.

Two long minutes went by. "What's he doing in there?" I asked.

"What do you think?" Neil asked dryly.

"Shhh," Diana said. "Here he comes."

The man took his time, looking around, and then he disappeared out of view beneath us. The others scattered to the other windows.

"I see him now. He's trying to open that wooden bench at the land end of the dock," Neil said softly. He had a better angle than I did. "It's locked."

The rest of us hustled over to stand behind Neil, watching, so he didn't have to explain. The man headed back toward the shack, then reappeared a moment later before we had time to panic. He had a shovel in his hand.

"That must have been in that pile of stuff under the tarp behind the shack," I said.

The man lifted the shovel and slammed the spade end down on the padlock. The sound ricocheted like a bullet through the clearing, and I think we all jumped. But the lock held.

Now we said nothing, held rapt by the upsetting inevitability of this stranger opening the box and violating Alice's trust. I figured the same rules didn't apply to us, since we knew her. Or maybe this guy knew her, too?

He hammered at it again and again. I pulled my phone out and took a couple of photos as he worked. Mark, apparently inspired, did the same with his camera.

Finally, it wasn't the lock that broke. The hardware that held it failed and hung loose, dangling by a screw. The man yanked off the latch and tossed it into the water. Then he froze, looking toward the shore. At what, I wasn't sure.

Finally, he hurled the shovel in the direction he'd been looking, reached down and flipped open the lid of the box.

"What's in there?" I whispered.

But there was no answer. And given his quick riffle through the contents—and the life jackets and coil of rope he tossed to the dock—not much. The man threw the flotsam back in and closed the lid.

"Picky thief?" Neil murmured.

The man stood up straight, turned and looked right at us.

We gasped and stepped back. "Did he see us?" Diana said.

I waited a moment, then crept forward and saw him reach the bottom of the steps. "I don't think so, or he wouldn't be coming this way after breaking open the box in full view."

"So now he's looking for something else to steal?" Diana asked.

"Or he wants to kill the witnesses," Mark said idly.

Diana elbowed him. "For breaking a lock on a box?"

"Or he realizes we just saw the killer return to the scene of the crime," I suggested. "Maybe we should hide." I pointed to the tiny loft where Alice had slept.

"Don't be ridiculous," Mark said, slinging his camera cross-body over his shoulder. "I'll lock the door."

But he was halfway across the floor when the knob turned.

One thing I'll say for Mark. He was always ready to wade into action.

And as the door opened, he rushed it, bellowing, *"What the hell are you doing here?"*

The man screamed and stumbled backward, his few remaining brown hairs flying about his head, and Mark slammed the door shut and locked it.

I clapped my hand over my mouth to keep from laughing out loud.

"Maybe we should ask him in a more civilized manner," Neil said, but it was too late. The man half ran, half fell down the steps, sprinted down the dock, freed his boat and cranked it up. He swept out of the clearing on a whine of overtaxed engine.

"I'd say that was a missed opportunity," Diana said coolly.

Mark shrugged. "I scared him off, didn't I? And after his stunt with the box, I doubt he'll tell someone about finding *us* here. He probably has no idea who we are anyway."

"Probably," I mused. There was something about the man ... "The thing is, he looked familiar. What if he already knows who we are?"

"Familiar? Tosh." Mark waved the notion away.

I looked at Neil. "I swear—"

"Holy hell." Neil's eyes widened. "It's impossible."

"What? Out with it," Diana demanded.

I nodded. "He looked like that little man from the treasure museum in Fort Lauderdale, the one with the shipwreck rum."

"Davy Jones's Locker," Neil said. "Could it be?"

Mark stood there with his mouth agape. "You're imagining things. It's Florida. How many sun-wizened old fellows in sandals, raggedy short pants and hairy chests are there here?"

"Thousands, but that's not the point," I said. "I think it was him. What was his name? Thor something?"

"Thor Roberts," Neil said. "What would a treasure museum owner be doing here?"

We exchanged a look.

"Treasure hunting?" I asked incredulously.

The roar of another motor in the distance brought us back to the windows.

Mark clapped his hands together. "It's Otter. Let's get out of here."

We practically sprinted for the door. Using his handkerchief, Mark pressed the button to lock it before he closed it behind us.

"I want to look at the box," I said as we hit the bottom of the stairs.

"There's nothing in it," Neil said.

"Nothing that guy saw. Go ahead. I'll be right there."

"I'll go with you."

I loved that about Neil. He always had my back, even if he thought I was nuts.

Mark and Diana had already turned right, toward the boat. I went left with Neil behind me and approached the box where it was mounted on a small platform at the land end of the dock.

I eased open the lid and looked carefully, but all I saw were the two life jackets and rope, a bilge sponge, two halves of a disassembled paddle—bright green like the kayak—and a bilge pump.

"Just kayak stuff." I recognized kayaking gear because I liked kayaking. I had no problem with small boats I could paddle. It was other kinds of boats that turned me into a frothing volcano.

"Innocent enough," Neil said. "You ready?"

I closed the lid to the sound of a loud *hissssss* and froze. "Neil?" I croaked.

"Look to your right," he whispered.

Not three feet from us, Phantom had appeared—that is to say, the giant alligator had moved, revealing his well-camou-flaged self among the leaf litter along the water's edge, just beyond the platform. Behind him was the shovel the interloper had thrown, which had probably ticked off the beast.

I took a step back, away from the box and the edge of the platform, which was only a shallow step off the ground. An easy step for a dinosaur like Phantom.

The creature eased forward out of the mud and halfway into the water next to us.

I turned and ran down the dock. Neil, laughing, followed at a brisk walk.

"How'd it go?" Captain Vance asked as we settled into the benches of the airboat a minute later, with me puffing for air.

"Uneventful," Mark lied.

I looked back toward the island. Phantom had entered the water and now glided slowly toward us. "Uh, Captain Vance?" I pointed toward the alligator.

"Phantom! Good to see the old boy." Weirdo. Otter eased the boat away from the dock, which was fine with me, because it put more distance between us and the alligator.

Diana pulled her buzzing phone from her bag. "How odd. Someone's texting me."

"Why odd?" Mark asked.

"I don't get many texts, especially when I'm traveling. Oh, dear."

"What is it?" Neil asked.

Captain Vance kept the boat on idle, listening in. "Detective Keene says they are now treating Alice's death as suspicious and she may have more questions for me."

"Then it's a good thing we got in here before they come back and do a real search," I said.

"Is it?" she wondered. "If and when the police come back here, they'll see what—they'll see we've been there." Ah, she didn't want to let Otter Vance know she'd taken the notebook. Probably wise. Besides, he wouldn't want to be accused of tampering with a crime scene.

"If they ask you, I think you should be straight with them. Tell them you came out here to see if you could save any of her work," Neil said. "It's unlikely they'll care we were here anyway. We left it pretty much the same as it was before."

Except we probably didn't, with all our tramping around. But I heard what he wasn't saying. It was unlikely Detective Keene and Game Warden Ernie had done a thorough search in the first place, given they thought Alice had died of an accident outside the shack. If they had, they didn't find the slim notebook interesting enough to take. Just the laptop. That is, assuming someone else didn't take the laptop.

But another thought popped into my head, and my head-mouth connection being what it was, I couldn't stop myself. "They'll see the box."

"What box?" Captain Vance asked.

Argh! I sighed. Might as well tell him. "Oh, that box at the end of the dock had its lock broken off. We didn't do it," I tried to explain.

"Huh," Captain Vance said. "I saw that lock on there when I dropped you off."

Well, wasn't he observant? We were in the middle of the clearing now, and Phantom drifted off to our port side to oversee our departure. But Otter Vance seemed in no hurry to crank up the engine. He wanted an answer.

"Oh, all right," Mark said. "A man came along after you left and smashed it open while we were inside the shack. I don't think he took anything. He was short and tan. Like a wrinkly Oompa-Loompa."

I snickered.

"See anyone like that?" Neil asked our captain.

Captain Vance shook his head. "Not that I know of. He might've gone off in a different direction. You don't know who it was?"

"We don't know," Neil said.

That was true. We didn't *really* know. It might not have been Thor Roberts. But we both had a feeling we recognized him.

Oh, yeah. And I took those phone photos. They might be crappy, but maybe if someone else recognized him, too ...

Who else had been with us that day when we toured the museum?

And would know about treasure hunting?

Captain Vance, his curiosity satisfied, went full throttle,

and the airboat jumped forward, leaving the Swamp Shack and Phantom behind. I pulled out my phone and texted Neil.

He pulled his phone from his pocket and looked at it, then tapped out a message. My phone buzzed in my hands.

"I agree," he'd replied. "We need to talk to Gramps and Cray."

Chapter Eleven

Reginald Rockaway—or as Neil called him, Gramps—had a two-story Mediterranean Revival house in tony south Bohemia Beach, where gorgeous oaks and palms shaded large lots teeming with tropical vegetation. His paver driveway encircled a fountain that featured a busty bronze mermaid. I'd previously learned she was a replica of a figurehead on a sunken ship whose riches Reginald recovered in his treasure-hunting days.

Our burglary crew had spent almost an hour looking through the notebook at Aunt Celestine's with no comprehension of its contents. Some of its sketches were obviously plants, and there were puzzling geometric diagrams of hexagons as well. But the rest was gibberish. Or code.

"I'd like to take a crack at it," Mark had said to our amusement. "Don't laugh. I was quite good at maths at Cambridge. Almost went the theoretical route before I was lured into crass commerce."

So we'd left Mark with Diana and Celestine and headed over to Reginald's. As much as I wanted to dig further into the notebook, right now Neil and I wanted to figure out if we were right about the guy we saw at Alice's shack. Could he really be Thor Roberts, treasure hunter and tourist-trap entrepreneur?

"My boy! And Pepper!" Reginald's smile got even wider

when he saw me. I thought he had high hopes of Neil getting a love life. I hoped Neil had the same idea. "Come in, you two. Cray and I were just having a pre-lunch cocktail."

At the mention of lunch, my stomach growled, and Reginald's eyebrows shot up. "Oh, you poor kids, working twenty-four seven. There's plenty for all. Let me fix you up with a drink. Sandwiches are self-serve. I got plenty of chicken salad at the market."

We walked through the archway of the front door, through the foyer and into the bright, colorful two-story space that was the main room, filled with bookshelves, artifact-stuffed displays, and elegant furniture. A gorgeous art-deco fireplace crackled with a fire, even though it was pleasantly warm outside. A four-foot-tall fake pine tree sat next to it, covered in lights and antique glass ornaments, the only evidence it was Christmas Eve.

An open staircase on the wall opposite led upstairs, and other archways led to a dining room and a Florida room green with plants.

"Neil! And Kayanne Pepper!"

I turned to greet Cray, who'd set his drink on a coffee table in the seating area and stood to greet me. He was about the only person who ever used my given first name.

"Great to see you again." I gave him a hug. "We didn't get much of a chance to talk at the party."

"You were busy. That's quite all right," he drawled in that Savannah accent, which had survived his many years in New Orleans. He smoothed his flyaway white hair. "Reginald and I have so much to talk about."

"Product of living to a ripe old age." For an older guy, widower Reginald still had a decent physique, a couple of sizes bigger than the shrinking Cray, with just a bit of a paunch. His sun-ravaged skin might be a bit loose under his mustache, but he had a charming, mischievous grin. "Scotch?"

"I think a soda would hit the spot," I said. As I chatted with Cray, Neil went to rummage in the kitchen and came back with a tray of root beers, plates, chicken salad sandwiches and potato chips for everyone.

"Thank you, my boy." Reginald gestured to the coffee table, where Neil set down the vittles. Grandfather and grandson each took a soft chair, and I sat next to Cray on the couch.

"So what have you been talking about?" I asked Cray.

"Oh, this and that. Reg has quite a few interesting collections." His pale blue eyes twinkled.

I shook my head. "You're not referring to his ancient dildo collection, are you?"

Cray laughed. "Oh, my. I wouldn't discuss such a thing in mixed company. Don't tell me he showed it to you."

"He shows it to everyone," Neil said with a grimace.

Now Reginald chuckled and took another sip of his scotch. "It'll all be yours someday."

Neil groaned to our laughter.

"It's always nice to see you," Reginald said, "but I get a sense this isn't a holiday visit."

"No, it isn't." Neil glanced at me. "We saw someone today—"

"Wait." I pulled my phone from my bag and queued up the pictures I'd gotten of the would-be thief at Alice's. "I want you two to look at these photos and see if you recognize this man."

Neil nodded in approval as I handed the phone to Cray. While they looked, I bit into my sandwich. It was delicious or I was starving, or maybe both.

"Hmmm." Cray handed the phone to Reginald.

"If this is who I think it is, it's been a long time," Reginald said.

"Who do you think it is?" Neil asked as he took the phone from his grandfather and set it on the table.

The older men exchanged a look.

"Well," Cray said, "if I had to guess, I'd say it's that fellow who gave us the dubious rum at that treasure museum."

Reginald nodded. "You mean Thor Roberts, right?"

"That's what we thought!" I said.

"We remembered him from the museum," Neil added.

"Where did you see him?" Cray asked.

Neil and I were quiet for a moment.

I finally spoke. "OK, just between us, we were checking out the shack where Diana's friend was staying—the botanist who died?"

"I saw that in the paper," Reginald said.

"Right. Diana wants to try to save her research. So we were up in the shack, which is on stilts, and Thor Roberts comes along and breaks into a storage box on the dock with a bunch of kayak stuff in it ..."

I paused for a moment. Something still bugged me about that.

"And then he tried to get into the shack, but we scared him off," I concluded.

"Mark scared him off," Neil pointed out, and I giggled at the image of Mark rushing the door.

"How very peculiar," Cray said.

"He *is* peculiar," Reginald said. "The world of treasure hunters is pretty small. Most of us could've told Thor that museum he bought was a bad bet. Then it turned out most of the treasure had been replaced with fakes before he moved in.

And he's hardly found enough good stuff over the years to stock it himself."

"The museum was kinda lame," I agreed.

Reginald sighed. "It's a shame what's become of him. He used to be a scrappy worker. A good diver. I worked with him once. Then he got lazy."

"Meaning what?" I asked.

"He liked shortcuts. Namely, he liked to poach treasure from sites someone else had already discovered."

A tingle of excitement shot through me. "Is there any reason he might think there's treasure in the swamp west of Bohemia?"

Reginald chewed on a bite of chicken salad sandwich before he replied. "No good reason. I mean, there are stories. There are stories all over Florida. No wonder, given how many Spanish ships met their doom off the coast, how many pirates lurked offshore, and how many outlaws went to ground here."

"Anything specific to the St. Johns?" Neil asked.

"I've read about rum runners stashing their ill-gotten gains," Cray said.

"That was more in the Everglades, though we weren't without our moonshiners," Reginald said. "Stories of significant lost hoards go back centuries before that. I heard a tale once about the 1715 Spanish treasure fleet disaster off our coast."

Neil smiled. "You've told me lots of tales about that disaster."

"True, but this one is specific to the St. Johns."

"What happened in 1715?" I asked.

Reginald warmed to his topic. "Spain had long depended on New World treasure to function, but hostilities interrupted the usual flow of gold and silver its ships carried back and forth across the ocean. King Philip was desperate for funds after years of war and sent a fleet of ships to the New World to gather another round of riches to keep them afloat. So to speak.

"The squadrons loaded up with gold and silver bars, pearls, emeralds, exquisite porcelain from China that had come through Mexico, and so on. It's thought that some fifteen million silver pieces of eight—coins—were aboard these ships when they gathered in Havana and set forth in July of 1715. They had five days of beautiful weather, and then the big waves started."

I shivered. "A hurricane?" I guessed. Since my Katrina experience, hurricanes gave me the willies.

"That's right," Reginald said. "The fleet was running parallel to the storm. Then the hurricane changed course and slammed right into them, destroying the ships just a week after they set sail. Only a French warship that had accompanied them escaped after its commander opted to sail northeast through the storm. Eleven Spanish ships went down in the Atlantic, and more than a thousand men died. A few made it ashore in lifeboats.

"Some of the treasure has been recovered over the years. Once in a while, a coin washes up on shore even now. And here's where the story you're asking about strays into legend, in my opinion."

"On with it, my man," Cray said.

Reginald smiled. "One of these scrappy survivors is said to have grabbed a haul of gold, silver and gems from the wreck- age. Name of Casanova, or maybe that was just part of the legend. The men who'd washed up on shore had no supplies and no ships. No doubt they were preoccupied with survival. Amid the carnage, Casanova fled with his booty and scrabbled his way inland to the St. Johns. As the story goes, he found an island where he could bury the treasure to recover later."

Gold and gems! "Then what happened?" I asked.

"Supposedly he died of a fever before he could extract it. It's never been found, but I doubt it existed in the first place. Then again, you never know. I think there's a lot of treasure in Florida that's never been found, in spite of my best efforts." Reginald chuckled.

"Is there any other reason Thor Roberts would be poking around the marsh?" Neil asked.

"Fishing?" Cray asked with a hint of humor.

"No gear," I said. "Plus there's the whole breaking and entering thing."

"Maybe he's desperate enough to steal stuff even if it's not treasure," Reginald said.

"Life jackets and the junk we saw in that shack? Unlikely." I had an idea. "Barclay's taking Gina to spend Christmas with their families in South Florida. Maybe he can run by the museum, see how it's doing and get a sense of what Thor is up to. See if he really is desperate."

"That museum looked rather desperate when we visited it several months ago," Cray pointed out. "But I find it difficult to envision Mr. Roberts having enough initiative to hunt down a mythical treasure."

"But what if it had already been found? Maybe most of the work was done already." I typed up a text to Barclay as the others munched, noticeably quiet. Their lack of enthusiasm was getting to me. "Come on, guys. Why would he be here? Why the Swamp Shack? I bet he thinks the Casanova treasure is there."

Reginald took a sip of his scotch. "It's possible," he

acknowledged after a moment. "But where did he get the notion it's at this shack, specifically?"

"That leads us to another question," Neil said. "Did Alice know the stories? Did she actually find treasure or some clue that it might be there? Was she actively looking for it?"

"And following along those lines," I said, "could Thor Roberts have killed her for it?"

"Given he was still looking for something this morning, he hasn't found it. If she knew where it was, murder seems like a poor strategy," Neil observed.

"Maybe he just wanted her out of the way so he could have the site to himself," Cray said.

I took a sip of root beer. "Good luck with that. Raquel Tocks seemed excited to have her tenant gone off her juicy piece of property. Now that she's free of the lease, she won't want another renter."

"He might not have known about that," Neil said.

Cray sipped what my supernose told me was rum. "Seems like the point is moot if Dr. Dalworth's death was an accident. That's what the article suggested."

I thought back to the message Diana got from Detective Keene. "The police have changed their minds about that."

"Is there any way to confirm this Casanova story?" Neil asked.

"Many have tried and failed," his grandfather answered.

I finished off my root beer. "You know who might know of any rumors of treasure out there? Bill Boyle. That property was in his family for years, right? I think we should talk to him."

"If he thought there was treasure on it, would he have sold it?" Neil wore a hint of a smile.

I gave him the side-eye for popping my bubble. "He still

might know something about what happened. He's the one who leased the land to Alice in the first place, before he sold out."

Reginald set down his scotch and leaned forward, resting his elbows on his knees. His expression turned grave as he looked from me to Neil.

"I think you two should leave this alone. If Alice was murdered, it's dangerous enough to go poking around. But if there's a treasure out there and that idiot Thor knows about it, he's probably not the only one. And I know all too well that if treasure is involved, some people get so obsessed they'll kill anyone who's in their way. It may be they've already killed once. I don't want the next victims to be you."

Chapter Twelve

Neil and I left his grandfather's house a half hour later, pleasantly full of lunch and unpleasantly full of Reginald's warnings.

Neil had picked up on my train of thought as we got into his SUV. "He's been a treasure hunter his whole life. He knows the mindset."

"I'm not a treasure hunter, but I'm not that worried. I can't help but get excited by the idea of gold and silver and gems somewhere out there."

"That's how it starts." A corner of his mouth turned up as he started the car. "He stuffed my head full of stories. Somehow, I ended up on the mixology path."

"After a brief stint studying astronomy at Oxford."

He pulled out of the driveway. "Paths that go in a straight line are boring."

I knew Neil had a little subversion in him. Sometimes it peeked through. "Now I know what you're going to say, but I think we should talk to Bill Boyle."

"What am I going to say?"

"That it's a fool's errand, and it's Christmas Eve, and we should probably just let the police do their thing."

"Well, then, I can call Millie and tell her to cancel our appointment."

I gaped at him. "What?"

"I texted Millie and had her make an appointment for us to talk to Bill Boyle. Unless you don't want to." He was trying not to smile.

"Oh, you are crafty. When?"

"Right now."

"Yes!" I leaned over and kissed his cheek. I would've hugged him, but he was driving. Then I looked at myself, still in my casual airboat clothes. "Maybe I should change."

"No time. And you look great." Neil gave me a warm look that heated my body like a hot toddy. "It so happens he lives nearby."

"In one of these fancy neighborhoods? It's a long way from the swamp."

"He's a developer like Raquel Tocks. Well, maybe not *like* Raquel Tocks."

"I hope not." I pictured Raquel's predatory smile when she looked at Neil.

"He claims to be a green developer. Or he was—he's retired."

"That explains the solar panels on the Swamp Shack."

"Probably easier to use solar for the shack's meager needs than to run power out to that island."

"True," I acknowledged.

"Here we are." Neil turned past an open gate and rumbled down a long gravel driveway.

Bill Boyle's house was right on the lagoon. Oak trees dripping with Spanish moss and clusters of palms hid most of it from view until we were almost on top of it.

Neil stopped the car in a large crushed-shell parking area in front of a three-car garage. I couldn't tell if the Boyle home was remodeled from an original 1960s house or brand-new and inspired by the space age.

Natural stone panels and tinted windows broke up the creamy white of the stucco walls. Dramatically sloping metal roofs over the garage on the right and part of the house on the left started at a high point on the outside edges of the house, then sloped down toward the center to form a *V,* with a gap in the middle where the front door was. Over this central entranceway, a wooden pergola covered in a thick vine provided shade and softened the hard angles. Beyond the door, a more conventional roof sloped up and away from us, suggesting a large indoor space beyond.

"More solar," I noted, looking at the panels on the south-facing garage roof.

"Green development," Neil observed.

We strode under the dappled shade of the pergola, and I touched the doorbell, which had a built-in camera. Somewhere inside came an explosion of high-pitched barks.

"You make friends with the dog," Neil said.

"Don't I always?" I adjusted my glasses and showed him my dimples.

A burly man with thin, silvering dark brown hair, an inch or so taller than Neil, opened the door a minute later, and a beagle puppy shot out from between his feet and attacked my Skechers.

"Hey!" I said.

"Spike! Get in here!" The beagle barked once and ran back inside. "Sorry about that. We're still trying to train him. Neil and Pepper, is it? I'm Bill Boyle."

He smiled and stuck out his hand, and after a round of shakes, he let us inside.

In his pastel outfit, our host looked like he'd just walked off the golf course. Maybe he had.

"Thanks for seeing us," Neil said as Bill walked us through an open-plan living space filled with comfortable, contemporary furniture. Not fussy but, I suspected, expensive. And it was decorated to the hilt for Christmas, with a big, glitzy tree, garlands and gewgaws everywhere.

"I understand you want to talk about the old family property," he said. So Millie had told him that much.

"If you don't mind," Neil said. "One of our friends knew the woman who died out there yesterday."

"Ah," he said. "A sad business. She was a real nice lady. Why don't you come on through to the patio?" He turned his head and shouted in the general direction of the kitchen. "Tracy, can you bring out some iced tea?"

"We're fine," I tried to say, but a woman's voice came back, "Just a minute."

Bill led us through sliding glass doors and onto a paver patio. There was a fire-pit coffee table filled with glass gravel, an impressive outdoor kitchen, and plenty of chairs. Steps led down to a lovely yard full of more trees that stopped at the Indian River Lagoon, what we locals called the river.

Neil and I sat on a cushioned love seat while Bill took a big chair perpendicular to us.

"Beautiful place," I said.

"Thanks. We took an old 1960s house, added to it and renovated. Really we rebuilt it from the inside out to make it as energy-efficient as possible. It's comfortable."

Just then, Tracy, presumably, came out with a tray of glasses, the puppy bounding behind her. Spike hopped up on the love seat, climbed over a squirming Neil and settled between us. I chuckled and slid my hand along the beagle's silky back.

"Iced tea?" Slender with ash-blond hair, in jeans and a T-shirt spattered with paint, Tracy handed out the tall glasses. "I've got to keep working."

"No problem, honey. Thanks," Bill said, and she waved and headed back inside. "She's quite an artist. You can see her work in one of the galleries in the arts district."

"Nice." It felt like we'd been overwhelmed with nice.

"It's just as well," he said more quietly. "She always gets a little edgy when I talk about Alice."

I blinked. "Oh? Why is that?"

Bill sipped his tea and smiled. "We were friendly, Alice and I. Nothing untoward. But Tracy has a suspicious mind."

I wondered if he'd given her a reason to have a suspicious mind, but I didn't go there. "How did it come about that you rented the Swamp Shack to Alice? And that she stayed there after you sold the property?"

He looked from me to Neil. "Can you explain your interest again? Your friend knew Alice?"

"And my father is our friend's lawyer, so I'm doing a little research for him." *Ooo, nice little white lie, Neil.* "The police have questioned her, and we'd like to help her out, if we can, by understanding the situation."

"I see. I hated to sell that property. It's been in my family for generations, but I have kids and grandkids who have zero interest in it. And I want to help put my grandkids through school. Selling the property gave me the funds to do that." Bill looked at me. "But let me go back to your question. It was Alice who tracked me down after hearing about the shack. I'd never rented it out before, but I used it as a base for fishing sometimes since the main house has been closed up for years.

She said she was a researcher and was interested in rare plants and wildlife out there and wanted to know if she could rent it."

"When was this?" I asked, stroking the puppy's soft fur. His eyes drifted shut, and he snorted a wee snore.

"About eighteen months ago."

Neil traced a pattern in the condensation on his glass. "And you had a long-term lease that allowed her to stay as long as she wanted, even when you sold the property?"

"Well, that came along later. You see, Alice and I talked quite a bit, and she said she'd found some really interesting plants, but she also thought she'd spotted an ivory-billed woodpecker out there. She wanted time to document it. I loved the idea. They're supposed to be extinct, though there was a sighting in Arkansas not too long ago. Alleged sighting." He chuckled.

"So when you wanted to sell to Raquel Tocks—" I prompted.

"I adjusted the terms of the lease first so Alice could stay as long as she wanted. Raquel had wanted to get her hands on that property for years, so she was willing to roll the dice."

"You're known as a green developer," Neil said. "So energy-efficient houses and communities, recycling, low water use, solar, green spaces and so on?"

"That's right."

"Then why sell an environmentally sensitive property adjacent to the marsh to Tocks Development Corp.?" Neil's neutral tone masked a very sharp question.

Bill's eyes narrowed, but he nodded, acknowledging the point. "I know. I love it out there. And I know the true value of the marsh. Given my reputation, I didn't want to develop that property myself, but I also couldn't hold on to it anymore either. The taxes alone were killing me. With Alice as a long-term lessee, I knew we could at least delay the inevitable. And if she found the woodpecker, who knows?" A sly smile touched his lips.

"You mean because the bird is extinct—er, endangered," I corrected, "finding one there might stop the land from being developed?"

"Sneaky," Neil said.

Bill laughed out loud. "It's Florida, so there's no telling once the politicians get involved. They find it easy to ignore environmental issues. But yes, blocking development there was a real possibility, especially if the feds got wind of an extinct species there." His face hardened. "Unfortunately, now Raquel's going to get exactly what she wants. Nothing gives her a bigger thrill. She's the ringmaster of her little circus. In her mind, the rest of us are just the clowns."

Wow. What if Raquel had known what Alice was looking for, had possibly even found? A species thought extinct? Killing Alice would mean killing two birds with one stone, almost literally. Raquel would get rid of her eternal renter and any evidence of the rare species that could stop her project. A double motive for murder.

"Do you know if Alice was studying fish out there?" I asked. "Doing fish counts?"

Bill's face looked blank. "Not that I know of. She was a botanist primarily, wasn't she?"

I nodded. So we still didn't know why she had the electrofishing gear out there. "And have you ever heard of treasure being buried out there in the swamp?"

He stared at me for a second, and then he barked out a laugh. "Don't tell me you've heard those Casanova stories too?"

I ignored his mocking tone and scratched behind Spike's

ears, and the puppy gave a little sigh. "Do you think the stories are real?"

"If there was any treasure on our property, my brothers and I would've found it during our reenactments of bloody pirate battles on and around the island years ago. And to answer your question, no, I don't think the stories are real. Though every year or so when I was growing up, some numbskull would come onto our property out there looking for it, and my dad would scare him away with a shotgun."

After a moment's awkward silence, Neil set down his glass and stood. I reluctantly released the puppy and did the same.

"Thank you very much for your time," Neil said. "I'm sorry about what happened to your friend."

"I'm sorry, too," Bill acknowledged. He got up and showed us to the door.

"Thanks," I said. "Merry Christmas."

"You too. And look out for treasure hunters. They're idiots."

Neil snorted and turned after Bill closed the door. "They're not *all* idiots."

I walked with him toward the car. "Your grandfather isn't. But Bill Boyle seemed to suggest that anyone looking for treasure out there is."

"He gave us a lot to think about. It seems like he really set out to mess with Raquel Tocks. Do you think he has an axe to grind?" Neil unlocked the car, and we climbed in.

"It could be. If it's all right with you, I'll ask Millie to dig a little deeper."

"Fine with me."

"I'm surprised Raquel went along with the purchase agreement," I said, texting Millie to ask her to do more research into Bill Boyle's connections to Raquel Tocks. "Then again,

maybe she didn't think twice about it. She also has a reputation. And goons. Getting rid of Alice might have been her plan
all along."

Neil started the car, then reached into his pocket and
pulled out his buzzing phone. "Would you look at that?" He
showed me the caller ID.

Tocks Development Corp.

Chapter Thirteen

"Neil Rockaway," he answered his phone as I cringed, wondering who was calling him from Tocks Development Corp. "Yes, Lissa."

OK. Raquel's assistant. At least it wasn't Raquel.

"Sure, put me through," Neil said.

Crap!

"What can I do for you, Raquel?"

I watched Neil's face as I heard the vague purr of words on the other end of the line. "I was hoping we'd covered that in our meeting." His eyebrows slowly crept together. "I'm afraid that won't be possible. I work from noon to midnight every day after the holiday." More purring. "No, I have plans on Christmas." He turned to me and lifted an eyebrow as the purring became more clipped. "Is that something you'd like Enzo to talk to me about?" *Purr.* "OK. I'll make it work. Thanks very much."

But he didn't hang up, just waited for a moment. "Lissa? Raquel wants me to make an appointment to see her. Preferably Thursday. Early afternoon works for me." Pause. "That's fine. See you then."

He ended the call.

"That Raquel Tocks, working around the clock," I said.

"Tock around the clock," Neil agreed.

"One of my favorite hits by Bill Haley and His Comets."

Neil wheeled the SUV around and headed out of the driveway, then turned in the general direction of my neighborhood. We didn't say anything for a minute until I couldn't stand it anymore.

"What did she want?"

A corner of Neil's mouth lifted. "First she wanted me to meet her for a drink and 'talk about the menu,'" he said.

"But we already did that."

"I told her I thought we'd covered it. Then she suggested we meet just to talk about cocktails in general. She said she thought she could learn from me in a more intimate setting."

"Oh, barf."

Neil laughed. "You heard me. I told her I was busy."

"But then you made an appointment to see her."

"I can't completely ignore the client. She said she wants me to make the vodka punch for her."

"But it's a punch! What does she want, a whole punch bowl?"

"I can scale it down."

"Face it," I said. "What she really wants is to get in your pants."

"No chance. And if you're available, I want you to come with me."

"Am I available?" I didn't wait for him to answer my loaded question. "I'm not sure whether to be insulted. You don't need a bodyguard."

"No, I don't. But if you want to know more about whether Raquel had a role in Alice's death, an opportunity may present itself."

He had a point. "I guess I can come along. Jorge's covering for me whenever I can't be there this week, and at that time of the afternoon, we probably won't get anything more than a few exhausted post-Christmas bargain shoppers. But I'd better get in there this afternoon. He worked his buns off at the party last night."

"Great party," Neil said.

"Thanks." I smiled at him now that we had a plan to deal with Raquel. "Melody's asked anyone who's around to come by the hotel bar tonight for a drink. She has to work till ten. Can you make it?"

"We're closing early for Christmas Eve so our staff can spend time with their families, so yes, I can. Want a ride?"

"Desperately." I gave him what I hoped was a seductive glance. "But I have to work, too, so I guess I'll meet you over there."

He just chuckled. "It's a date."

CHRISTMAS EVE AFTERNOON, and it had already been a busy day. I was running on little sleep. I had to work. And I still didn't have a present for Neil. I'd considered making him one of those homespun coupon books filled with lewd acts, but I had a feeling he'd never cash them in. I needed something more creative.

Back at the house, all was quiet. Aunt Celestine was snoozing on a lounge chair by the pool with Astra snuggled up next to her. The dog lifted her head and sniffed, then settled back down and closed her eyes. I suspected Diana might be taking a nap, too. Nobody else was around. With luck, we'd catch up tonight at Melody's bar.

After changing into jeans, a black suede vest over a button-up white shirt—generously open at the collar—red Christmas ball earrings and black boots, I headed to downtown Bohemia. First stop: The Knick-Knackery, an antiques store filled with a jumble of goods from collectible toys to old signs to kitchen kitsch to vintage jewelry.

I combed the crowded shelves until I found something interesting enough for Neil. It wasn't romantic, exactly, but it was very him. I hoped I had chosen wisely. Melody's advice about making sure I got him something that was on the level of what he got me had me freaked out. How the heck was I supposed to know what that was?

And what if he didn't get me anything? Then we'd strayed into super awkward territory. I mean, could we even keep dating?

Were we dating? I thought so. We saw each other on an irregular basis. But we were still wading in the kiddie pool. I was ready to dive into the deep end.

Neil's gift fit into my messenger bag, though it was crowded with more than my usual flea market's worth of junk.

Oh, yeah. That little package from the other day was still in there. I'd wait to open it at home. There was no use in opening a dog toy when Astra wasn't around to enjoy it.

I walked to Nola. It was a gorgeous day, cool and bright. Or at least it was till I saw Mr. Mixy lurking on the sidewalk outside.

"There you are!" he called as I got near the front door.

Rats. I'd parked in back, but since I'd strolled to the antiques store, it had seemed silly to walk all the way around to my back door. Until now.

"Stephan. What do you want?"

"Do I have to want something?" He trailed me into the bar, which was surprisingly busy for a holiday afternoon. Or maybe not surprisingly. Some people had off on Christmas Eve, and it being Florida and near the beach, there were always a lot of people loafing with no visible means of support. That was fine with me, as long as they paid their tab.

"Hi, Jorge! How's it going?" I waved at my business partner, who was wiping down the bar.

"Great! I think I'm getting the hang of this. Though most people just want beer this time of day." He noticed Mr. Mixy following me and shot me a questioning look.

"Why don't you go home? Relax? You must be exhausted."

"I don't have anything to do, really. My parents are having a bunch of the family over for dinner tomorrow in Miami, but I opted to stay up here."

"Oh no. Don't you want to be with them? We're closed tomorrow. You could go."

"I'm good. Honestly, I'm having so much fun, I'm questioning my chosen career. And down there it's all screaming nieces and nephews, and my parents treat me like a pariah for being single. Gina and I are the only single ones left, and now she has a serious boyfriend." *Barclay.* "And I'm the oldest of five. I don't think I can take the pressure."

I chuckled. "You could come over to Aunt Celestine's for dinner tomorrow. There's going to be plenty of food."

His brown eyes shone. "Really? I'd like that."

"Great!" Mr. Mixy said from behind me. "I'll be there."

Finally, I turned to acknowledge him. "No, you won't."

"Pepper! You wouldn't leave me an orphan on Christmas, would you?"

"Honestly, Stephan, I don't even know why you're here in Bohemia. Don't you have a life in L.A.?"

"Sure. It's a great life. But Raquel Tocks invited me to be a celebrity at that New Year's Eve benefit, and it was all-expenses-paid."

It was funny how celebrity often fed on itself until it blew up way beyond any real reason the fame existed in the first place. "But that's a week away."

"I know, but I'm doing research for my book. I thought it might be good to get the feel of the place again." He sat on a barstool, pointed to one of the taps, and Jorge drew him a beer. "And you're here."

Whoa no. He did *not* just say that. I threw out his cheating hide back when I was young and naive and finally figured out that he was the worst boyfriend ever, and nothing would ever make me respect him again.

I stared him down. "I have no idea what you mean."

"I'm trying to get insight into your character," he said. "I mean, I know you said I can't identify you in the book, and I won't, but I have to have some kind of—what do they call it?—analog for you. A Pepper character."

"*Not* named Pepper."

"Of course not!"

OK. This I understood, him being in Bohemia for purely selfish reasons. But I didn't like the idea of a "Pepper character" in his allegedly nonfiction book. Especially after the horrible interview he did with me back in Kentucky in which he took whatever I said and twisted it for his own purposes.

I tried not to think about him as the afternoon wore on. I hated that I felt even one second of pity for him. Yet I really didn't want him ruining my Christmas at my aunt's. Then again, I could ignore him and work on getting onto Neil's naughty list, in the best way possible.

But maybe I'd get points on Santa's nice list if I were kind to Mr. Mixy? *Argh*.

Jorge and I kept busy making drinks for a light but steady stream of customers, some stopping for cocktails and a snack during their last-minute shopping, some having an early dinner with friends. Our talented kitchen staff did fantastic work, but I knew they were looking forward to getting out and enjoying a free evening and a whole day off. So when I flipped the sign on the door to "closed" at 6 p.m., we tended to the last customers, gently sent them on their way and cleaned up faster than kids tearing open presents Christmas morning.

"You coming to the beach?" I asked Jorge, who knew about the meetup at the hotel bar.

"Naw. The last two days have finally caught up with me. But I'll see you tomorrow."

"Great. Good night!" I looked around as Jorge went out the back, following the rest of the crew.

Mr. Mixy was still at the bar. Somehow I'd hidden him in a dark, dusty corner of my brain, even though I'd been vaguely aware of Jorge serving him several beers and a bowl of gumbo as the afternoon turned into evening. And I'd watched carefully to make sure he paid the bill, given Mr. Mixy wasn't great around money.

"Give me a ride, Pepper?" He slurred his words.

Oh, joy. "How'd you get over here?"

"Rideshare." He burped. "You're going to the hotel anyway, right? We can party." His teeth flashed in a grin through the giant beard. He had a future haunting shopping malls as a demented Santa if he played his cards right.

I could make him get a taxi back to the beach, but what was the point? He'd still show up at the bar. He always did. At least this way I could minimize the amount of trouble he'd get into.

I maneuvered him out back and into the passenger seat of the Angry Orange, where he immediately started snoring, and set out through the festive lights of downtown and over the causeway bridge toward Bohemia Beach.

I didn't want to party with Mr. Mixy. But I did want to see Neil, see if anyone had figured out Alice's notebook, and hear what Millie had to say about Bill Boyle. So over the river and through the palm trees, to the bar we went.

Chapter Fourteen

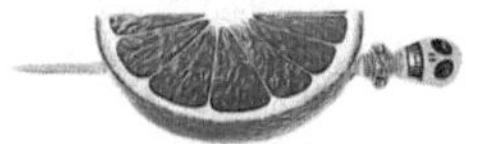

"Mark! Thank God." Under the lights of the high-rise hotel's parking lot, I spotted the muscular Brit stepping out of his silver Jaguar I-Pace. This had to be the electric car he'd mentioned earlier. To my surprise, Diana and Celestine rolled out of it, too, along with Royce and a grumpy-looking Alastair. Mark must've volunteered to be everyone's taxi tonight.

"Hot Pepper! I'm so glad *you're* glad to see *me*." He grinned as he walked over to where I stood next to my Honda.

I quirked my mouth and pointed to the passenger seat. "I can't get him out of there."

Mark peered inside at the snoring bearded one. "Tsk, tsk. Dallying with that Mixy fellow again, eh?"

"Oh, shut up," I said to his teasing tone. "Can you pull him out? I'm sure he'll wake up if you can just get him going."

"Royce? Alastair?" Mark called.

"Not me," Alastair said, blowing one of his wavy blond locks out of his face, but Royce helped, and together, the two got Mr. Mixy on his feet and lugged him into the hotel.

Diana and Aunt Celestine walked in with me. "How do you keep ending up with him?" my aunt said. "Don't forget how he treated you back in the day."

"As if! He follows me around. He's like a puppy but not as

cute." Which made me think of that adorable beagle of Bill Boyle's. And how devious his plan was to foil Raquel's development of his childhood homestead. I hoped Millie would be here so I could see what she found out.

A minute later, I joined the burgeoning crowd at the hotel bar, almost all people I knew.

The bar wasn't bad-looking—modern, with cool lighting, though the frozen-drink dispensers made me cringe. Melody did her best to guide guests to decent cocktails, but too many tourists opted for the icy sugar bombs that stained their tongues with neon colors and, no doubt, gave them horrible hangovers. She'd been making noises about finding another job, but the tips were good here.

"You look gorgeous, as usual," I told her. She wore a clingy, sleeveless ice-blue dress that complemented her blond good looks. Her up-do showed off dangling, frosted blue glass earrings that seemed to glow. "And those earrings are fabulous."

"Thanks," she said as she worked on a Mai Tai for Luke, who was already ensconced at the bar. He was such a Melody groupie. I hoped his presence meant Neil would be here soon. "I made them."

"You what!" Then I remembered Melody had been taking crafty classes in her spare time. Probably when I was working on the bitters I made with my aunt. "Is this the side business you hinted at?"

"Yep. I'm making recycled glass jewelry. These are made from gin bottles. I have an online shop and everything."

"Sweet! Maybe I could carry a few of those at my bar?"

"I'd love that!"

"Those will fit right in with the T-shirts and Bohemia Bitters in my Nola shop. We'll talk."

"Sounds good." She spanked a fluffy tuft of green mint, added it to the fragrant Mai Tai, pushed the glass over to Luke and looked at me. "What'll you have?"

"Let's keep it simple. Old-Fashioned?"

"You got it."

"Did I hear Old-Fashioned? Make it two," Royce said as he and Mark approached the bar.

"Three," added Mark.

"What did you do with Stephan?" I asked.

"We dumped him in his room. At least I hope it was his room," Mark said.

"If not, someone's going to have a very hairy surprise," Royce added.

I giggled. Then Royce caught an interested glance from a handsome guy down the bar I didn't know, winked at me and headed off in that direction to say hello.

I spotted Oleanna arriving and waved. She wore blue jeans with tall high-heeled boots that matched her draped black top with loose, flowing sleeves. Her hair was down, too. Only a movie star could make a casual look so glamorous.

"How's the vacation going?" I asked.

"Great! And it's turning into more than a vacation."

"You mean a romance?"

She smiled. "Oh, I wouldn't say that. Business first. Enzo's made me a very nice offer to be the face of the Desjardins champagne brand."

"That's great publicity for you, too."

"That's what I thought."

"So business first—romance second?" I waggled my eyebrows.

She bit her lip in a comic gesture and looked up as if she were thinking about it. "It's the time of year when the world falls in love, or something like that. Who knows?" Then we both startled as the man himself glided up to the bar, his dimples showing.

Oleanna looked flustered for only a moment. "Enzo! I'm glad you could make it."

"*J'ai la banane,*" he said.

Oleanna looked at him with a puzzled expression. "You have the banana?"

He laughed. "*Non.* Well, yes, but no. I could not be more delighted. It is like, I have the smile. The big smile on my face."

He was happy to be here and away from Raquel, no doubt.

Melody had glided over to see what they wanted after serving our drinks. "Did I hear someone say banana? I can make you a banana cocktail that will drive you wild. Ever have a Puhi Split? With macadamia nut liqueur, rum, cream, coffee liqueur. Total panty-dropper."

Oleanna looked embarrassed, but Enzo laughed heartily. "I am *very* interested."

"Let me whip you up a couple. It's a blender drink, but don't be afraid." Melody winked and got to work.

I toasted them. Then I spotted Neil entering the room, and my heart did a little flutter. He wore one of his nerdy bow ties, a button-down dark blue shirt and a big smile as he came over and gave me a quick kiss on the lips. *More, please!*

"How was your afternoon?" he asked.

"Other than Mr. Mixy holding down a barstool at Nola for hours, fine. You'd better get a drink so we can talk to Millie."

He chuckled. "My day was fine, thank you."

I gave him an embarrassed smile. "Sorry. I'm eager to find out if she learned anything. Of course I care deeply about your afternoon."

"Cray and Gramps stopped in to have a drink. We weren't busy. It was fun." He headed toward Melody, who was serving up the Puhi Splits in tiki mugs.

She used a chef's torch to flame three discs of banana on a skewer and laid the garnish across the top of each, then added a fat straw. The caramelized banana was like dessert to my nose.

Neil gestured to the blender. "Is that spoken for?"

"Just enough for one more." Melody poured it into a ceramic mug and did the thing with the banana, then slid it across to him. "On the house."

"Well, that's sweet," I said after she moved off to help another customer.

"She owes me," he said cryptically.

"Do tell," I replied as he and I drifted down the bar toward our organizer, Millie, and her boyfriend, Bennett.

"I have to have *some* secrets." He took a sip and closed his eyes in pleasure. "Damn, that's good."

Hmm. He was such a tease. "Do I get a taste?"

He paused and handed me the drink, and I had my taste: a swirl of sweet nuttiness, the almost vanilla tang of the banana, both doing a happy dance with the other liquors. "Oh, she's so right. Total panty-dropper."

"What?" His exclamation was half laugh.

My face heated as I handed the drink back. "Just something Melody said."

"Really." He leaned in. "Let me taste it again." Then he kissed me, lingering this time, and when he pulled away I was dizzy.

Total tease!

Feeling the buzz of his kiss and my Old-Fashioned, I drifted after him down the bar, where Millie and Bennett were already drinking. They were so cute together, her with her Betty Boop haircut and him with his sandy hair and scruff. Millie, a lightweight when it came to alcohol, daintily sipped a glass of champagne, but Bennett quaffed something dark and dangerous-looking.

"Doing any sand-sculpting?" I asked Bennett.

"I fly out to Hawaii the day after tomorrow. Going to spend Christmas with Millie's family first. I can't miss the Italian feast."

"We had the seven-fishes dinner after church tonight," Millie said. "I'm stuffed."

"I ate a little something at Nola," I told her. I looked around and lowered my voice. "Have you had a chance to see if there's any history with Bill Boyle and Raquel Tocks?"

"Actually, yes." She slid off her stool and gestured to a square table away from the crowd, and the four of us sat around it.

"I called a few friends of friends who know something about behind-the-scenes real-estate shenanigans around here," she said in a low voice. "Boyle and Tocks have had a low-level feud for years, stealing deals out from under the nose of the other and that kind of thing. One of Raquel's plans—to knock down a historic building in downtown Bohemia and build an office building—was held up for five years while Bill Boyle clung to a lease for the parking garage on the lower floor, even though no one was really using it anymore."

"So he's tried tricks with leases before," I said. "But where does the animosity come from?"

"I think part of it is simply philosophical differences." An amused expression took over Millie's face. "He once called her the devil incarnate in a newspaper article for her plan to build a development on top of a crucial gopher tortoise habitat.

Apparently developers have been hounding the critters out of existence."

"Devil incarnate? No idea why she would find that offensive," Bennett joked.

"She might actually like it," I said to Neil's chuckle. "Anything else?"

Millie nodded. "This isn't widely known, but Bill is Raquel's uncle."

"No way," I said.

"Why would he hate his own niece, aside from the difference in philosophy?" Neil asked.

"I haven't been able to verify all this, but the story is that Bill had three brothers and a sister."

I cocked my head. "Had?"

"I'm getting to that." Millie sipped her bubbly. "At some point, Bill's father gave each of his children a choice piece of land. Though the old man had a rep for being an ornery cracker, an angler, and a swamp guy sometimes on the wrong side of the law, he was actually a savvy businessman. He quietly accumulated real estate for years, picking up properties during the busts between Florida's booms. Bill's sister got the choicest of the properties, a sweet house on a beautiful long stretch of beach, a popular turtle nesting site. She kept it even when she married a shady developer—Raquel's dad—though he pressured her to develop it. As the story goes, she wanted to save that little bit of natural Florida her father gave her. When she died of cancer shortly after her husband died of a heart attack, Raquel, then twenty-two and new to the business, sold it immediately. It became a resort. The beach was 'restored' as part of the construction."

"In other words, destroyed," Neil said.

Millie nodded. "It appears so. Bill was furious. Since then, he's done everything he can to throw roadblocks in her way."

"Hence his tricky lease that let Alice stay on the family homestead indefinitely, even when it was sold, preventing Raquel from developing it," I said. "But maybe he has some family feeling for her after all, if he sold it to her in the first place. He had to know that Alice wouldn't be there forever."

"More to the point," Neil said, "Alice being gone blows up his plan to delay Raquel. So I don't think he would have done Alice any harm."

I had to admit that Neil was probably right.

"Unfortunately, his fears seem to be justified," Millie noted. "Rumor has it Raquel Tocks submitted plans for the Boyle Lakes development to the planning commission this morning."

"Already?" I couldn't believe it. "And she's calling it Boyle Lakes?"

"Talk about adding salt to the wound," Bennett said.

I shook my head. "She must have had them drawn up for a while. This makes me suspect her more than ever. Maybe we should see if Diana's had any luck with the notebook."

We thanked Millie and Bennett and found Diana, Celestine and Mark at a table on the beachfront deck just outside the hotel bar. The lights out here pointed down and were subtle enough I could see stars twinkling overhead. A fresh, salty breeze and the sound of waves hissing up the sand infused me with energy. Sometimes I got so busy, I forgot how magical the ocean was.

"Just who we wanted to see," Mark said.

Neil pulled up an extra chair, and we squeezed around the square table. "What's up?"

"Diana wants to go back to the shack tomorrow."

"You're kidding," I said. "We were just there."

"But we didn't get a chance to look around before that man scared us off," Diana pointed out.

"Speak for yourself," Mark said. "He didn't scare me."

"And you don't need to come with me," Diana told him.

"Nonsense. You need a protector."

"Oh, please." Diana cocked an eyebrow at him. "I've made my way through jungles all over the world without a bodyguard. I don't need protection."

Neil interrupted the squabble. "Numbers should be protection enough. A group will discourage bad actors."

"And Otter is armed, if he takes us." I flashed back to Captain Vance's carefully secured pistol.

"We think we know who that guy was today," Neil told them. "In fact, you should probably know what we discussed with my grandfather this afternoon." And we filled in Mark, Diana and my aunt on the Casanova treasure legend and Thor Roberts.

"Treasure?" Mark asked with interest.

"It might be bogus," I said, "but why else would Thor be there?"

"Well, I won't be there," Celestine said. "I'll stay home and work on dinner. Besides, one airboat ride a year is plenty for me."

I knew the feeling. "What if the police are there? Now that this is a homicide investigation, won't they be poking around?"

"It's Christmas tomorrow. They probably did all their poking today," Neil said.

"I find holidays a lovely time for poking," Mark joked, and we all groaned.

Neil's mouth twitched with a smile. "I'm not saying they won't be working on the holiday, but I doubt they'll be working that hard. And it's not like there's anything to guard out there."

I went to sip my drink, but it was empty. I frowned at the glass and set it down. "What are you hoping to find?" I asked Diana. "Did the notebook give you ideas?"

"Not exactly. The only clues it's given me are the drawings of plants. While we work to crack it, I want to get a few samples analyzed in case Alice learned something interesting. And I need to water the other specimens. I can't just let them die."

"You didn't think of this yesterday?" Mark asked.

"We were interrupted," Diana insisted.

"I think you just can't tolerate the idea of the plants suffering on their own. You see," Mark said to me, "the way you feel about Astra is the way Diana feels about plants."

Aunt Celestine and I laughed.

"How do you intend to get out there?" Neil asked. "Is Otter Vance willing?"

"For an even more exorbitant sum, yes," Mark said.

Diana waved away his remark. "Oh, I'll pay this time."

"You will not. Consider it my Christmas present." Mark looked at Neil and me. "You in?"

I resisted the urge to clutch my belly. "Only if I get eight hours of sleep first."

"That can be arranged," Mark said. "We don't need to get out there at dawn. Besides, we need to see what Father Christmas brought."

"Well, don't feel obliged to bring anything but yourselves to Christmas dinner," Aunt Celestine said. "You all are coming over?"

"Yes, and I'm most grateful for the invitation," Mark said.

"So when am I picking up Pepper and Diana in the morning?" Neil asked. "Nine?"

I mouthed "thank you" to him.

Neil nodded. "Then Mark at nine fifteen."

"I could drive," Mark said.

"He's ghastly," objected Diana. "Always drifting to the wrong side of the road."

"It's no problem." Neil looked from one to the other, a twinkle of humor in his eyes. "We might get killed in the swamp anyway. No sense in rushing things."

Aunt Celestine elbowed him as the guys chuckled. "You'd better not."

"Isn't it quicker to drive to the old Boyle house and take a boat out from there?" I asked.

"Not really," Neil replied. "You'd have to trailer a boat out there, for starters. And driving there is a lot less direct than taking the airboat. Lots of winding around."

"Fine." I scowled. "Just keep us away from Phantom."

I wondered whether I should wear my gator-tooth bracelet on another trip to the swamp. Wasn't that tempting fate? Its luck hadn't failed me yet, but Phantom might not like it. Or maybe he'd like it too much. Maybe he was drawn to it. I'd be a tasty morsel for an alligator, especially since I joined the cheese of the month club.

I had another thought that I felt a little guilty about. What if there really was treasure out there? Sure, we could pick up a few plants for Diana. But shouldn't we maybe stick the shovel into the island here or there, just to be sure?

I caught Neil looking at me, his gray eyes turbulent.

Stop reading my mind. I figured if he *was* reading my mind, he'd hear me and stop. And if he wasn't? He probably knew I was on a collision course with trouble anyway.

I usually was.

Chapter Fifteen

Christmas morning. Somewhere, happy kids were opening their front door and flying into the snow with their new sleds.

Here in Bohemia Beach, Florida, where the air was barely cool, I opened the door on the worst present ever.

"Hey, Pepper!" Clad in black pinstripe pants, a thin black sweater, a draped red scarf and hideous red boots with purple trim, laces, buckles and shiny gold toes, Mr. Mixy grinned at me and held out a wilted poinsettia.

I scowled. Sorry, not sorry—my dopey ex didn't put me in the holiday spirit, and I didn't feel as kind today as I did yesterday. "What are *you* doing here?"

Diana, apparently hearing me emerge, had come out of Aunt Celestine's door, which was adjacent to mine. I'd already entrusted Astra to my aunt, who planned to spend the day cooking tonight's dinner.

"What are you doing here?" Diana also asked Mr. Mixy.

He deflated a bit. "Don't you like the poinsettia?"

"It looks like it's seen better days." I wasn't inclined to cut Mr. Mixy any slack. "Like it's been sitting in a hotel lobby for a few weeks."

His eyebrows met and he paled slightly before setting the

foil-wrapped plastic pot on my doorstep. *Holy crap!* He *had* stolen it from the hotel!

"Christmas is almost over," he tried to explain. "They won't miss it."

I rolled my eyes. "You already invited yourself to dinner. Why are you here now?"

"I thought it might be fun to spend the day with you."

I exchanged glances with Diana, who knew Neil and I were trying to get our dating act together. And that Stephan was a menace.

I groaned softly as Neil rolled up in my driveway and waved. Then his expression grew puzzled as he saw Mr. Mixy loitering by my front door. He stepped out of the SUV, looking good in jeans and a black Junction Box sweatshirt.

"Merry Christmas. You ladies ready?"

"Of course." Diana had on her adventure khakis and carried her backpack.

"Ready," I agreed. I wore jeans and a light hoodie over a T-shirt, along with waterproof boots, in case I had to dig for treasure. I also had my messenger bag. It could probably hold a couple of gold bars.

"Oh, are we going somewhere?" Mr. Mixy asked.

Some things were inevitable. Death. Taxes. Ketchup stains on my shirt whenever I ate a hamburger. And Mr. Mixy worming his way into a situation where he wasn't welcome.

My phone buzzed with a text, and I pulled it out of my pocket and glanced at it.

Aunt Celestine: "I see he's back. He can't stay here."

Oh, she was tricky. I glanced at her front window to see the curtain fall back into place. "Trying to get rid of him," I shot back via text, then told Mr. Mixy, "You should go back to the hotel and sleep off your hangover. We're going back to the

Swamp Shack. There's a homicide investigation now, and we could be in danger of being killed, eaten or arrested." I didn't think that was too far off. "This isn't a pleasure outing."

"Sounds like fun to me!" Mr. Mixy went to the car and climbed into the third-row seat of the SUV as if Neil was his limo driver.

"How did that just happen?" Neil asked.

"I don't know. He's like a wandering black hole. We just keep getting sucked in."

"We could always throw him to Phantom first and make a run for it," Neil mused.

I giggled. It wouldn't be that hard to push Mr. Mixy overboard, would it? Even though Captain Vance liked to tell us how alligators were rarely aggressive unless provoked. All I knew was that Phantom had been around a long time and likely had a lot of reasons to want to eat people.

When we stopped outside Mark's condo building, he started with "Happy Christmas!" followed by "Oh, God" when he saw Mr. Mixy.

"And I guess I should tell you that Royce wants to come along," Mark added as my half brother poked his head out of the lobby door and grinned.

"Great!" I hadn't spent enough time with Royce, and even though this wasn't a pleasure cruise, having another person along made it feel more like one—and perhaps made us a little safer in case we ran into any sketchy people.

Neil just sighed next to me, and we were on the road again with our original airboat crew minus Aunt Celestine.

"So tell me about this treasure legend," Royce said. Mark must've told him about it.

"What treasure?" Mr. Mixy asked from the back.

And there was the problem. But I didn't see any way to

avoid telling him now, so I filled in Royce and my ex on the little we knew.

Otter Vance seemed pleased to see us at Whirlwind Airboat Tours, holiday or not, especially when Mark handed him a fat envelope. And then we were off.

The wind created by our speed added to the chill of the morning, but the sun was winning the battle, and by the time we reached the clearing that held the shack, I'd unzipped my hoodie. I looked around as we neared the dock but didn't spot Phantom.

"I'm not leaving you this time," Captain Vance said as he stopped the engine and blessed silence ensued. "You do what you need to do, and I'll be right here. But don't dawdle, all right?"

"No problem," Mark said. "But I think we'll need at least thirty minutes."

"Go." Our captain reached for his fishing poles as we climbed out.

I looked up as we walked down the dock. "Crime scene tape on the door."

"So they've been here," Neil said. "Let's try not to disturb anything."

"I don't want to get in the way," Mr. Mixy said. "I'll go to the outhouse and then hang out down here."

At least I didn't have to be near Mr. Mixy when he used the outhouse. I put bad memories out of my mind as we climbed the steps. The yellow crime-scene tape had been tied across the door from one railing on the landing to the other. We all looked at one another before Neil, Mr. Responsible himself, carefully untied one end of it and let it flutter.

Mark tried the doorknob with his handkerchief. No luck.

So I repeated my trick with the Cheesy Does It card, and we found ourselves back in the shack.

Lit only by window light, the room was bright enough to see there'd been activity—furniture moved and that kind of thing. The whole place looked, well, ruffled. Not messy or overturned. Just as if a thorough search had been made.

Diana and Mark headed over to the screened porch and the plants there, where Diana pulled on surgical gloves and began her extraction. Royce began a slow circuit of the room.

Neil and I stepped closer to the desk with its two shelves above. The books looked a bit askew but basically intact.

"Think they missed it?" I asked. "Noticed it's gone, I mean?"

"The notebook? Probably not. I don't think they knew about it. But it looks like another one is missing. The blue one."

"The one with the grocery lists and expenses."

"Right." He leaned in and looked more closely. Then, pulling the sleeve of his sweatshirt down to cover his hand so he wouldn't leave prints, he pulled open one drawer after another, giving the contents a good look as he went.

"Normal desk stuff," I said.

"She didn't stuff the drawers with much. She was living light out here."

"Made it easier to leave if she wanted to. I can't believe she stayed as long as she did."

Neil closed the last drawer. "Passion for science, I guess."

"Or obsession." But was it with science? Woodpeckers? Treasure?

"Hey, Pepper?" Royce's voice came from the kitchen area. "You might want to see this."

We exited the desk alcove and entered the kitchen. Royce

had opened the door of the small fridge, with a towel covering his hand. We were getting good at this "don't leave finger-prints" business, but at this point, it probably didn't matter.

The fridge had a few ginger ales and condiments, a half-eaten six-pack of eggs, a quart bottle of skim milk, a cardboard takeout box stamped with the logo for the Whirlwind Airboat Tours restaurant, and a dark green bottle with a gold foil label and unmistakable wrapped cork.

"Champagne?" I couldn't believe it. "She barely has enough in here for breakfast, and she had champagne?"

"If she had orange juice she'd be in business for mimosas," Royce commented, then grimaced. "Sorry. Bad joke. This place is so quiet, it's easy to forget she's dead." He looked up. "Sorry, Alice."

Neil did his trick with his sleeve and pulled out the bottle. He set it on the old Formica table and turned it slowly around.

I goggled at the seal. In a handsome serif font on the gold and white label, it read DESJARDINS in all caps.

"Coincidence?" I asked. "I mean, it's Enzo's label. But you can buy this anywhere, right?"

"You can buy Desjardins, but not just anywhere. Enzo's champagnes are highly sought after and carried by only the most exclusive wine shops." Neil bent and looked more closely. "And this one? You can't even buy it in Florida. We're using his flagship champagne at the New Year's Eve event. This is one of his more obscure bottlings. Goes for five hundred dollars a pop if you can find it."

"So Alice had a taste for pricey, collectible champagne?" Royce didn't sound as if he actually believed it.

"Maybe. She'd have to have a way to get it," Neil said.

"She had a way. The most direct way." I knew they were thinking the same thing. "Enzo."

"Put it back," Royce said. "They might be looking for that later."

"I think we should get out of here," Neil said.

Royce set off toward the porch. "I'll see if they're ready."

Movement out the window caught my eye. I took a step closer and looked down. "Oh my God. What the hell is he doing?"

"What?" Neil stepped up next to me. "Is he digging?"

Mr. Mixy had found the shovel Thor used and was digging chunks out of the dirt. Several holes already surrounded him. He worked fast!

And yeah, I'd thought about looking around for treasure. But I hadn't intended to dig enough holes to open a golf course.

"Let me get down there." I headed for the door. "See if they can wrap it up."

I had a feeling Neil was grateful I'd taken on the task of reining in Mr. Mixy, who was sweaty and excited when I got to him.

"I found a beer bottle!" he said. "I wouldn't be at all surprised if there was treasure here. I bet the guy who buried it was drinking the whole time."

"In 1715?" I looked at the bottle he'd found. "I don't think they had Corona back then."

"This is fun. I'm so glad you brought me along." He walked a few feet away from his current shallow hole and stuck the shovel into the dirt again.

"Would you stop that? Now everyone will know someone was out here looking around, including the police."

"Aw, come on, Pepper. What if we found silver and gold and all of that?" He turned over the shovelful of dirt, lost interest and walked a few feet away, poised to dig again.

"Stop it!"

He froze and looked at me. "What?"

"We're not even supposed to be here. It's a crime scene. We have to get going. The others are almost done."

"Just a couple more holes. Let's look for something really promising."

He traipsed off toward the water, and I trailed after him, wondering if I could grab the shovel and whack him on the head with it.

"Oh, look at that." Mr. Mixy had reached the edge of the island, not far from the dock. "There's a little indent in the bank. And you can see a hole right in the riverbank! It's like a mini cave. I bet there's all kinds of treasure in there!"

He set the tip of the shovel into the ground, stuck his boot on it and stomped down hard.

Hisssssss. The rough, eerie sound floated up to us from the hole.

"Uh, Stephan?" I took a step back. "I don't think that's such a good idea."

"I can feel it breaking through. Let me just take a quick look." He positioned the shovel for another big dig, and I stepped back again as I heard the door opening above us.

Stephan pushed down hard with his foot, and the shovel's blade crashed through the soil so quickly, he stumbled forward and fell onto his knees—just as the earth exploded beneath him with a deep, rattling growl.

Chapter Sixteen

"P hantom!" I shrieked at the sound of the massive gator's roar.

I turned and ran up onto the dock as Mr. Mixy slid forward in a collapsing mess of wet earth and leaves.

Yelping, he dropped the shovel and scrambled for purchase, but the ground liquefied around him, shooting him half into the water. Beneath him, the gator emerged, the crumbling remains of his cave shedding from his bumpy hide. The white scars on his face glinted in the patchy sunlight as his throat puffed out in a guttural bellow.

Pushed up by the beast, Mr. Mixy screamed. He lurched to the side and out of the way of the creature, scrabbling to get back onto land as the bank's edge dissolved into the water.

Phantom whirled to see who had destroyed his lair. The gator opened his mouth wide, water dripping off his sharp teeth. His bumpy tail followed his head around like the thong of a whip, whacking Mr. Mixy on the leg. Stephan lost any purchase he had and slid farther into the water, even as he clutched handfuls of dirt in his effort to climb out.

"Pepper!" he cried, just as a deeper voice called "Pepper!" from the stairs.

Neil. I looked up. He and the others rattled down the stairs, and at the sound of pounding steps on the dock, I swiveled my gaze to Otter. The airboat captain sprinted toward me, his gun in his hand.

I looked back at Mr. Mixy just as Phantom spun the other way, incredibly fast for such a big beast, and clamped down his teeth on the mixologist's foot. Mr. Mixy cried out, grasping handfuls of dirt in vain as he tried to get away.

Whoa no. Had my murderous thoughts manifested into Stephan actually being killed by Phantom?

Was I enjoying this just a little bit?

Of course not! This was really bad. "Shake off your boot!" I yelled.

Mr. Mixy jiggled his leg even as he clutched at the scrub along the bank. He managed to grab ahold of a thick vine as Phantom tugged. And then, like a jet-powered log, Phantom launched into a roll, spraying water everywhere.

The death roll!

In that moment it was as if everyone oozed forward in slow motion, even as everything happened at the speed of light. I remained glued in place, like those dreams when you know you have to run but can't move an inch.

Mr. Mixy screamed again as he was flipped and rolled, but somehow he clung onto the vine. About to be twisted into a pretzel and tenderized for dinner, he howled as his boot popped off in the gator's mouth.

At the same moment, the sound of a gunshot blasted through the clearing. I ducked and turned to see Otter behind me, panting hard, pointing his gun at the sky.

The huge gator, oblivious to the shot, rolled even faster without the drag of Mr. Mixy, attempting to kill his prey— now, just Stephan's egregiously fashionable boot.

Phantom's spins abruptly stopped, and he wriggled away

from the bank and submerged, leaving naught but a ripple behind him.

Neil grabbed me by the shoulders. "Are you OK?"

My adrenaline crashing, I nodded. Honestly, I felt like a coward, but then my rational brain intervened: What was I supposed to do, wrestle the alligator? I looked over at Royce and Mark, who'd made it to Mr. Mixy. They hauled him out of the water but didn't stop there. In a moment, they'd dragged him through the brush and over to the relative safety of the wooden dock.

"Are you all right?" Royce asked me as they dumped him next to me. Mr. Mixy's beard was askew and filled with leaves. His clothes were trashed.

I gave Royce a thumbs-up as Mr. Mixy erupted in a whine.

"He took my BOOT!" He grabbed his bootless foot and held on to it as if it were his favorite stuffed animal.

"He could've taken your foot," Mark said. "Calm down."

I eyed the purple accents on the surviving red boot. "Is the trim on that boot made of gator hide, by any chance?"

Mr. Mixy caressed his remaining boot and didn't reply. I touched my lucky gator-tooth bracelet. Clearly, the boots weren't as charmed.

"Are you injured?" Neil tried to get a look at the foot, but Mr. Mixy had contorted himself into a ball.

"I don't think so?" he said in a small voice.

"Show us the foot," Diana commanded, her tone brooking no refusal.

Mr. Mixy slowly unfolded, then stretched out his foot.

"Take the sock off," she said. "I'm not touching it."

"Wise move," I remarked.

Royce snorted, and Mr. Mixy drew off his wet, muddy

sock. His hairy foot looked a little grubby, but the skin wasn't broken.

Otter stepped closer. "You idiot. You could've been killed. And harassing gators is a felony. What were you doing digging in his gator cave?"

"I was looking for treasure!" Mr. Mixy put his wet sock back on and assumed a pathetic "pity me" face covered in mud.

Otter shook his head, furious, his mouth working like he was trying to contain himself.

"What is it, Captain Vance?" I asked him.

"Alice," he said. "We'd have a beer now and then. She told me she'd found something really special out here. I wonder how many people she told. Or if somebody overheard us at the Whirlwind bar and thought maybe she found that stupid Casanova treasure and wanted to help themselves. Like you," he said to Mr. Mixy. "Pathetic."

Ouch. Also, accurate. We suffered in uncomfortable silence for a moment before Otter spoke again. "Let's get going. Someone was bound to hear the gunshot and might come looking."

Mark hauled Mr. Mixy to his feet, and the bedraggled mixologist limped his way down the dock and climbed into the airboat.

I sat as far away from him as I could. I couldn't help thinking this fiasco was my fault. Otter might just as well have been yelling at me. I'd let Mr. Mixy hear the story about the treasure. I should have known better. He always had an eye out for an easy buck, and he followed me everywhere. I could've just said no this morning and left him behind, no matter what my aunt said. So I really was responsible.

Neil slipped his arm around me, and I leaned into him as

the airboat flew down the waterways and back toward the fish camp. His warmth made me feel better and a little calmer. Phantom's attack had scared the hell out of me. But it could've been worse. Much worse.

In all the commotion, I'd almost forgotten about the shack and what we'd seen there. Champagne in the fridge. A hard-to-get boutique champagne whose auteur was right here in Bohemia.

And now we had to consider that Enzo Desjardins might've known Alice as well. Had he visited her? Were they friends—or more? And just what was his business with Raquel Tocks?

I looked up at Neil to find him gazing at me with a little smile playing about his lips.

"Enzo?" he mouthed.

I nodded, then slipped out my phone so I could text Neil instead of shouting over the roar of the airboat. "Let's talk to him today."

He texted me back. "It's Christmas. He might have plans."

"If his plans are with Raquel, he might be glad to break them."

OUR CREW WAS quiet when we disembarked at the fish camp. While Mr. Mixy limped off to the bathroom, Mark thanked Otter and handed him what looked like a generous tip.

"You're all right," Otter told him, then looked around at the rest of us. "I agreed to take you out there today because I want to know what happened to Alice, too. She was a friend. I'm invested. That said, never bring that furry guy with you again."

"Understood," Mark said, and we all thanked him and headed to the gravel parking lot. Neil stepped aside to make a phone call—to Enzo, I hoped.

"Did you get what you needed?" I asked Diana.

She opened her backpack and let me have a peek inside, where, next to Alice's notebook, a handful of labeled, zip-closed clear plastic bags held moistened paper towels and little wisps of green. "These samples might give me an idea of what she was working on. I think I parsed her organization system, but I didn't find a key or log. Everything's numbered. So I just took a few specimens, labeled everything with their positions in the trays and the numbers on each pot."

"And I took photos with my phone." Mark must've given up on the fancy camera.

"I wish we had her laptop. I would expect her to keep records about the plants there," Diana said.

"What about her notebook?" I asked. "Maybe she recorded her findings in there."

"It's just so odd." Diana closed up her bag and looped it over her shoulder. "The cryptic record-keeping. The notebook."

"She must have been trying to keep a secret." I thought of the treasure. "Maybe it was about more than plants."

"Our priority has to be unraveling the notebook," Mark said.

Diana patted her backpack strap. "Mine is looking at these plants and getting a sample off to a friend at the technical university in Bohemia. He's willing to do a rush DNA analysis on anything I need."

"Is he now?" Mark teased. "Special acquaintance, is he?"

Diana glowered at him. "Professional colleague."

"So he's a professional, is he?" Mark lowered his voice. "Is he for hire by the hour?"

Diana smacked Mark on the arm.

"Ouch!" He rubbed his arm with extra drama, but he was grinning.

Neil strolled back over and shook his head at me. No luck with Enzo? Maybe Oleanna knew how to get ahold of him.

"After you sort out your plants," Mark told Diana, "I can take you to deliver your samples if you like. I think Celestine is busy preparing the holiday meal, correct?"

"Correct," I said, charmed by Mark's devotion to Diana.

Hmm. Devotion?

"I suppose that would be all right," Diana said, "if you have a place to work."

"Plenty of room. And it's quiet. Alastair is spending all his time on the beach. Though perhaps I can get him to make us a drink. I could certainly use one after witnessing that wildlife special back there."

"I'll drop you both off at Mark's then," Neil said as Mr. Mixy emerged from the restroom. The furry one had cleaned off his face, though I felt bad for Neil's upholstery when Stephan climbed into the rear seat of the SUV and lay down. As we all got in and the car rolled out, I could smell the swamp funk he'd brought with him and tried not to gag.

At least the hairball wasn't dead. I mean, I wouldn't say there weren't times when I wished he were, in a general revenge fantasy kind of sense. But him actually torn apart by a gator and eaten for lunch? Gross. And we'd have had a hard time explaining to the police why we were back at the shack. As it was, they'd see all the holes Mr. Mixy had dug and wonder what was going on.

I pulled out my phone to text Oleanna. No way was I going to have a phone call in the car where Mr. Mixy might hear me.

"Hey," I wrote. "Merry Xmas. Looking forward to seeing you this evening. BTW, we wanted to talk to Enzo but he's not answering. Any idea where he is today?"

There was a minute of nothing, then bubbles showed she was composing a reply. When it came, I might've released a little gasp.

"He's here at my hotel. Want to meet us for lunch here? The restaurant's open till two."

"Great. Half an hour?" I typed, all the while thinking, *Did Enzo ever leave after last night's drinkfest?*

"See you then," Oleanna replied.

Oleanna and the Frenchman? Hmm. How was I going to ask all the girl-talk questions I wanted to ask with Neil and Enzo right there? Even though the big reason we wanted to see Enzo was to ask him about Alice.

And to figure out whether he had a reason to kill her.

Chapter Seventeen

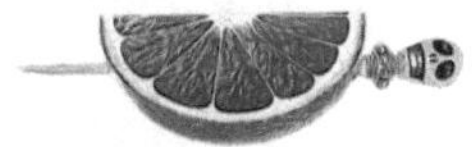

Neil and I made sure Mr. Mixy got into the elevator to go to his room at the hotel, then we went to the restaurant to meet Enzo and Oleanna.

They were already seated opposite each other at a table by the big windows that looked out on the Atlantic Ocean, bright blue and sparkling under the sun. Even dressed casually, they both exuded beauty, like a commercial for a high-end car. Their cocktails caught the light: She had a mimosa—a champagne drink, of course—but the champagne guy had what looked like an Old-Fashioned garnished with a slice of bacon. I was sure it had been smoked; the scent was pleasant, and the bacon had my tummy rumbling.

Neil shot me an amused glance. He could hear that?

"How are you doing this morning?" I asked Oleanna and Enzo. "Or is it afternoon?"

"Afternoon, barely. I'm great," Oleanna said.

I sat next to her, and Neil sat next to Enzo, who lifted his glass in salute.

"No champagne for you?" I asked him.

He offered a one-shoulder shrug. "Their selection leaves something to be desired. I find it is better to drink good champagne or none at all."

"And mine is drowned in orange juice, so it tastes just fine."

Oleanna smiled and lifted her glass. "Of course, from here on out I'll only be drinking Desjardins." She turned to Enzo. "Cheers."

Enzo smiled at her. *"À ta santé."* They sipped while gazing into one another's eyes. So they must have made the endorsement deal. At least.

"I understand the French believe if you don't look each other in the eye during a toast, you'll have seven years of bad luck," Neil remarked.

"Or bad sex," Enzo said, one eye fluttering, and we all laughed.

We looked at the menus that were already on the table, and a young woman came over and took our orders. She was back momentarily with club soda for Neil and a cola for me; those airboat rides dried me out, and I needed the caffeine. We chitchatted about the weather and our holiday traditions or lack thereof before I dug deeper.

"So ..." I prompted Oleanna.

"Yes, we have reached an agreement." She looked at Enzo, her eyes shining.

Enzo nodded. "She will be the beautiful face of my champagne. I could not be more delighted."

"Congratulations to both of you." I looked at Enzo. "Does this mean you'll be expanding production?"

He looked surprised. "Why do you say this?"

"Well, you told me a little bit about how you grow your grapes and bottle them. I got the impression that you don't produce a lot of bottles. Am I wrong? Hiring a movie star to promote your brand suggests you want to reach a wider audience, and that means more bottles."

A corner of his mouth lifted. "You are quite right."

He didn't have a chance to say more, because just then, the

food arrived. Oleanna got a salad with a slab of sesame-encrusted seared tuna. Enzo had scampi. Neil had a Cobb salad, and me? A cheeseburger topped with bacon. I had bacon on the brain. I would need to take Astra on an extra-long walk later.

"You're known as a grower," Neil said to Enzo as we ate. "Will you still be using your own grapes as you expand production?"

"Indeed. I have also acquired more property. I won't be putting out so many bottles like you think. You will not see your football teams spraying it around the room when they win the big game."

I chuckled at the idea. "Though they could probably afford it. What's your thinking? Are you worried people won't take you as seriously?"

"Eh, champagne is not so serious. And I want to do as much as I can with this little life, make as much as I can of it. Why not be excellent and famous, too?"

"Too much of anything is bad, but too much champagne is just right." Neil smiled.

"Who said that?" I knew Neil was witty enough, but he always had a quotation in his pocket.

"F. Scott Fitzgerald."

"And he is correct!" Enzo took a sip of his whiskey drink. A bit ironic, that. "Oleanna says you wanted to speak with me? Is this about the party?"

"No." I hated to break the mood, but this was why we came. "It's about Alice."

"Ah, poor Dr. Dalworth." Enzo's eye twitched as he took another sip of his drink.

"Did you know her well?" I asked.

He hesitated. "Not well, no."

Now the loquacious winemaker didn't have so much to say. "We thought maybe you did, since you visited her in her shack."

Neil's eyes snapped to me in alarm, even as Oleanna stiffened. OK, so we didn't know Enzo had been there, but the champagne sure was.

"Once or twice," Enzo said, seemingly unfazed. "I was interested in her work. Though of course I knew it was going away sometime, since Raquel has plans for the property."

I washed down a bite of burger with my cola. "I understand she's already filed papers with the local planning commission."

Enzo nodded. "That is correct. In fact, I delivered them for her."

Now this was news.

"If you don't mind me asking," Neil said, reading my mind, "what business do you have with Raquel?"

"I am an investor in the Boyle Lakes development."

"Why?" I asked, stunned. "I mean ..."

"Why does a grower from Champagne invest in a development in Florida? I don't want all of my eggs in one basket. Or should I say grapes?" Enzo smiled. "I like the climate—for visiting, not growing. I was looking into opportunities in Florida and sought out Raquel."

"And gave Alice a very nice bottle of your best," I prodded.

His pursed lips seemed to quirk from side to side as he swirled his glass. Finally, he looked up, his colorful hazel eyes cool. "I met her during one of my visits several months ago. I then sought her out at the shack. I was trying to win her over." He glanced at Oleanna, who looked away, then returned his gaze to me. "She is a botanist. I thought she might have advice for me on the new land I have acquired. A different terroir means different growth, different taste. I wanted a thorough analysis."

I didn't know much about growing grapes for champagne, but wasn't France full of experts? Why would he want to talk to a botanist who specialized in endangered species in the Americas?

"Was she receptive?" I asked him.

"Not as much as I hoped. She was busy with her research."

Her research. "Did she give you an idea of what she was working on?"

Enzo's eyes seemed to wander before they landed on me again. "Not in so many words. She said it was too early for results and she never liked to discuss a scientific investigation until it was over."

Convenient. Ha.

"How did you get out there?" I asked him.

"Raquel has kindly loaned me a small motorboat with a trailer. I just attach it to one of the trucks from her business and can indulge in fishing whenever I wish."

Whoa. Talk about access to the scene of the crime.

"I'm surprised the police haven't talked to you," Neil said.

"Oh, they have. They talked to Raquel and me together," Enzo answered.

I got over my surprise quickly. Of course they wanted to talk to Raquel. She had the most to gain from Alice's death.

I looked at Enzo. "Did they ask for an alibi?"

"You mean where I was when she died? Of course. It so happens ours is the same. A business meeting that morning that went on for more than three hours. We were discussing the development."

Also convenient if he was working with Raquel to hasten Alice's demise. But then why did he get chummy with Alice?

Was he really hoping to hire her as a consultant? Make her feel better about the development? Get her out of there as soon as possible?

"Speaking of Raquel, I have promised to be her sommelier this afternoon and help her prepare for her dinner tonight. I will tell the *serveuse* to put lunch on my bill. Please let me know if you have any concerns about New Year's Eve, all right?" He stood and cast a warm look on Oleanna. "It is always a pleasure. We will talk again tomorrow?"

Oleanna hesitated only a moment. "Of course. Thank you, Enzo." She smiled at him, but I had the impression her acting skills had come into play.

Enzo stopped by the bar and spoke to our server, then left the room.

"Boy, you two are definitely deflating my bubbles," Oleanna said.

"I'm sorry." Neil looked truly contrite.

I also gave her my best sympathetic frown. "I didn't mean to mess up the mood, but we had to ask after we saw that champagne in the shack. Who knew he was working with Raquel? I mean, we knew he was staying with her and in town on business, but I never really put the two together."

"Pardon me," Neil said, heading for the bathroom. Or maybe he was just giving us a minute.

"I didn't know the details either," Oleanna said. "He mentioned he was staying in her guest house. I guess I didn't really care while he was wining and dining me. Last night, we walked under the stars on the beach. Then we curled up on the lounge on my balcony and he said sweet nothings in French and kissed me. We fell asleep there until the sunrise woke us up. And—just between us?"

"Of course."

"Let's say it would have gone further if housekeeping hadn't banged on the door at oh dark thirty."

"Oh, I hate that! And I'm sorry. He's probably telling the truth. You don't have to throw the baby out with the bathwater."

"I'm not throwing out either, especially the deal," said Oleanna. "It's sweet. But I'll proceed with caution. Oh, gosh— you don't think he killed her, do you?"

"Of course not!" *Maybe.* "The police are treating the death as suspicious, but that doesn't mean it's for sure murder anyway. Maybe it was an accident after all."

"Maybe."

"Right." That said, I didn't think Enzo was telling the whole truth, either. "You know, not to be a Debbie Downer, but champagne and business might not always mix."

"Except when champagne is your business." She sighed. "I have a quote, too. Jay Leno said it. 'Show business is like champagne. You'll appreciate it more if you don't drink it every day.' I need a break. And another source of income."

"Then enjoy yourself and get that contract signed. You're going to be perfect. Elegant. Beautiful. Smart. And you have this energy about you that is going to sell *lots* of champagne. He's lucky to have you."

She set her jaw and nodded at me. "Yes, he is." She lifted her mimosa and clinked it against my soda glass. "Bubbles up."

We drank, and Neil returned. After we said our goodbyes— or *au revoir,* since Oleanna was coming to dinner—and got out to the car, I turned to Neil.

"I'm going to ask Millie to see what she can find out about Enzo."

"Go for it." Neil sounded resigned. "I just hope he wasn't into treasure hunting."

Chapter Eighteen

Florida was the perfect place to have a poolside dinner on December 25.

Well, not always. Once in a while we touched freezing this time of year or got a week of cold, miserable rain. But not today. If anything, our lovely coast basked in the bright sun all day, guaranteeing our Christmas dinner would be just cool enough to wear a sweater around the fire bowl but not cold enough for discomfort.

Aunt Celestine and I each had our sliding glass doors open to the patio so people and dogs could move in and out easily, visiting my bar or her yummy buffet, sitting wherever they wanted to land with their plates. She'd made a variety of dishes, from traditional ham to a fantastic vegan thing that took advantage of her vast herb garden, and a few of our guests arrived with decadent desserts. Mark brought a supply of his distillery's liquors. Royce donated a bottle of his primo Penny Brilliant bourbon. I'd made a champagne punch, and Neil gave us a wicked eggnog he'd been aging.

He and I hadn't talked about Christmas presents yet. I'd wrapped my gift for Neil and put it under the rosemary tree sitting atop my art-deco bar. The little tree had rainbow lights and a silver ribbon at the top, but that was it. I'd been so busy working, I hadn't had time to do much decorating. Fortunately,

Aunt Celestine had bought a dozen of these trees for inside and outside our houses, so everything sparkled and smelled fresh and delicious, like a pine forest crossed with a pork roast.

My aunt didn't make a big deal about the holiday usually. We were both more into the cultural aspects of Christmas than the religious ones. But she and I had exchanged books earlier, a nice tradition that made us both happy, and she'd put on this fantastic spread for our friends, which was about the best gift she could've given me. This was my family, and I could feel the love. A few folks gave each other gifts if they wished—Cray brought me a beautiful old bottle of rum from his precious collection—but there was no formal presentation or crazy exchange where people stole each other's presents. Low-key was the name of the game tonight, and we all needed an evening like that.

We were missing a few folks who had other obligations, but we had a very nice crowd—Neil's grandfather, Reginald, and Cray (Neil's parents were at some fancy dinner with their friends). Jorge, Royce, Mark and Alastair were here, and of course, Diana was staying with my aunt. Oleanna and Melody came with Luke, and to my surprise, Mr. Mixy showed up, though he appeared more subdued than usual. He was lucky the only souvenirs he had from the gator attack were small scratches on his face, muscle pains he emphasized with dramatic groans whenever he moved, and a slightly trimmer beard. But it was still bushy enough to hide a bird in.

When we'd all stuffed ourselves, we settled in chatty little groups with our drinks. What I'd come to think of as the airboat crew gathered in chairs around the fire bowl on the patio, away from the others: Royce, Mark, Diana, Neil, and myself ... with Victoria in Mark's lap, snoozing, and Astra in mine, trying to grab the strawberry that garnished my champagne punch.

In the big rust-colored fire bowl decorated with leaf cutouts, logs crackled, their undersides glowing orange. They released bursts of bright sparks that drifted and died in the light breeze. A variety of offbeat and classic holiday music played through the speakers. Astra was warm, as was my festive, scoop-neck black sweater decorated with silver sparkles and a small offset silver bow at the neckline. The punch was delicious. And Neil's chair was almost close enough to mine.

"Did you get the plant samples to your friend?" I asked Diana.

"Yes, I did, thanks to Mark," she said, her arms crossed over her gorgeous green wool sweater. "We'll see if they can tell us anything about what Alice was working on. I think I recognize a couple of the specimens, but it can be especially difficult to identify young plants visually, especially if they're something I'm not familiar with. I'm wondering if she had a mature sample in that plant press."

I really hoped she didn't want to go back and find out.

"And how's the journal coming along?" Neil asked.

"That bloody notebook," Mark said, and we all laughed. He scratched behind Victoria's ears, and the spaniel shifted with a sigh. "We need to know what kind of cipher it is, and then we need to figure out the key. I have to admit, it's far beyond my ability."

"But you said you were good at maths," Diana teased, and we laughed again.

Something Mark said flared a spark in my brain. "You said you need a key? Surely Alice had to have a key somewhere. Maybe even in the notebook itself."

Royce leaned forward, his glass of bourbon catching the firelight. "But she wouldn't have wanted to make it that easy. Otherwise, why would she have had the notebook in code in the first place?"

"True," I said.

Now Neil sat up. "She might have left the key with someone she trusted."

I looked at him. He focused on Diana.

"Oh my God. You're a genius," I told him, then to her: "Do you still have the letter?"

Diana shot out of her chair and ran into Aunt Celestine's side of the duplex as Neil berated himself. "I'm not a genius. It was in front of us the whole time."

"I should have thought of it earlier," I argued.

"Don't be silly," Royce said. "Mark should have thought of it. He's the genius at 'maths.'"

Mark said something extremely rude to Royce as we all chuckled and Diana came back to the fireside, carrying the letter and the pretty green notebook, which she set on the pavers next to her.

"Read it again?" I asked, hugging Astra. "The weird parts, anyway?"

"I love the weird parts," Mark teased.

Diana struggled with the envelope. "If I can get it out of here without tearing it."

"Easy. You don't want it to end up in the fire." Mark's golden irises reflected the flames as he sipped his eggnog.

Diana harrumphed and finally slipped the folded card out of the envelope, which Royce took and examined before he set it safely atop the notebook.

"All right," she said. "It begins with her thanking me for

being interested in her work and saying she didn't think she'd be doing it for much longer."

"Eerily prophetic," Neil noted.

"Indeed," she agreed. "Then she goes on: *The winds are changing, as are the seasons. Beware the Ides of March, as they say. It's getting a bit too hot for me. And after a few setbacks, I find I don't want to prove the adage that bad things come in threes. Sometimes life is a puzzle, but the prize is worth it. I hope my work will live on.*"

"There's a lot there, if we see it as a code," I said. "The Ides of March? March is three months away. March fifteenth, right? Is that date significant in some way? And I can see things getting hot if she was feeling pressure from someone. And she tells us right there it's a puzzle."

"And that she thought she might not survive," Royce said softly.

We were all silent for a moment as a song about snow drifted eerily through our tropical backyard.

"All right. Read the rest," Mark prompted her.

"Very well. *I feared we might not get to see each other, and so I have written you this note. How I miss our salad days together. But the key is to concentrate on what's next, not what is left behind, and I wished to express a dear wish that you will move ahead. And that's what letters are for.* Then she signs off 'with respect and affection.'" Diana's voice cracked a little. Mark reached over and rubbed her shoulder for a moment.

"Well, speaking of maths, she does include a number. Three," Mark said.

"Um. Yes," I said.

"What about the salad days? Is that a reference to anything in particular?" Royce asked Diana.

"We knew each other at school, but we weren't terribly close," she said. "Friends, yes. Salad days seems a little poetic."

"So you weren't sitting around growing lettuce and eating Caesar salads?" Mark joked.

"Wait," Neil said. "Isn't there something called a Caesar cipher?"

"Good God!" Mark said as I burbled, "The Ides of March! Julius Caesar!"

"That has to be it," Diana said excitedly. "How does it work?"

Neil already had his phone out, tapping the screen. In a moment, he said, "It's one of the simplest ciphers. Each letter in the coded message is assigned a letter a set number's distance away in the alphabet. So if the number is two, *A* would mean *C*. Or *Y*, depending which way you went."

"Three!" I shouted, and a lot of people looked our way before they laughed and went back to their conversations.

"But which way?" Mark said. *"C* or *Y?"*

"It's right here." Diana waved the letter at us. "She says, *I wished to express a dear wish that you will move ahead. And that's what letters are for.* Moving ahead means *C.* Rather, *D*—three letters. She even said 'that's what letters are for.' I must say, she put an awful lot of faith in my figuring this out."

"She knew you'd have intelligent friends," Mark quipped, and Diana smacked his arm with the card. Victoria raised her head and let out a low *woof.*

"Not only did you have to figure it out," Royce said, "but it's almost a miracle you walked away with the notebook."

"Which means she *really* didn't want this falling into the wrong hands," I suggested.

Mark's face was alive with more than the firelight. "Let's work on it now. Just get a flavor of it. I've noted words that were repeated several times. Maybe we can get a taste of those before we really get into it."

Neil was tapping on his phone again. "There are places online where you can type in the key and then the passages and it will translate for you. But it might take forever, and if this is sensitive—"

"We'll start the old-fashioned way." Mark turned to Diana and set a sleepy Victoria on the patio.

Diana granted him a huge, genuine smile. "Let's go into Celestine's kitchen."

"Report back!" I called after them as they moved inside, the dog trotting after them.

"Well, I'm going to get some of that eggnog and see how Mr. Mixy is doing," Royce said. "I feel sorry for him. He looks so pathetic curled up on the lounge chair, listening to Cray."

"Maybe he'll learn something," I said, and Royce chuckled as he walked away. To my surprise, Astra jumped off my lap and followed him. Maybe I shouldn't have been surprised. She loved Royce.

"And that leaves us," Neil said, sipping his eggnog.

"Yes, it does." I held up my glass and clinked it to his. "Merry Christmas. I—I have something for you."

"You do?" His gray eyes, rimmed in that dark blue I loved, sparkled. They even matched his navy-blue sweater—no bow tie tonight. "I have something for you, too."

"You do?" Then I felt silly for echoing him. "Mine's on the bar."

"Let's go."

Chapter Nineteen

Neil and I passed Royce and Astra coming out of my house as we went in. My sleek little bar sat in the living room, opposite the couch and a comfy chair. With the bar's wings open, it appeared as a semicircle of shining reddish-brown wood inlaid with silver-colored trim. The cabinet doors in the front featured what looked like a porthole—actually two silver semicircle handles—in the center. Its streamlined symmetry was totally deco. As were the two red leather barstools in front, each with a chrome frame base shaped like a *Z*.

Bottles were scattered over the top where people had been making cocktails, next to the punch bowl and the rosemary Christmas tree. I put down my champagne flute, picked up the small package wrapped in red tissue paper and silver ribbon, and handed it to Neil.

He set down his drink and shook the package, making me laugh. Then he tore it open. His eyes lit up.

"Oh, wow. This is Prohibition-era, isn't it?"

"Yes." I tried not to get too excited at his look of delight as he turned the silver flask over in his hands. Its walls were slightly curved, as hip flasks were, but the coolest part: The metal vessel was shaped like a closed book, with a molded cover and pages, etched with the title *Dry Stories* in a funky art-deco font. At the top of the "book" near the binding was the flat silver stopper.

"This is one of the coolest Prohibition collectibles I've ever seen. And you know I love Prohibition stuff."

"Because you're a very strange bartender," I joked. *He likes it!*

"I'm not too strait-laced for you?" he asked. It took me a second to realize he wasn't joking.

"Oh, Neil. Never."

And then he leaned in and kissed me, just long enough to make my toes tingle. "Thank you."

"You're welcome." We stared at each other for several seconds before I spoke. "Well?"

He laughed. "You want your present?"

"Yes, of course I want my present!"

"All right." He reached behind my bar and pulled out something thin and almost flat wrapped in gold paper.

What could it be? A string of pearls? A fancy bottle opener? A—a—

As soon as he handed it to me, I ripped it open and found, beneath the gold paper, more gold paper with print on it. "A chocolate bar?"

"A very fancy chocolate bar. Go ahead. Taste it."

I gave him a puzzled look. I loved chocolate, but this seemed a little odd. Whatever. He knew what he was doing. I popped open the wrapper, and inside was a dark chocolate bar —with silver paper wrapped around it. I looked up at him and grinned as I unfolded the layers to reveal the inner paper wasn't just plain silver. In the shape of a ticket, it also had writing on it.

"Is it a silver ticket?" I exclaimed. "Not a golden one?"

"Golden tickets make me think of that thing at Hookahakaha."

Oh, yeah. Bad memories. "So what's the ticket for?" I read the printing on the ticket as he watched me with a silly grin. *"Good for one weekend getaway to anywhere of your choice.* A weekend away? With you?"

"Yes. I'll book the rooms and a flight if we need a flight, or we can drive. How does that sound?"

Wait. "Rooms?" I asked.

"Yes. A ... romantic getaway." He looked so eager for me to like his gift.

Oh my God. He was such a nerd. And what I wanted to hear was *room*. Room, singular! A room we shared!

This man was such a project. But the gift was sweet. And promising. "I love it. Thank you," I said. And I kissed him back. At least he'd progressed to "romantic." We were getting somewhere. Then I took a bite out of the corner of the chocolate bar. *Mmm.* Salted dark chocolate.

We stood there awkwardly for a few seconds smiling at each other as I savored the rich chocolate, and then with all this thinking about gifts, a new thought popped into my head. "The toy! That thing for Astra! I totally forgot to put it in her stocking."

"What toy?"

"I have no idea. It came in the mail. I ordered a bunch of things. It's still in my bag. Hang on." I set down the chocolate bar and the silver ticket and ran to my bedroom, then came back with the box I'd been carrying in my messenger bag. "Astra!" I called.

When my dog didn't make an appearance—no doubt she was socializing with Royce—I retrieved a knife from behind the bar and cut open the box anyway.

"Here we go," I said as I folded back the flaps. Whatever was inside was wrapped in purple tissue paper. I paused. "That's pretty fancy for a dog toy. I can't remember what I ordered."

"Wait." Neil put his hand over mine, and I froze. "Maybe you should open this slowly."

A chill shivered through me. Then I relaxed. "Oh, Neil. You don't think it's him, do you? I haven't heard anything since Kentucky. He's probably forgotten all about me."

"Just be careful. You've already cut it open, so I don't think it's going to explode."

"That makes me feel better," I said dryly. I went ahead and eased the contents of the box into my hand. "See, it's a toy. A ball, I think."

But as I pulled the tissue paper away, the ball revealed itself to be something else: a plastic pink Easter egg.

"That does seem like an odd Christmas present," Neil said.

I swallowed. This was definitely odd. "I'm afraid to open it."

"Let me."

"No. It's fine." I wouldn't put Neil in danger, though maybe it was too late for that. I held it as far away from me and him as I could and popped the two halves of the egg apart.

Something fell to the floor. It made me think of a gum wrapper, but it seemed to be plain paper. For a moment I let my mind run wild, imagining it was tainted with poison or might spontaneously combust. Then I told myself to get a grip, reached down and picked it up.

The piece of white paper had been folded several times so it would fit in the egg, so it was crisscrossed with creases when I unraveled it.

"What is it?" Neil asked, moving closer to look over my shoulder. "Looks like a poem."

The words were written in a small, blocky hand. I swallowed. "It's not Shakespeare. Listen to this."

And I read it aloud.

> *In her trusting little mind,*
> *Mama's eggs are scrambled.*
> *Who's to say just who she'll find*
> *in NOLA while I ramble?*
> *Brothers come and brothers go*
> *but mother, she'll stay true*
> *to the man she knows as Beau.*
> *The yolk will be on you.*

I uttered a curse word I'd been trying to work out of my vocabulary. "Beau. It's him."

"Looks like it." Neil's tone was grim. "It sounds like he's telling you he's in New Orleans."

"And threatening my mother. She sounded like she was completely under his spell when it all went down in October. I thought the police had filled her in on what a con man he was."

"You haven't talked to her any more about this?"

"Neil, you know we don't talk. Hardly ever. And I didn't want to have a big chat with her until Royce talked to her."

As we'd learned in Kentucky, Royce found out he was the baby my mom had given up in her wild-child days before she turned to religion, but Royce hadn't met her yet. He told us the truth after Beau claimed to be my brother.

"I did talk to my father once after all that happened." *After Beau tried to kill me.* "I asked if they were doing OK and if they'd heard from him. Dad was kind of vague. It was almost like he didn't believe me. I reiterated how dangerous Beau was and how they should call the cops if they heard from him again. Do you think they've heard from him and didn't want to say?"

"Well, he is a con man. Maybe he has his claws in them again or plans to."

"They came into all that money. They're still a ripe target. I have to warn them."

"You have to consider another possibility," Neil said.

"What?"

"This is a trap, set just for you. He's told you where he is— or where he wants you to think he is."

"And in so many words, he's promised to get back at me for spoiling his plans the first time." I stuck the message back in the egg and put the egg back in the box. I looked at the address. Creepy. He knew where I lived. But at least it had been mailed—it had postage and a postmark. So he hadn't dropped it off here. "There's a return address. Dauphine Street."

Neil looked worried. "Pepper—"

"We have something!" Diana's voice snapped me out of my racing thoughts as she and Mark burst into the room. She carried the green notebook.

They halted when they saw our faces. "Is everything all right?" Mark asked.

"Fine," Neil and I said together. I put the box behind my bar. I wasn't ready to discuss the egg or even think about it yet, and it seemed Neil didn't want to get into it now either. But I would have to figure it out soon.

"What do you have?" I asked them.

Mark's eyes glittered. "Sit down and we'll show you."

"Let's go back to the fire." I didn't like the idea of having to watch what we said whenever someone came in to get a drink. So Neil dipped up fresh glasses of punch for him and me, and we returned to our seats at the fire. Royce came over, too, carrying a sleepy Astra.

"Where's Victoria?" I asked Mark.

"She's occupying your aunt's lap. I think she's trying to get the edge in a territorial dispute with Astra."

I chuckled and added a log to the fire. "All right. Whatcha got?"

"We focused on words that seemed to appear more frequently and recognized several right away," Diana said, "including plants and marsh and Florida, that sort of thing."

"But that's not why you're excited," I concluded.

"Right." Mark sat forward. "There's one in particular that has our attention."

I swear, he was dragging this out on purpose. "Go on."

Diana glanced at Mark, then at us. "This may sound strange, but she frequently wrote the word *emeralds*."

I almost dropped my glass. "Treasure?" I asked in a hoarse whisper. "The Casanova treasure?"

"We don't know yet, but why else would she write that?" asked Mark. "The question is, where did she keep these emeralds?"

"And did she find anything else?" My mind raced. "And did someone else find them after she died or know about them beforehand?"

"We don't have any context yet," Diana cautioned. "And who knows how much she gives away in this?" She held up the notebook.

"Did you say Alice had a grant for her work?" I asked Diana.

She nodded. "She mentioned it in an email. I don't know the details."

"She sure wasn't spending much on her life in the shack. Unless the rent was crazy. Where was the money going?"

"It might not have been a very large grant," Diana replied, "but that's a good question."

"Maybe she needed money," I speculated. "A few precious gems might go a long way."

Royce smiled as the sound of Astra snoring cut through the music and chatter on the patio. "Did you ever have the sense Alice was hiding something?" he asked Diana.

"Recently? We weren't really close enough for me to get a feeling one way or another, and she had been much less in touch over the past year. I was surprised she was so eager to see me, but I suspected she had something interesting to show me. Not necessarily a secret. She certainly didn't give me the impression she was digging for treasure. But clearly she's been keeping secrets in this notebook."

"I guess you have a lot more translating to do," I said to Mark and Diana.

"Not my favorite activity," she confessed.

"Come over to the flat. I'll have lunch brought in. We'll make a day of it," Mark told her.

"Why are you so interested?" she asked him, a hint of suspicion in her voice.

"How could I not be? Besides, we're not going to let that nasty Thor Roberts get ahold of her treasure." Mark sounded both enthused and earnest, but I wondered if he was holding back something.

"All right," Diana said. "I'll come over in the morning."

"I can drive you over on my way to Nola," I told her.

"And then we'll see you all tomorrow night at The Junction

Box, I hope," Neil said. "I'll have Boxing Day specials for everyone. The bar is open to the public, but I don't expect a ton of customers the day after Christmas."

"I can't wait," I said. And not just to hang out with Neil. I really wanted to find out what else was in that notebook, and Millie and Barclay should have information for us, too.

Neil smiled at me. OK, I *really* wanted to hang out with Neil. I leaned over to him, and we exchanged a quick kiss.

"Oi!" Mark made a face like a schoolboy who'd eaten something sour. "Get a room, you two."

Royce and Diana just laughed, and I chuckled. Little did Mark know how much I wanted to get a room with Neil. *One* room!

But I was happy with my gift, even if events—and that evil egg—had overshadowed it. Tomorrow, we would learn a lot more about Alice Dalworth.

Chapter Twenty

Pain before pleasure. That's what I told myself as Neil drove us back to Raquel Tocks's office, early afternoon the day after Christmas. We'd have to endure the pain of seeing her again before we enjoyed our Boxing Day gathering at Neil's bar tonight.

I'd had a rough night, plagued by nightmares. In the worst of them, I dreamed that I rode on Phantom's back, pushing through the water of the swamp. Only it wasn't the swamp. I looked around and found the gator and I were moving through one of those carnival games that usually features rubber ducks floating in an oval track. You know, you pull a duck out of the channel, look at the bottom and see what prize you've won? Then I realized I was surrounded by alligators, all carrying people I knew—my friends and others, too: Raquel. Enzo. Lissa, who carried a laptop computer on her gator. Mr. Mixy, wearing gator-skin boots. And a huge hand descended from above and began plucking gators and their people out of the water. I screamed when it took Neil. I couldn't see who the hand belonged to. When it came for me, blotting out the blinking carnival lights, I woke up.

At least sitting next to Neil helped chase away the disturbing memory. Both of us were quiet after he picked me up. I nursed a coffee, and he nodded his head to some obscure indie rock band playing on his stereo. It was nice. Comfortable.

The tail end of a cold front had tickled Bohemia overnight, with rain showers my aunt loved for the garden. Now the scudding clouds had started to clear, but a nip in the wind gave me an excuse to finally wear a fluffy sherpa fleece jacket I'd picked up in a bargain bin. The cut was cute, and the light green color matched my eyes and went nicely over a black mock turtleneck, but I had a strong suspicion I resembled a wayward sheep.

Whatever. I was owning it. I loved any chance to wear layers. In Florida, I usually dressed according to what would make me sweat the least.

After Neil parked outside the Tocks Development Corp. building, he reached over and rubbed a hand down my arm.

"Soft," he said. "I've been wanting to do that the whole way over here."

I smiled at him. "You might want to check out the whole thing. It's soft all over."

He made a low sound in his throat. "Don't tempt me. Not when I have to face Lady Caca in there."

I laughed as we disembarked. "Oh, I'm going to keep tempting you if I can."

He grinned as he grabbed a soft-sided cooler and a smaller than usual bar bag. "You do. Always."

Well, that was good to hear. I guessed I had to figure out how to make him act on his temptations.

We went through the ritual handoffs from one assistant to another until we found ourselves back in Lissa's antechamber outside Raquel's top-floor office. Today, Lissa, her hair only slightly neater than last time, was bent over two bowls on her desk. She bit her protruding tongue in concentration as she used shiny silver scissors to snip—what *was* that?

She looked up at us. "Oh, it's you. I mean, good afternoon."

"Is that lettuce?" I asked.

She looked down at the two plastic bowls as if she'd already forgotten they were there. "Oh! Yes. I'm preparing Ms. Tocks's afternoon snack." She cut the lettuce leaf in her hand into several square pieces and dropped them into a bowl. The other bowl, I realized, held long, uncut pieces of romaine. "She likes all of her lettuce to be the same size. I'll announce you." She pressed a button on her phone. "The Bohemia Bartenders for you, ma'am."

There was a pause. "Neil, you mean?" came Raquel's voice over the speaker.

Lissa gave me a questioning look.

"Pepper," I supplied.

"Neil and Pepper," Lissa said into the speakerphone.

Another pause. "Send them in." Raquel didn't sound happy.

Lissa led us into the office, then shut the door behind us. There were no goons in sight.

Raquel came out from between the two halves of her glass UFO desk, stood in front and leaned against it, crossing her long legs. Her short, white dress clung to her like a coat of Elmer's Glue. Her slick, short hair and makeup were perfect. She kept her silver eyes on Neil.

"Are you ready to make me a cocktail?" she said in a low voice.

"I can help," I cut in, forcing her to break her seductress vibe.

She stood a little straighter and looked at me. "Actually, if you don't mind, would you talk to Lissa about the favors? She needs help finishing those up so we can get them to Milkweed Mansion this afternoon."

What was I, assistant No. 2? I exchanged a glance with Neil.

"Surely," Raquel said, "you don't need two bartenders to make every cocktail? That doesn't bode well for service at the event."

Neil laughed as if she'd made a joke, not insulted us. He was more diplomatic than I was. But he cut off my smart remark with a gentle, "Go ahead, Pepper. I'll just be a couple of minutes." If he hadn't worn such a pleading look, I would've said no. He didn't want to stress the client, and I didn't want to stress him.

Though I kind of wanted to punch the client.

"I'll be right out here," I said ominously as he started to unpack the cooler on the bar top at the side of the room: juices, vodka, a small bottle of champagne ...

I headed into the reception area. As I closed the door, I heard Raquel say, "You didn't bring a full-size bottle?"

"A split is sufficient for a cocktail," Neil said.

"Or two," Raquel murmured. Then the door shut, and I really couldn't hear any more. I resisted the urge to stay there with my ear pressed to the smooth wood finish.

Lissa dropped the last of the cut lettuce leaves into the bowl, then produced a small box of cherry tomatoes and sliced cucumbers from the mini fridge that had been hidden in the cabinets behind her. She combined everything, popped a lid on the salad bowl and stowed it all in the fridge before looking up at me. "Can I help you?"

"I'm supposed to help you, apparently. Something about favors?"

Lissa looked at me blankly, then snapped her fingers. "The

ribbons! Yes! Oh my gosh, that would be a lifesaver." She jumped up and disappeared through another door—a supply closet, apparently—then emerged with a big cardboard box. She brought it into the middle of the reception area and set it on a coffee table. "We have to tie these zebra-stripe ribbons around the stem of each one." Out of the box she pulled rolls of ribbons and trays of miniature champagne coupes made of gold-colored plastic. "They're going to put truffles in these and put them on the tables. We just have to add the ribbons. For the zoo, you know?"

"I get it," I said. "Animal print. And the black and white will go with the tuxes."

"I didn't even think of that!" Lissa exclaimed. She grabbed a couple of pairs of scissors from her desk—not the silver ones she'd used for the lettuce, I noted with relief—and handed me one. "We can get this done in no time! There are only maybe two hundred and fifty."

Oh, great. Neil better not take that long to make his damn cocktail. By the time we were done, Raquel might have made him pregnant.

"And I already did at least half of them," Lissa was saying. "I think we only need about a hundred more."

I sighed and sat. "OK. You cut, and I'll tie."

"Great!"

We started the factory, and the work went fast. I realized I had an opportunity. "Hey, Lissa."

"Yeah?"

"Where was your boss Monday morning?" Monday morning, the day Alice died.

Lissa paused in her ribbon-cutting, squinting as if trying to see her calendar in her mind. "What was the date? Hang on." I loved that she didn't even ask why I wanted to know. Pure stimulus-response. She got up, went to the computer on her desk and tapped the keyboard. "December 23. She had a—a private meeting."

"Oh?" I asked as she returned to the chair in front of me and cut another ribbon. "With whom?" Enzo had said he and Raquel met for three hours that morning, but I wanted to hear Lissa confirm it.

"Mr. Desjardins."

There you go. "Do you know the topic of the meeting?"

"Probably Boyle Lakes. That's a development they're working on."

"I've heard of it." I tied off another ribbon and set aside the mini coupe. "Was it a long meeting?"

She lifted her brown eyes to mine and smirked. "I think it went all night."

"Oh!"

"Not that you heard it from me." She kept snipping. I was having trouble keeping up, but we'd turned the corner on the favors.

"Of course not." But this news complicated things. For one thing, Oleanna might want to know her would-be beau had other pokers in the fire. *Ew, not the best metaphor, Pepper.*

And if Enzo and Raquel really were together, then would Raquel have been able to get to the swamp to kill Alice? Then again, she had goons for that.

But ... if they were each other's alibi, then neither of them had a very good alibi, did they? Especially when they both stood to benefit from the development going forward and Enzo had been visiting Alice—and giving her pricey champagne. Was Raquel jealous? There was another motive.

I jumped as the door from the hall burst open and Enzo

himself came through it. He pulled up short. "Lissa. Pepper." Then he launched toward the office door.

"Wait!" Lissa cried, but he yanked it open and barreled right in.

I was kind of relieved.

"Raquel!" came his French-accented voice, loud in spite of the closed door.

A minute later, Neil came out toting his cocktail luggage, looking less than his usual calm self. Was that—was that lipstick on his cheek?

I stood, ready to tear somebody apart. I just wasn't sure who.

A loud bump, then a thump came from inside Raquel's office.

We all looked toward the closed door. Then another sound came through. Like a cow softly lowing. Or a woman enjoying herself very much.

"Gah." Lissa shook her head. "Those two. At it again. Go ahead, Pepper. I can finish up here and take these over to Milkweed Mansion. I could use some air."

Neil nodded his head toward the outer door, asking me to go with him. He looked like a wildebeest trying to outrun a hyena. I almost laughed, then got up and followed him out. "Later, Lissa."

We found our way to the elevator without an escort and headed down.

I gave Neil a sidelong glance. "You have lipstick on your cheek."

"I do? Damn it." He pulled a handkerchief from his pocket —of course he had a handkerchief—and started rubbing the wrong cheek.

"The other one. Have a good time, did you?"

"No!" He got it right this time and erased the hot pink lip stamp. "I danced around the furniture in there for five minutes of her 'tasting' the drink and stalking me before she caught me and laid this on me. Then Enzo came through the door, thank God."

"Oh, Neil. I'm starting to think you don't like being kissed."

He looked at me wild-eyed, and I laughed. The elevator dinged. I strode out, straight through the lobby and into the now beautiful chilly day. He was right behind me, and after he'd packed his stuff in the back of the SUV, he came around to my side to let me in. Only he didn't. He pressed up against me, all six feet or so of him, and I sucked in a breath at the weight of his body against mine. He grabbed my soft jacket by the collar and yanked me to him, then laid a kiss on me that just about made my head explode. Not to mention my ovaries. I wrapped my arms around him and moaned into the kiss, happy to have him mess up my lipstick.

He let me go almost as fast as he'd tackled me, and I looked up at him with breathless joy.

"I like to kiss *you,* Pepper. Don't forget it." He gently moved me aside so I could get into the car, then helped me in. He wore a small smile of satisfaction.

I still couldn't get no satisfaction, to quote the Rolling Stones. But this was a start.

Wooooo, baby. This was a start.

Chapter Twenty-One

Neil was wrong about crowds being sparse on Boxing Day. Now that the holiday was over, people who still had time off were eager to celebrate, meet old friends or escape their houseguests. So The Junction Box was packed with people, including many of our friends, by the time I got off work and let Jorge deal with closing Nola. Neil and Luke were both behind the bar, mixing multiple cocktails at once. And, thank goodness, there was no Mr. Mixy.

Though the bar still sparkled with holiday lights, rock music played over the sound system. This place wasn't as fancy as Alastair's Dandy Tipple in London, but it might have come from the same era. It had Victorian touches, dark wood accents, antique-looking lights and a stage, empty tonight except for the baby grand piano. The rectangular bar was an island with the bartenders working in the middle, and guests sat all around it. Most of the tables were full, too.

I spotted Mark, Diana and Royce at the bar, already drinking, so I pulled up a stool next to them, said hello and grabbed a menu. I was starving. I looked up to find Neil standing before me, resplendent in suspenders, bow tie and a handsome smile. "Hi," he said.

"Hi." I smiled back, remembering our kiss this afternoon. "What'll you have?"

"Are *you* available?"

"I'm taken."

I chuckled, feeling all warm inside. "You said something about Boxing Day drink specials?"

"I have a Berry Festive cocktail."

I raised my eyebrows. "Puntastic. I saw that on the menu for New Year's Eve."

Neil shrugged. "I've come up with a lot of cocktails this week. I ran out of names, and the name suits the drink: Chambord, champagne, gin, lemon juice and fresh raspberries. Want one?"

"Yes, please. And the mini charcuterie board?"

"You got it."

Mark interrupted. "Go ahead and get the large charcuterie board. My treat. We're hungry, too."

"I don't know how you can be hungry," Diana said. "You were eating all day."

"I need to feed these, don't I?" Mark bent one arm and flexed his muscles, which popped under his gold sweater. Royce and I laughed, and Diana tried not to, but she ended up chuckling, too. And maybe her eyes lingered for an extra second on that very impressive arm.

"OK, the large charcuterie board," Neil said, sliding over to tap the order into a screen.

"And send a small one to Alastair, will you? He's pouting because he has to take a commercial flight back home tomorrow."

We all glanced at a slightly sunburned Alastair, nursing a cocktail at the end of the bar. The corner of Neil's mouth lifted. "No problem. And I should be able to take a break in a few minutes. Don't start without me."

"I can *hear* you, you know," Alastair said to Mark. "I'll be glad to be done with you. Bloody boring, watching you trans-late gibberish all week."

Mark and Diana exchanged a merry glance.

Luke, busy behind the bar, grinned and waved at the door, so I turned to look. Barclay and Gina had come in, wearing matching sweaters—Christmas presents?—with Melody right behind them in a hip leather jacket and jeans, her blond hair loose. I waved them over. "How's it going?"

"Great," Barclay said. "We stopped by your bar first."

"You did?"

Gina smiled. "I wanted to say hi to my brother. It's nice to see him so happy."

"Jorge works too hard, but he loves it." I turned to Melody. "Did you work today? And did you see Oleanna?"

"Yes to both. The bar's dead, and Oleanna has a date. Fortunately, I didn't get stuck with the late shift."

Oh, boy. I wondered if Oleanna had a date with Enzo. I was a bad friend for not warning her already of what we saw today. Or heard.

Movement caught my eye, and I spotted Millie entering the bar. I tried to keep myself from pouncing and asking her what she'd learned as she came over to us. "Hi! No Bennett?"

"Already on his way to Hawaii," she said with a regretful smile. She looked cute in a red sweater dress.

"Oh, that's right. Maybe we should grab a table?" I suggested.

"Good idea," Mark said. "I also ordered nachos and a couple of the flatbreads and that fish dip when you weren't looking."

Excellent. At least we wouldn't go hungry.

We nabbed a big table not far from the bar as another group left. Luke delivered drinks and took more cocktail orders. In a few minutes, Neil came over and joined us, presenting more cocktails just as two servers set down the food. There was barely enough room on the tabletop.

"Tuck in," Mark said, and we did. Man, Neil's food was getting better all the time. Fortunately, my chef was at least as good as his, and I had an idea they were quietly trying to one-up each other, a competition that benefited both of us.

"My favorite." Neil took a bite of the prosciutto and fig flatbread.

"I need to try that." I helped myself to a slice and took a bite—savory with a hint of sweet, with tangy Gorgonzola cheese on a thin, crispy crust. "Mmmmmygawd."

He grinned. "I know."

"OK, where do we start?" I asked after a few more bites. The bar traffic had slowed a bit, and Luke moved to work closer to us so he could hear some of our conversation.

"I'll start," said Barclay, who sipped a rum concoction. "Thor Roberts's treasure museum is closed."

"Not just closed for the holiday?" I asked.

"*Closed* closed. The sign said something about Davy Jones's Locker getting renovations, but we peeked in the windows and looked around the parking lot, and there were no signs any work was going on. We checked on our way out of Fort Lauderdale this morning, so it wasn't just closed for the holiday. Even the emporium was closed."

Gina concurred. "I talked to the people in the hair salon next door, and they said they hadn't seen anyone around for at least a month."

"So it's temporarily closed and they have the money to do renovations, or it's closed for some other reason," Neil said.

"A reason like they have no money and no business," I

suggested. "Or maybe Thor closed it while he's off treasure-hunting."

"So Thor is on the loose and possibly desperate," Neil said.

"Which brings us to emeralds," Mark said. "Diana?"

She nodded, looked around to make sure no one could hear her, and talked so quietly we had to lean in. "We've found a few references to 'emeralds' in the coded notes, but we're still not sure what Alice was talking about or where they might be. Decoding this thing is terribly slow. She has a lot of research notes on different plants she's found and catalogued: descriptions, location, right down to GPS coordinates. In fact, there's a page that's outlined in a box where she has several GPS coordinates listed—at least, that's what we think they are—with room for more. But she doesn't say what is at those locations. It's very frustrating."

"How many locations are we talking about?" Neil asked.

"On that page? Nine, I think," Diana said. "We should probably check them out."

"So they're local?" Millie asked.

Diana nodded as she munched a nacho chip. "Around the marsh, yes."

"Maybe that's where the treasure is," I whispered.

"In nine separate locations?" Mark huffed. "Only if Alice dug it up and reburied it. Seems like a lot of trouble when one could simply rent a safe deposit box."

"Maybe it's too big for that!" I imagined piles of loot. "And she didn't want someone else to find it."

"Unlikely." Neil's tone suggested he still doubted the treasure theory. "But it makes sense to check out the locations."

"The police have delivered my rental boat back to the fish camp," Diana said. "I can take that."

"That's a good sign," I said. "I guess they didn't find any

evidence that got their interest." It was also a good sign that she said "I" and not "we." I'd had enough of boats.

"The airboat would be faster," Mark suggested.

"It's a lovely way to see the backs of fleeing animals," Diana replied.

He smiled. "Then I'll go with you on the little boat."

"What? No, you won't."

"Of course I will. What if these really are places where Alice buried treasure? You'll need protection."

I suppressed a laugh, and Mark looked at me. "What?"

Then everyone else started laughing. Sure, Mark was game for anything, and he was a strapping fellow. But he was such a goofball.

Diana seemed torn, but I think she took pity on him. "All right. You can come along."

"That's better." Mark gave us all the stink eye.

"Weren't y'all talking about Ponce de Leon earlier?" Royce asked Mark. "I thought I overheard something."

"Oh, that's right," Mark said. "Alice had a lot of notes on Florida history."

"Was she studying the treasure fleet?" I asked.

"She did write about that," Diana said. "She also had some notes on the Fountain of Youth. Ponce de Leon supposedly landed at Bohemia Beach."

"There's a statue in the park downtown," Melody said.

"Every town on the east coast of Florida claims a landing by Ponce de Leon," Neil scoffed.

"The Fountain of Youth. That's what Ponce de Leon was looking for, right?" Millie asked.

"That's the legend," Diana said. "I looked up a bit about him while we were trying to decode that blasted notebook. He heard of a magic fountain or river from the Taíno people in the

Caribbean while he was gallivanting about with Christopher Columbus. He rewarded this confidence with a vicious suppression of their rebellion and generally abusing native peoples hither and yon on behalf of the Spanish crown. On one of his missions for the king, he anchored off the east coast of Florida in 1513."

"And in fact called the land 'La Florida,' correct?" Mark asked.

"That's right," she said. "Presumably, this is when he might have searched for the rejuvenating waters. But there's not a lot of mention of him actually searching for the Fountain of Youth until a bit later. That's the story historians and writers developed, first as an insult—"

"Apparently, he was looking for a little magical Viagra," Mark said to chuckles.

Diana rolled her eyes. "I'm sure that report was as untrue as the others. It all became a myth that's built over the years. He was killed eight years after this visit by a native arrow on the other side of the peninsula."

"Just desserts," Barclay said.

"Sounds like it," Melody agreed. "Even eternal youth isn't much defense against an arrow."

"Surely a scientist didn't believe in the Fountain of Youth," Neil remarked.

I took another sip of my tasty cocktail. "Maybe not, but Alice was interested in Florida history, judging from her bookshelves."

Diana looked thoughtful. "Perhaps it was her way of understanding the land. Florida once looked quite different. She has notes on explorers that talked about a lot more water here. Natives told Franciscan monks they could paddle all the way across the peninsula. Early maps showed Florida as a collection of islands. That's hard to imagine now. And of course, that would mean more wetlands and plants, many of which were lost to drainage schemes and development." She took a sip of her gin and tonic. "I just don't know, honestly. Anyway, we're still a long way from figuring out what she was working on. She had wide interests, even if her speciality was endangered plants."

I looked around. "Just to make sure everyone's caught up, we found a bottle of one of Enzo's best champagnes in Alice's shack, and he admitted visiting her more than once. He's also partnered with Raquel Tocks on the Boyle Lakes development, which is planned for the old Boyle property that Alice lived on. What else am I forgetting?" I looked at Neil, wondering if I should go further.

His eyes met mine. "That's all, I think." OK, for now we wouldn't mention Enzo's apparent affair with Raquel.

"He's been busy, hasn't he?" Royce raised an eyebrow at me. I wondered if he guessed there was more to the story.

"Apparently." I smiled at him. I'd tell him the rest later. "Millie, did you get anything else on Enzo?"

She took a sip of her club soda with lime and pulled a tablet computer out of her bag. "So glad you asked."

"Oh, boy," I said, and titters rippled around the table.

"As you know, Enzo Desjardins owns the Desjardins champagne house. He inherited it from his parents," she said.

I nodded. "He told me he inherited it at quite a young age."

"His parents died relatively young. Enzo once mentioned in an interview that his father died of a stroke. That was six months after his mother died, and he's never said in public what happened to her. Her obituary left that out but mentioned illness. At least that's all I got with the web translation. I'm working on my French, but it's not that good yet."

Hey, I was impressed she was working on her French. "Anything weird about that?"

"The fact they both died within six months of each other at a relatively young age is a little weird," she said.

We all looked at each other before I asked the obvious question. "Could their deaths be—suspicious?"

Millie's eyes danced. "These things happen. But there's more."

"Go on," Mark said, leaning forward.

"Enzo is a widower," she replied. "And his wife's mysterious death is still unsolved."

Chapter Twenty-Two

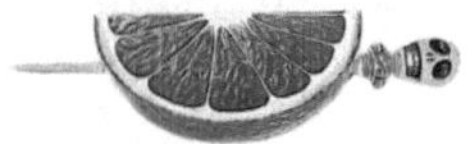

"Whoa," I said. "How did Enzo's wife die?"

Millie's tone grew dark. "She fell off a cruise ship."

"What? Where?" I asked.

"In the Mediterranean," Millie said. "It was a big news item. Tragic death and all that. She was twenty-nine."

Holy crap. I was about to turn twenty-nine.

"Was it investigated?" Neil asked.

"Yes, and deemed an accident," Millie said, tapping on her screen. "Though there was speculation in the press about whether Enzo was a tragic figure or something more sinister."

"I've heard about cases like this before," Barclay said. "Ships don't always have cameras where things happen. And at night, in the dark, someone can go overboard and no one might know anything until the next day. By then, it's usually too late."

Millie nodded. "That was the case here. A search was attempted, but it was hard to narrow down the area given they didn't know when she went overboard. Her body wasn't recovered. Apparently, cameras confirmed Enzo was in the casino that evening, after passengers had seen him and his wife arguing at dinner. When he went back to their cabin, she wasn't there. That's what he told the police. He said he thought she'd just gone out for some air. He fell asleep. When she hadn't come back by morning, he went to ship security. A significant detail was that her high-heeled shoes were out on the balcony, suggesting that was the last place she'd been, though it was never clear. He claimed he didn't notice them there."

"You'd think if he did it and wanted to divert attention from himself, he'd have put her shoes away," Mark said.

"But the shoes suggest she did fall," Diana mused, "rather than someone pushing her. She might've been drunk and fallen overboard."

"If Enzo was involved, what did he have to gain?" I asked. "Millie?"

"She brought considerable wealth to the marriage," she said. "She came from a prominent family. Now he has it all, no strings."

"Maybe his artisan champagne isn't as profitable as it looks?" I asked. "But it seems like she would've supported him in his endeavors. Was he already bottling under the Desjardins label when they got married?"

"I think so," Millie said. She scrolled through her screen again. "Yes. She married him at least five years after his father died, and he was already producing his first bottles. And she died just a few years later."

Melody shivered. "Well, it's a terrible tragedy. And if he didn't have anything to do with it, I feel sorry for him. Look at how much he's lost."

She was right. But there were a lot of questions swirling around Enzo.

"Any thoughts on what he's getting out of working the development with Raquel?" I asked. *Besides getting laid on the regular.* Was he in love with her? Or was she going to get pushed off a balcony, too?

"Remember I told you the development plan has already been filed with the planning commission?" Millie looked around at all of us. "The clerk gave me some more details. The nice Frenchman who dropped off the plans told her he was excited because he was going to have a place in the development. He even pointed it out to her. The lot included the old Boyle house."

"He's going to *live* there?" I asked.

"And he's going to knock the old house down?" Neil frowned.

"Not sure about that," Millie said. "But the clerk said it was a big lot and the old house appeared on the plans."

"Wait." Melody waved around her Berry Festive glass. "Why would a man who lives on and runs a beautiful, successful vineyard in France want to move to the swamp? I mean, you know, I'm cool with Bohemia, but *really?*"

A corner of Mark's mouth lifted. "I bought a place here. There must be something in the water." His eyes strayed to mine for a microsecond before he turned back to his Old-Fashioned.

I was sure Mark didn't buy his condo here because of me. Well, pretty sure. And he had a point. There *was* something about Bohemia that drew you in.

"But it's the *swamp,*" Luke said from the bar, where he was between customers. It was late, nearly closing time, and a lot of guests had slipped out already, so he'd moved closer to listen in. The servers were settling bills and starting their cleanup.

A few chuckles greeted his point. Why the swamp, indeed?

"Treasure?" Royce suggested.

"Why now?" Neil leaned back in his chair and crossed his

arms. "Like Melody said, Enzo's got a pretty sweet situation back home. And usually the treasure-hunting bug bites early."

"Maybe treasure was never this easy or close at hand," Diana said. "Maybe Alice told him something that made him believe it was there for the taking. An irresistible temptation."

"Does he need the money, then?" Gina piped up.

"He has enough to invest in the development," Royce said, "which suggests that he's doing OK."

"Or he isn't, and he needed a faster return on the investment, and Alice was in the way." Mark's voice had lost all its humor.

We all fell silent. Could Enzo have killed his parents? His wife? And now Alice?

Neil looked around, then stood. "Last call. Anyone?"

There were no takers, and he returned to the bar to help Luke wrap things up.

As the group chatted in twos and threes, I turned to Millie. "Thanks for doing this."

"You know I'm always up for helping you out. This is fascinating." Millie stuffed her tablet back in her bag. "But there's something very wrong here. I don't like it, Pepper. I don't like it at all. Please be careful."

"Hey, bro!" A few days later, I welcomed Royce into Nola for lunch. I was back into my busy work schedule, hardly seeing my friends—or Neil. My half brother and I hadn't spent as much time together as I wanted before he headed back to Kentucky. He'd probably seen more of Aunt Celestine than he had of me. So I'd invited him to visit me in the restaurant.

"Pepper!" He gave me a hug. "Uh, I should probably tell

you that I'm not alone." He smiled at my puzzled look. "When Mark heard I was going to lunch, he invited himself along, and he also invited Diana."

"Diana, eh?" I smiled back.

Royce nodded as if he knew what I was thinking. "They've been working hard on that journal. I think they've made some progress, so you might want to hear what they have to say. Unfortunately—"

Mark and Diana came through the door then, followed by the Unfortunately—Mr. Mixy.

"Oh, Royce. Couldn't you get rid of him?" I murmured to my brother.

"He ran into us outside, and it was hard to say no. We'll figure it out," he said, unperturbed. Royce was a lot more laid-back than I was. And I seriously doubted Mr. Mixy "ran into" them by accident.

I sighed in resignation and turned a smile to my guests. "Hey, everybody. Would you like to start with a drink?"

A few minutes later, I'd hooked up Mark with a G&T, Diana with a Singapore Sling, Royce with a Boulevardier, and Mr. Mixy with a Moscow Mule. They sat at the bar and perused the food menu.

"So, how are you feeling since your—encounter?" Royce asked Mr. Mixy.

Mr. Mixy took a long sip of his ginger beer, lime and vodka drink, then set down the copper mug and turned a serious look on Royce. "I'm a changed man."

"Really?" I couldn't help myself. One, I didn't believe it. Two, any change in Mr. Mixy was probably for the better, even though everything he did had a tendency to make things worse.

"Yes." Stephan didn't seem to notice my skepticism. "I've

been thinking a lot about what happened. I think me losing my boot was symbolic. A symbol of the sacrifices I've made so I can make other people happy. This is truly my mission, to entertain people. And you're a key part of making this happen, Pepper. I had a dream about it."

Whoa no.

"I don't have all the details yet," he continued. "But I've been visualizing. Walking on the beach and reaching out to the universe. And you know what? The vibe I'm putting out there is working. I just got good news. My book synopsis has fallen into the right hands. We have interest in a movie."

"A film?" Mark said. "Would you star in it?"

"Oh, I don't know. I don't have control over that kind of thing." But Mr. Mixy showed his teeth, and I wondered if he'd be cast as the lead in his own made-up autobiography. Oh, geez. His head couldn't fit through normal doorways as it was. "But it's a very serious offer. I need to finish writing it. Problem is, I'm having trouble sitting for any length of time. My back is killing me. I'm all beat up from what that gator did to me."

"Sounds like you need a chiropractor," Diana said. "Did my mother a world of good when she hurt her back."

"Oh yeah?" Mr. Mixy turned to me. "Know of anybody good, Pepper?"

"Not really. Maybe Neil does." I texted him.

After I took everyone's food orders and put in a shrimp po'boy for myself, my phone pinged again.

Neil texted: "Talked to Gramps. He said Mixy should try Dr. Bretzel. He's just down the street. You OK?"

"Great. Can't wait till tomorrow," I typed back. Tomorrow was the day before New Year's Eve, and I planned to help Neil with any prep we could do a day in advance—which wasn't a lot, but I wanted to see him.

I gave Mr. Mixy the info.

"Awesome! I'll go right now. Maybe they can squeeze me in." He drained the rest of his drink and shuffled awkwardly out of the bar. I guessed somebody else would eat his muffuletta.

"He really doesn't look very comfortable," I said.

"He's lucky to be alive, given what Phantom did to him," Mark said.

"Speaking of the swamp ... shall we move to a table and talk? Lunch shouldn't take long."

Nola wasn't busy, and Jorge came out of the back office to take over for me at the bar as I settled us into a table near the Christmas tree, which would come down soon enough.

"Are you having fun?" I asked Royce.

"Sure. Mark's place is great. I saw that rocket launch last night from the beach—amazing! And I've been exploring and hanging out with Aunt Celestine." He smiled. "I like having an aunt."

"Me too." I grinned, then my smile faltered. "There's something I should probably tell you. I might as well tell you all, too." I looked at Mark and Diana, then I told them about the weird plastic egg and the ominous note.

"Oh, no." Royce had turned pale. "Maybe you shouldn't engage with him at all. It sounds like what he wants. Turn it over to the police."

"I could do that, but what are they going to do with a little piece of crappy poetry? There's no explicit threat, just an implied one against my parents. I'm afraid of what he'll do."

"We'll figure it out." Royce echoed what he'd said earlier about Mr. Mixy.

"Do you think he's watching you?" Mark asked.

"Ugh. Not till now," I said.

Diana chuckled. "I'm sure you're safe. But you might want to proceed with caution."

No kidding.

Our food arrived with the delicious scents of garlic and seafood, and we dug in.

"So I hear you might have more info about Alice's journal?" I asked Mark and Diana.

Diana nodded, finishing a bite of her étouffée. "Tons of information about plants. She's noted rare ones and has a lot of observations. In fact, we found some of the plants she noted when we checked out the GPS coordinates. I snipped a few to examine later."

"The mysterious coordinates?" I sipped my Sazerac. "No treasure?"

Mark shook his head. "I had a waterproof metal detector, but it turns out that every spot on the list was on land adjacent to the water with a bunch of scrubby plants, and the detector didn't find anything. We didn't go digging."

The front door opened, letting in a blast of light, and I glanced over to see who it was. "Uh-oh."

Detective Cleo Keene and Ernie Alder, the wildlife officer, stood there blinking, their eyes adjusting to the dark, plush interior of Nola. And neither looked happy.

Chapter Twenty-Three

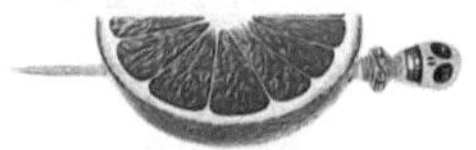

I jumped up and went over to them. "Detective Keene. Officer Alder. Can I get you a drink or lunch? On the house."

The wildlife officer, in his khaki uniform and FWC billed cap, sniffed the air and peered over at the dishes on our table, but Detective Keene, sleek in a black suit, shook her head. "No, thank you. We got a burger down the street and ran into your boyfriend on the sidewalk. He told us you all were here."

They ran into Neil?

"Stephan Sully," she said to my puzzled expression.

"Oh! *Not* my boyfriend."

"Then maybe you should get your stories straight." Her sharp brown eyes met mine, then she assessed our lunch bunch as I silently cursed Mr. Mixy. "We need to talk to Mr. Fairman. And all of you, actually."

"Um, sure. Please pull up a—hang on a sec."

Jorge had come out from behind the bar, and following his lead, I helped him drag over a two-top table to the end of our four-top so the officers could sit down easily. Even if they had us hemmed in.

"Waters? And a box for the muffuletta?" I whispered to him, and he nodded and brought out the to-go box and glasses tinkling with ice a moment later. We would be hospitable in spite of their protestations.

When we were all settled in, half of my po'boy crying out to be finished, Detective Keene looked right at Mark.

"I understand you were at Alice Dalworth's home."

We sat there silently for a minute. We had been there. More than once. What did she know?

"That's right," Mark said in his forthright way. "I escorted Diana so she could try to save some of Alice's work."

His easy response seemed to take a bit of the frost out of the air, but the detective was still plenty chilly as she looked around. "We understand it wasn't just you."

"I was there, too," I said. "We thought there'd be safety in numbers." *And Neil was there both times after the first visit. And Royce was there once.*

Royce didn't say anything, waiting to see what she knew, and I wasn't going to throw Neil under the bus. It wasn't like we'd committed a real crime, but I supposed it might look that way. Breaking and entering with the Cheesy Does It card and all.

And how did she know?

Then it hit me.

"Thor Roberts, right?" I said. "He told you. We saw him break into that box on the dock while we were there."

Ernie Alder looked at me. "You did, did you? And you didn't think to report this?"

"Maybe because you weren't supposed to be there?" Detective Keene piled on.

"We weren't sure who it was then, and besides—"

"We meant no harm," said Diana. "Alice was a good friend. I couldn't let her work just be swept up and dumped as rubbish. At the time, we didn't know you were treating the shack as a crime scene. I'm so sorry."

Her sincerity went a lot further than my babbling. The other good news was that they hadn't mentioned yet that Neil had been there, too. Probably because Roberts barely had a glimpse of us when he opened the door and didn't get a good head count.

"Have you spoken to this Roberts fellow, then?" Mark asked.

Detective Keene seemed to relax slightly. "We caught him inside the shack. It appeared he'd broken in. He told us a big guy with an accent yelled at him when he tried to visit the shack before. He said he thought it was a ranger station." Her tone relayed her disbelief. "We're holding him for now. He said he didn't know what happened to Dr. Dalworth but didn't have a good explanation for being there. "

"I'll give you an explanation. He's a treasure hunter," Mark said. "We've heard rumors about some sort of Spanish treasure or something?"

Yeah, and we have a notebook that talks about emeralds.

Officer Alder smirked. "Not that Casanova foolishness again. That explains all the holes."

Oh, God. Mr. Mixy and his digging. "You don't believe the story?" I asked him.

Then I regretted it, because he turned his piercing blue eyes on me. "So far I've seen no reason I should. Bill Boyle owned that land his whole life, and he agrees with me. Would you like to enlighten me?"

"Oh, I don't know anything either." I swallowed and tried to look cool. "It's just kind of interesting. For someone like Thor Roberts, I mean."

"How do you know Mr. Roberts?" Cleo Keene asked.

"We toured his museum in South Florida a while back," I said. "Didn't recognize him right away. Later on, we figured out it was him."

"That's right." Mark backed me up. "I got a few photos of him that day at the shack. I'll send them to you, all right?"

"You'd better," the detective said. "Mr. Roberts might have killed Alice Dalworth to get at this treasure." She looked around at all of us, then landed on Diana. "Unless someone else had a motive."

We all just sat there, uncomfortable, and speaking for myself, too scared to say a thing. Diana had zero motive.

"Perhaps you wanted to steal her work," Officer Alder said.

"Preposterous!" Mark exclaimed just as Diana shot them an icy glare and said, "Impossible. I actually have ethics, unlike this Roberts person."

"Then what did you find at the shack?" Ernie asked.

"We saw her notebooks and her plants," Diana said, not blinking at his gaze. *Smooth.* It wasn't a lie. And we'd left all the notebooks but one. "I presume she had a laptop computer, but we couldn't find it. But I did take a few of the plants. I can provide you with a list." *Very smooth.* She took the plants later, but saying so was a calculated risk. They might not care if she had some of Alice's work or plants. Would they care that she'd been there twice after Alice's death?

"We have her laptop computer," Detective Keene said. "With her email exchange with you on it."

"Then you know exactly where we stood," said Diana, her voice still coldly furious. "I hope you will preserve her work. It may be that I or another of her colleagues can put together her findings and publish anything of value. A final tribute. She was a good person."

"And you didn't notice the fish in her freezer when you visited her home?" the detective asked.

"I did not. We did not." Diana seemed taken aback, and none of us mentioned the champagne. Would they look into Enzo, too? "So now you're implying she wasn't murdered? That she electrocuted herself while fishing?" Seeming to ignore that this theory would take suspicion off her, Diana plunged on. "She was a conservationist. She would have never engaged in illegal fishing."

Ernie Alder seemed almost amused, then looked at Detective Keene, who nodded slightly and said, "You may be right. We think the killer put the fish in her freezer to throw us off. Someone at the scene likely knocked Alice out before electrocuting her."

We all stared at her after this ghastly revelation. It was Royce who finally spoke. "So she *was* murdered? You already have the autopsy results?"

"Preliminary conclusion," she said. "A blow to the head and damage to the heart consistent with electrocution. And we have a weapon."

"Dare I ask?" Diana was getting snippy now.

"Kayak paddle," Ernie said. "We found it tangled up in the weeds near the island. We're having it analyzed, but it appears to have been used in an act of violence. There's physical evidence."

Yuck.

"Native plants are not weeds," Diana snapped. "And my fingerprints are not on the paddle because I didn't know it existed."

Mark placed a hand gently on her arm. Diana twitched, then took a breath.

"That's terrible," Mark told the officers. "The way she died, I mean."

"What color was it?" I asked.

"What?" Detective Keene, startled, looked at me.

"The paddle. What color was it?"

"Yellow and black. Why?"

"Just wondered. I noticed a paddle was missing from the dock box. We, uh, looked after Thor Roberts left," I said in response to her glare. "Alice had a bright green kayak for two and one bright green paddle. But maybe her paddles didn't match."

The detective appeared nonplussed. So was I. *That's* what had bugged me about the dock box. One paddle for a two-person kayak, and Alice had even emailed Diana that she wanted them to go kayaking. But was it Alice's paddle that had been stuck in the weeds? Er, vegetation?

Just then, Jorge arrived at the table with a plate of beignets. "Please help yourself," he said, then gave me a questioning look and went back behind the bar.

Ernie took one and bit into it. His mouth twitched with a smile as powdered sugar fell onto his khaki shirt like a light dusting of snow.

Detective Keene looked at the fried dough treats with something like longing, then stood. "We'll be in touch," was all she said to Diana, but she swept us all with her gaze.

I stuck Mr. Mixy's untouched muffuletta in the box with a couple more beignets and handed it to Ernie. He smiled and took it silently before following Cleo Keene out the door.

"Is it just me, or are we in trouble?" Royce said.

"You aren't! Not yet, anyway," I said. "Though you are withholding information."

"So are you!" he said.

"All of us are. I still think we're doing no harm," Diana said. "But if we find treasure, we're going to have to tell them the rest. It's definitely motive, especially for Thor Roberts."

I pushed my plate away. I couldn't finish my po'boy now, not after thinking about Alice struck down by a paddle, then electrocuted by the fishing equipment.

I helped Jorge make another round of drinks for the table —not for me, since I had hours of work ahead—and we were halfway through them and deep in theories when the door opened again and a familiar ash-blond woman walked in.

She looked around, then spotted me and came right over. "Can we talk?"

"Tracy? I mean, Mrs. Boyle?"

"Tracy's fine." She looked at my tablemates, then back at me. "Alone?"

Chapter Twenty-Four

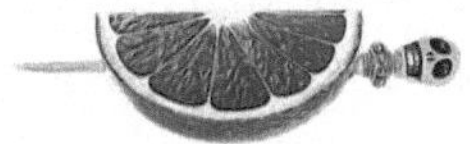

"OK. Let's step outside for a minute," I said to Tracy Boyle. I couldn't imagine why she'd sought me out, but it was that kind of day.

I glanced at Royce and shrugged before following Tracy out the door. It was a gorgeous, breezy day in Bohemia, just cool enough to be pleasant. We ambled toward the arts district. "What's up?" I asked her.

"Did my husband have an affair with that woman?"

"What?" Her direct question startled me. "Oh, Alice, you mean? Alice Dalworth?"

"Yes, *Alice Dalworth.*" Her tone was bitter as she looked straight ahead. "He could never stop talking about her. About everything she was studying and endangered woodpeckers and how he was getting back at Raquel. Do you know what I'm talking about?"

"He told us a little bit. And I learned that Raquel is his niece."

"See, this is why I'm here. I heard you're good at finding things out." Tracy glanced over at me. Her shirt today didn't have paint spatters, but it was a casual black knit, and she wore jeans. She seemed like a cool person. But now she was angry.

"Well, I don't know anything about Alice having any affairs

with anyone." Though my mind strayed to Enzo again. That champagne was suggestive.

We paused outside the entrance to a small park. Ponce de Leon Square. How about that? The fountain at its center featured a brass statue of the explorer, a cocky look on his face as he pointed east. As I watched, a pigeon alighted on his head and pooped on his feathered hat. Karma.

"I think he was in love with her." Tracy's anguished voice brought me back to the moment and twanged my heartstrings.

I turned to her. "I can't tell you anything about that. I just don't know. But we've seen no evidence of anything between them." Other than Bill Boyle's fond remembrances. And Mark and Diana hadn't said anything about him appearing in the journal. I'd have to ask them about that. "Anyway, he's with you. That means something," I finished lamely.

Her face grew blank, as if she was somewhere else, seeing something I couldn't see. Something dark.

"I just wanted to know for sure," she finally whispered.

"I'm sorry."

After another moment, she walked away, still heading for the art school. Maybe she had classes there.

I turned around and headed back to Nola, where my friends stood and chatted with Jorge at the bar.

"There you are!" Mark said. "I thought we might need to send out a search party."

I smiled ruefully and shook my head. "Speaking of parties, there goes more of our party time foiled by this horrible Thing. I'm sorry lunch wasn't more relaxing."

"It was great." Royce hugged me. "We'll figure it out. I keep saying that, don't I?"

I laughed. "Yes, you do."

"And we need to figure out that egg from Beau and what to

do next." He cut off my protest. "I will be there for you, Pepper. We'll talk later, OK?"

"OK, bro." I liked calling him that. I gave him another hug. "Mark? Diana?"

"Yes?" they said in tandem. *Cute.*

"Did Alice mention Bill Boyle anywhere in the journal?"

They exchanged a look. "We've seen, what, one or two references?" Diana asked Mark, then turned to me. "For one thing, she seemed to feel guilty about lying about a woodpecker. I wasn't sure I understood."

I thought I did. "She'd told Bill she saw the elusive ivory-billed woodpecker—and he'd pinned all his hopes of stopping the development on that. Maybe she was stringing him along so that she could stay as long as possible at the shack."

"How odd," Diana said. "According to the entries so far, he was full of advice on alligators and overall quite helpful."

"Alligators?" Royce asked.

"Phantom made her nervous," Mark said.

"I can see why, since she shared the island with the beast," I replied. "Tracy Boyle was concerned that Bill and she might have been—you know."

"Oh, no, there was nothing like that," Diana said. "At least, I don't think so. She also mentioned having beers with Otter, meeting Officer Alder, and occasionally encountering curious visitors. Now that you mention it, she talked about a skinny man who wanted permission to dig around the place, and she refused. Not surprising, given she was studying the plants."

"That could've been Thor Roberts," Royce said.

Diana nodded. "Perhaps. She also mentioned someone firing off a gun outside the shack one night. She thought they might be trying to intimidate her. There's an increasingly paranoid tone in her entries."

"Tell her about the last entry," Mark said.

"Yes." Diana looked sad. "She wrote, 'I can't keep this to myself anymore. Something isn't right. Someone is watching. I don't know how much time I have.'"

"Scary," I said. "That might explain the ominous stuff in her letter and why she wanted to talk to you right away. So this isn't just a plant journal?"

"It's a curious mix of personal and professional," Diana said. "I suppose it was her friend, in a way. A diary can be like that, especially when you're alone a lot. It was her confidante. I know a little about that."

Mark gave her a tender look.

I pretended not to notice. "Any mention of Enzo?"

"We just ran across something about him," Diana said. "She said he stopped by and that it was a long, interesting afternoon."

Was "interesting" code for something else? Something sexual? Or threatening?

"She seemed charmed by him," Diana continued. "Though she said something peculiar. Something like, 'Now I know I'm searching for the right thing, but I must work faster.'"

"Ugh." I crossed my arms. "You'd think she'd be more clear."

"Or just the opposite. Remember, this blasted journal is in code," Diana pointed out. "She didn't want people knowing her thoughts or her research until she was ready. And even though the code probably became second nature to her after a while, it must have been painstaking to write in that way. So the entries are usually brief."

"I'm glad you're figuring it out," I said. "Thanks for coming to lunch. Let's make sure we get together again."

"Oh, you'll see us," Mark said. "I'm taking Diana to the New Year's Eve event."

"Oh! That's awesome!" I looked at Diana, whose face had pinked.

"It seems so frivolous," she said.

"But it's supporting the zoo. They're really into conservation." I tried to sound cool, but wow! Could Mark really be interested in Diana?

"Mark asked me first, but I already have a ticket." Royce looked mischievous.

"OK, great." What was my brother up to? "Let's keep in touch. Share if we find out anything."

"Righto," Mark said. "Thanks again."

They headed out after more quick hugs, then I got a text from Royce ten minutes later. "I didn't have a ticket at first. Not until Mark asked me if I wanted his spare ticket. Then I told him I had one and bought my own so he'd ask a certain someone. I think those two would be cute together, don't you?"

"You are devious," I typed back. "And I think you're right, though they are opposites." *Kind of like Neil and me, but in a totally different way.* "And I'm happy you're going to be there."

"So am I. I've asked Aunt Celestine."

"Perfect!"

"Astra and Victoria are going to have a playdate while we're out."

"I hope the fur won't fly." Victoria seemed fine with Astra, but Victoria had a dopey sweetness about her. Astra also could be sweet, but she was smart and territorial when it came to me and my aunt. She seemed to see Victoria as a trespasser.

Not long after, as the post-lunch crowd thinned and Jorge

had retreated to our office, Mr. Mixy came through the door. I'd almost forgotten about him, given our police interrogation.

He walked like a monkey whose underwear was too tight. He practically needed crampons and pulleys to climb up on a barstool, and he groaned the whole time, drawing glances from customers at the other end of the bar.

"I need a beer," he barked.

I didn't even ask him what kind, just poured a Bohemia Brewing Red Ale from the tap. He grabbed it and sucked half of it down, leaving foam awash in his mustache and giant beard as if he'd just been overwhelmed by a rogue wave.

I couldn't tamp down my curiosity. "What happened to you?"

"Chiropractor."

"I thought they were supposed to help?"

He gulped more beer. "Well, they have this machine. They tell me it's called flexion distraction or something. Maybe it distracts you from the pain?" He took another sip. "This old doctor guy told me to lie down it, on my stomach, and then he strapped in my legs. That seemed kinda weird, but I figure he knows what he's doing. My face is down in this open ring like a massage, so I figure it's going to be awesome for my back. He starts pushing and prodding and that's OK. Then he says he's going to start up the machine and a timer will go off in about ten minutes and I'm going to feel much better. So the machine starts grinding, dropping and lifting in the middle, pushing my back up and down. At first it was good. Weird, but good. They had this mellow music playing. I heard people chatting in the other offices, then it got real quiet. Then the timer went off. At least I think it was the timer. It beeped. But nobody came. The table just kept going up and down, and I think, I'm getting my money's worth here! But then it started to get uncomfortable, so I called for the doctor. Nobody came. Then I just yelled for anybody. I screamed, Pepper. I screamed, and nobody came!"

"Uh-huh." I nodded and tried very hard not to laugh. *I know. I'm terrible.*

"And my legs are strapped in, so if I try to get out, I might fall halfway off and bang my head or something. 'Cause I can't flip around and do a sit-up. I'd just have to throw myself toward the floor and hope for the best. I figure after what that alligator did to my ankle, that's not a great idea either. So I'm stuck. An hour later, one of the attendants comes in and screams, literally screams! She says they went to lunch and didn't know I was there!"

"Oh no!" *Don't laugh, Pepper. Don't laugh.*

"Yes!" Mr. Mixy wore his best pity-me expression. "I said they had to know I was there because the doctor put me there. And she said, 'Oh, he's retired now and just came in for the morning. It's his son who does most of the work, but he couldn't be in the office this morning.' And I guess Dr. Bretzel Senior didn't mention that I was still on the table. But the woman was cute, so I asked her out, and she said no. Can you believe it? After all that?"

"Truly unbelievable." I was shaking from my pent-up laugh. "Excuse me a moment."

I practically ran back to the office, where Jorge sat at his neat desk opposite my chaotic one, and I burst into hysterics.

"Oh my God! What is it?" Jorge leapt to his feet.

I held up a finger until I got under control, which took a minute or two of gasping and crying. "Mr. Mixy ... got strapped ... to a mechanical table at the chiropractor for an hour. Couldn't get off. Now he walks like a monkey."

Jorge looked shocked at first. Then he smiled. Then he

laughed. "That is terrible," he said through his chuckles. "Is he out there?"

"Yes, of course he is." I took a few deep breaths. "I could have laughed in front of him, but I didn't want to lose it in front of the other customers."

"I think, deep down, you didn't want to humiliate him any further."

"I'm not that good of a person."

"You're better than you think," he said. "You OK to go back out there?"

"Yes. I'm fine. Thanks." I burst into another fit of giggles, and Jorge grinned at me. Then I went back to the bar, got Mr. Mixy another beer, and let him decompress until he wiggled his way out of Nola an hour later.

At least he didn't stay all night. We had a decent supper crowd, still festive, some exchanging late Christmas presents, others enjoying family get-togethers. I liked that our place had that comfortable but special feeling for people. I also liked that they kept me busy making good cocktails. One high roller ordered two very pricey comparison shots of Pappy and Royce's Penny Brilliant bourbon, and a group of young guys having some kind of reunion tipped extravagantly well. They kept me late—I was the last one to leave—and I was exhausted by the time I looped my bag over my head, locked the back door and headed through our lush tropical courtyard to our small employee parking area.

I was still three empty spaces away from the Angry Orange when a car opposite me purred to life, its lights blinding me. I didn't recognize it, and I halted. Then it crept forward.

"Oh, shit," I said.

Chapter Twenty-Five

A thousand thoughts went through my head at that moment, but some had priority: Was this a coincidence, having a stranger in our employee lot, or was this car after me? (Paranoia pushed me toward the latter.) Could I get back into the restaurant before someone jumped out and grabbed me? (No.) Could I get to my car and unlock it and get in and get away before they smashed into me? (Not likely.)

So I ran. I cut through the spaces, under a couple of oak trees and up the narrow, dark, empty street that was essentially a back alley for many of the businesses on this stretch of the main drag in downtown Bohemia. If the car wasn't after me, it wouldn't pursue.

But I heard the squealing tires and looked over my shoulder as it whipped around, shot out the exit of the lot and accelerated down the alley after me.

If I could just find a doorway, a small lot, another alley—but nothing materialized right away, and I couldn't run as fast as the car. Unlike Nola, most of these businesses were built right up to the back street—no courtyards or lots to hide in.

Just before the car caught up to me, I spotted a skinny corridor between buildings that wasn't gated. I took a hard left and sprinted down it, heading for the main street. The car couldn't pursue me down here, but its driver could if they got out and ran. Still, it kept rolling down the back street. And I couldn't imagine them going after me on the main street. There would be too many people around.

Or not.

It was maybe twelve thirty on a Sunday night—and while a handful of bars stayed open that late on Sunday, traffic was light when I popped out onto the sidewalk, breathing hard. No one blinked these days when a speedster jackrabbited their car between stop signs. They wouldn't look twice at someone racing down the street. And what if this person had a gun? What if they got out and chased me on foot? I'd be doomed.

Neil. I could get to Neil's. I spotted the car two blocks away, making a swift turn onto the main street. Did they see me? I heard the chirp of its tires, but the otherwise quiet, dreamlike scene just made me even more frightened. Instead of running down the street, I dashed across it in front of another car that honked at me and slammed on the brakes as its driver yelled out the window.

I didn't care. I went up one alley and down another, checking around corners, working my way east, doubling back on where the car came from. I headed toward the tracks or just shy of them—to The Junction Box. It closed at midnight. Was Neil home yet? He lived in an apartment above the bar.

Instead of banging on the front door of the bar and hoping someone would still be there and let me in, I aimed for the alley next to it instead. It had become a landmark in downtown Bohemia, lined with climbing hot pink bougainvillea and strung with fairy lights that zigzagged above my head.

I ran for the metal staircase that hugged one wall. I scampered up it and reached the windowless door painted the same terra cotta color as the stucco wall. I banged on it, looking around for the car. I couldn't see it. I couldn't hear it. If the driver didn't see me—

The door opened, and I almost fell in.

"Pepper?" Neil caught me and pulled me inside.

"Close the door! Close the door!" I bent over, my hands on my knees, gasping for breath.

"Are you all right? What happened?" Neil smelled vaguely of the bar, an aroma I liked. He was still in his work clothes.

"There was a car after me. I don't know." I was starting to question my own imagination. "Maybe they were just trying to scare me."

"Come into the bar. Tell me what happened. I'll make you a drink." He locked the door, then checked his phone. I knew he had security cameras and an app that showed the feeds.

"Anything?"

"Nothing in back. A few cars rolling by in front. Nothing unusual."

"OK." I still gasped like a fish that had been tossed out of the bowl and tried to get myself together. I didn't want Neil to think I was a total wimp.

I caught my breath and followed him through the ornately carved wooden door of his home tiki bar, and he flipped on the colorful lights—glass floats in nets and bamboo-framed, cloth-sided lanterns that dangled from the ceiling. Then he turned on some Martin Denny, and the relaxing music meshed with all the Polynesian-inspired art and textures. I was on Neil's island now.

I set down my bag and took a stool. As he made me a Mai Tai with great care, with his homemade orgeat and freshly squeezed lime juice, the ritual calmed me, and I told him what happened.

"What kind of car was it?" he asked.

"Not sure. It was a light color. Silver or white."

"So no one said anything to you? No one came out of the car?" he asked, spanking a tuft of mint and popping it into the top of the beautiful tiki mug. I recognized it from Pau Hana, where we made drinks at Hookahakaha.

I took it gratefully and sipped, basking in the rums and other flavors that made it so perfect. "No, no one actually threatened me. But that car was chasing me. I'm sure of it."

"Maybe they saw you run and decided to mess with you. People are weird."

"They are, but they made—well, threatening gestures first."

"With the car?" Neil's eyebrows lifted.

"Yes, with the car! It was waiting for me." But now I wondered if I'd imagined the whole thing.

"It's all right. I believe you." He came around to the front of his little four-stool wooden bar, with its surface made of matchbooks, coasters and swizzle sticks from famous tiki bars sealed in a smooth, clear resin. He stood next to me, reached for my mug and took a sip of my drink before setting it on the bar. The intimate gesture warmed me. He smiled. Then he put his arms around me, pulled me off the stool and held me close for a long time.

I might have sniffled into his nice vest.

Then I looked up at him, and he gave me a quick, soft kiss. "I'll take you home."

"No. I—" I wasn't going to ask to stay. We were still playing the game, and the ball was in his court. "Just walk me to my car."

"No way. If someone out there is after you, I'm not giving them another opportunity. I'll take you home. And I'll pick you up tomorrow and bring you here so we can work on the special garnishes. OK?"

I got on my tiptoes and gave him a quick kiss back. "OK. But what does it mean, Neil? That car? We've upset somebody."

"Yes, *you* have. You have a gift." He chuckled. "Did something in particular happen today?"

A sudden giggle bubbled out of me.

"What?"

"Oh my God. Who was that chiropractor you recommended? They wrecked Mr. Mixy."

"Some friend of Gramps's. Not good?"

I laughed out loud. "Definitely not."

His eyes sparkled. "You can tell me all about it on the drive over to Bohemia Beach. And until this business is over, don't go anywhere alone, OK? Call me, and I'll be there."

IN THE MORNING, I called off Neil's taxi service because I got a ride with Diana in my aunt's small SUV. My aunt and I had talked her into an expedition to downtown Bohemia to buy a dress for the New Year's Eve benefit.

She parked on the main drag. I looked around with caution as we disembarked, but I didn't see any threatening light-colored cars. Heck, most of the cars these days were white or gray or black. It would be hard to pick one out.

"This all seems like so much puffery. What's wrong with wearing trousers?" Diana had on a white blouse and khakis, as she often did, and seemed much less confident than usual.

"Don't you ever dress up?" I asked her as we walked down the bustling sidewalk toward The Junction Box.

"Oh, I've worn a nice jacket to academic gatherings and that sort of thing."

"Do you own a dress?"

"I think I own one. It's at home. I purchased it for a fancy dress party."

"A costume party?" I smiled. "Maybe you should think of this as a costume party. I mean, in a way, that's what all dress-up occasions are. We're dressing up for a role. I like my comfy work clothes, but it's fun putting on a cool retro dress."

She sighed. "All right then. What should I wear?"

I thought for a minute, then pulled out my phone. "I know who would know."

Ten minutes later, Melody met us outside The Junction Box with Oleanna in tow.

"That was fast," I said.

"Oh—I was downtown already." She had a secretive air about her.

"Not working?"

"Not today."

"We met for breakfast," Oleanna said. She seemed in on the secret, whatever it was.

Hmm. I let it go. "Diana needs us to help her find a dress for the New Year's Eve ball."

Melody lit up. "Really?"

"I'm going with Mark." There were so many layers in Diana's tone, I wasn't sure what to think. Annoyance. Worry. Anticipation?

"Yum, yum," Melody said, and I laughed. "I know just the shop."

"We'll make you red-carpet-worthy," Oleanna promised with glee.

"Are you going to the benefit?" I asked Oleanna as we headed toward Melody's chosen boutique.

"No. Enzo asked me, actually, but I told him I didn't think it was a good idea."

I shot her a guilty look. "I'm ashamed that I didn't tell you what Neil and I learned. He's been seeing Raquel Tocks."

"Oh, *c'est la vie.* I'm not invested in him in that way, at least not now. Besides, your hint that he might've been seeing Diana's friend cooled my interest." Oleanna shrugged. "We're friends, and now we're business associates. The contracts are signed, and I'm heading home to L.A. And tomorrow I'll go to a little party at my friends' beach house in Malibu. We'll stay up all night and greet the new year in style."

"Sounds wonderful," I said, "but we'll miss you."

"Oh, you'll see me again." She smiled. Maybe that date she had the other night would lead to another visit. And if not, we'd invite her for another holiday.

"When will the champagne ads come out?" Melody asked.

"We're shooting the first campaign next month."

"It's going to be so fabulous," Melody said. "I can't wait to see it."

I bit my tongue. Enzo probably wasn't a killer. Right? But worry took some of the fun out of our shopping expedition.

An hour later, Diana left with a full shopping bag, Melody went off to who knew where, Oleanna headed back to her hotel to pack for her flight, and I entered The Junction Box.

The staff was busy prepping for lunch, and Neil wasn't there. He took Mondays off sometimes, but his bar was open every day, unlike mine. It was a bigger operation than Nola, with live music and more capacity. I didn't know how he did it. When you owned a business, you tended to work every day anyway—I often went in on my day off—but I needed breaks and took them when I could.

Luke came out from the back. "Hey, Pepper."

"Is Neil around?"

"I think he's expecting you upstairs." He waggled his eyebrows. "Something about a special project?"

I smirked at him. "Special garnishes."

"If that's what you want to call it."

"Down, boy." But I grinned.

"Was that Melody I saw outside earlier?"

"Yeah, we helped Diana buy a dress for the New Year's Eve event."

"Really?" He had a look of longing. "I wish I could be there. But someone has to run the party here."

"That's a big responsibility. Neil trusts you."

"I know. But I'd rather hang out with you guys."

"We'll all get together New Year's Day. How about that? We'll make it happen."

"Sounds good. You'd better go see Neil. He's on a schedule." Luke gave me a knowing smile and started prepping the bar.

I found the inside stairs in back—I knew the secrets of this place now—climbed up and knocked on the door.

The peephole darkened for a second, then Neil opened it with a smile. "Pepper." He leaned in and gave me a quick kiss, and I followed him into his apartment. "Where'd you go with the girls?"

"Spot us on the camera?" I teased. "You'll see tomorrow night." Melody and I had taken advantage of our shopping time and bought little black dresses for ourselves, since the "help" had to wear black. Raquel's orders. It might as well be *chic* black. I'd pick up my dress later once I'd reclaimed my car from the Nola lot.

"Mysterious," he mused.

"You said it yourself. You have to have a few secrets." But

there were a few too many floating around for my comfort right now.

"You ready to make tiny paper airplanes?" He pointed to the coffee table in his living room, which was covered with a bunch of colorful printouts and two pairs of scissors.

"Are you serious?" My bag buzzed, and I fished around inside to pull out my phone.

"What is it?" Neil asked, sensing my interest.

"Text from Diana. She says her plant guy at the university told her he's supposed to get the DNA results from the samples back tomorrow. He'll bring them to the benefit to keep the results on the down-low at her request."

"At least she might be able to save some of Alice's work."

"That would be one good result out of this mess, since the marsh out there is going to turn into Boyle Lakes suburbia."

Neil snorted. "Maybe Phantom will have a say."

"Are you kidding? Raquel Tocks will eat him alive first."

He laughed, then sobered. "Unless Raquel killed Alice or arranged her death. Then all bets are off for Boyle Lakes."

"If she's caught. You don't think the cops are still interested in Diana, do you?"

"I guess it depends on what they find on the kayak paddle you told me about."

"Crap." I looked at him. "You don't think Diana *did* have something to do with it?"

"Of course not." But he didn't sound so sure.

"We can't doubt our friends." I slipped my arms around his waist.

"You're right." He brushed my hair away from my face and tapped the center of my eyeglasses. "Friend."

"Gah!" I pulled away as he grinned. "OK, what are we doing here?"

As he explained, more worries distracted me. I'd ticked someone off, probably by getting too close to the truth. Whatever that was. Which meant I was closer than I thought. We had to figure it out before the next car found me in the middle of the night.

Chapter Twenty-Six

It was easy to get sentimental on New Year's Eve. *Auld lang syne* and all of that. This had been the wildest year of my life and maybe the best. I'd joined the Bohemia Bartenders, met Neil and the gang, and faced my own mortality more than once. I was ready to drink champagne and toast a happy new year.

But at the moment, I was opening another bottle of Desjardins champagne. We needed a lot for all the cocktails we were making for the benefit. With Neil, Barclay and Melody, I shook and poured at our bar in the huge refreshment tent, filled with festive tables and kiosks featuring various restaurants offering tasty morsels.

The tent was set up among the old oaks at Milkweed Mansion, on a large piece of land on the lagoon. A profusion of white fairy lights among the trees and deep blue spotlights and special-effects projectors in the tent added a touch of magic.

Out of a gorgeous antique crystal punch bowl, we dipped the Poinsettia Punch, with cranberry juice, orange liqueur and vodka to please Raquel. We added cranberries, pomegranate arils, and rosemary sprigs for garnish. And it wasn't bad, partly because we'd used Enzo's superb champagne. And we had one more potent vodka drink to appease our client, the Atomic

Cocktail, which featured brandy and sherry with the champagne.

There was a French 75 punch with gin and champagne; the Berry Festive with Chambord, champagne, lemon, gin and imported raspberries; a bourbon cocktail of my invention (the only one without champagne); and the classic Air Mail. It included rum, honey syrup and fresh lime juice, served with crushed ice in a Collins glass and garnished with the wee paper airplanes Neil and I made. Folded from enlarged copies of old canceled Air Mail stamps, the planes were colorful and made for great Instagram moments.

There were plenty of pretty people taking photos of themselves. They posed in front of the backdrop provided by the zoo, sometimes with a zookeeper and whatever animal they were toting around—a sloth, a parrot, an alpaca in a bow tie on a leash. Sometimes they posed with someone equally furry, Mr. Mixy.

My ex was hard to miss in his outrageous leopard-print suit with black lapels. He wore it over a white turtleneck, with a shiny gold scarf. A pair of mini braids in his voluminous beard were tied off with leopard-print ribbons. At least the ensemble was on-theme.

Mr. Mixy made the rounds, talking to his phone as he live-streamed his semi-famous face, occasionally stopping to interview guests. I kept forgetting he was a rising reality TV star with his cocktail show. Today he didn't walk like a monkey so much as a stiff cyborg in need of oil. He'd evolved since his bad turn at the chiropractor's office. But once in a while, when he was near and moved suddenly, I heard him groan.

Not surprisingly, he also stayed far away from the young female zookeeper who cheerfully carried around a baby alligator.

Barclay and I went into the historic house with a cooler to hit the kitchen up for ice, and I snuck looks into as many rooms as possible to soak in the ambience. Landon and Kayla had done a stellar job fixing up the place, from the chandelier-dominated foyer to the sparkling ballroom, where guests danced to a DJ. Tables stuffed with auction items filled the parlor, which had a glowing fireplace that opened into the ballroom on the other side of the wall. The kitchen was a pleasant mix of vintage and modern, with a black-and-white floor of hexagonal tiles, mint walls and shiny new stainless-steel appliances and work surfaces. Someone had roped off the fabulous library, but I still goggled when I peeked inside the open doors. Life goals!

"Bummer you can't be with Gina tonight," I said to Barclay as we carried the cooler back to the tent. He looked sleek in a black jacket, black shirt, black tie.

"She understands. We're going to meet up later at The Junction Box, after closing, probably. I think their party ends at one."

"Of course it does, because Luke has been messaging our group all night telling us to come over there," I said.

Barclay laughed. "Yeah, I don't know how Neil feels about that. I don't think he'll mind, as long as it's not a big party."

"I'm getting my fill now. I think I'll be too tired to party later," I confessed.

We got back to the tent, and Neil, dressed a lot like Barclay in black but with a bow tie, shot me a warm smile. "Have I told you how beautiful you look tonight?"

"No. And thanks. So do you. I mean, you look handsome, in a ninja bartender kind of way."

He laughed.

My black velvet dress, with its flaring skirt, off-the-shoulder Bardot neckline and short sleeves, would've looked perfect with black gloves, but work didn't permit such a luxury. And my shoes were rather sensible, with low heels. But still, I knew I looked good with my rhinestone necklace, earrings, sparkly cat's-eye glasses and, of course, the gator-tooth bracelet.

Melody paused in her lime squeezing and put one hand on her hip as she stared at Neil.

"You look great, too," he told her.

"Gee, thanks." She rolled her eyes, but she grinned as we laughed. Her short, tight black dress was so Melody, showing off her tattoos, and she rocked it.

"You know who else looks amazing? Diana," I told them as we worked.

"Are they here yet?" Barclay asked.

"I don't think so. Mark and Royce came over to pick up my aunt and Diana for dinner just before I left. It was very satisfying to see Mark's eyes get as big as Jupiter when he saw her."

"So a rhinestone safari outfit, then?" Barclay joked.

I elbowed him. Then I caught a glimpse of their party entering the tent. "There they are!"

There was something just a little bit Cinderella about Diana tonight. There were no khakis. While Mark wore a black tux and Royce a good-looking blue suit, and my aunt had her own version of a little black dress, Diana wore a gown in dark red that perfectly complemented her deep tan skin and matched her lipstick. I'd never seen her in lipstick before.

Fabric draped across the low neckline and at the short sleeves, leaving her shoulders bare. The heavy material flowed like silk over the slender, shapely body she usually hid in her khakis, and her toned left leg peeked out of a high slit as she walked (Oleanna had advocated hard for this dress for this very feature). Her short hair had a bit of fluffiness tonight and was pinned up on one side with a barrette sparkling with red and white stones—I'd bet Aunt Celestine had something to do with that. Then, unconventionally, and mostly because Diana refused to wear towering high heels, her feet were clad in sturdy, low-heeled shoes in the same deep red, but with rhinestone buckles that glinted under the fairy lights. And she totally carried them off.

"I feel like a fairy godmother right now," Melody said.

"Stunning," Barclay murmured.

Mark had his arm looped through Diana's and wore a beaming smile as they approached. Their obvious sparks gave me a thrill. These two had something together, even if they didn't really know it yet. Maybe I could help fan the flame.

I slipped out from behind the bar and hugged Royce and Aunt Celestine, then grinned at Mark and Diana. "Who wants a drink?"

Mark's smile was almost shy for a moment, and then his boisterousness came through. "I want whatever features my gin. Diana?"

She looked up at him, her smile shy, too. "Perfect."

I tried not to squee. "Done. Royce? Auntie?"

Once we'd hooked them up with drinks, they went off to explore the auction items and the rest of the house.

Then Raquel and Enzo came our way, with Raquel's mustachioed bodyguard hulking in her wake.

She'd poured herself into a long, clingy white dress beaded with crystals, so she twinkled every time she moved. Enzo wore a classic black tux that seemed tailored to his very nice form. I could see why he turned the heads of so many women. But did he use that power for evil?

"What can I get you?" Neil asked.

"Atomic Cocktail," Raquel ordered.

"Appropriate for that *bombe* of a dress," Enzo said into her ear, though we all could hear him.

"Enzo?" I asked him.

He turned his charming smile on me. "Whatever you recommend."

"I'll make you an Air Mail." I started on it as Bill and Tracy Boyle stepped up to Barclay and Melody's end of the bar.

Awkward!

"Raquel," Bill said with a nod to her.

"Uncle Bill," she said back, never looking at him.

"You have some nerve," he said. "Boyle Lakes?"

She turned to him. "It's traditional to name developments after their historical origins."

"You mean after what they destroy, don't you?" Bill said.

"The development will be very natural." Raquel took her drink and watched me with icy eyes as I finished Enzo's. "Several water features are in the plans."

"It *is* a water feature," Bill said. "It's called a marsh."

Raquel's goon took a step forward. Without looking back at him, she waved her hand. "Get lost, Alph."

The goon snorted and walked away as Bill continued, "Did you hear what I said? Don't you care what you're doing to this beautiful place?"

"My friends," Enzo interrupted, "please—"

"You are not my friend," Bill cut him off.

Raquel turned to her uncle. "And you are no longer the owner of Boyle Lakes. By choice, as I recall. And what were you thinking, sending someone else to rent the shack? How long do you hope to delay me?"

"Someone else came to you about the shack? Who?" I probably shouldn't have asked, but I couldn't help myself.

Raquel gave me a cold look. "Some wrinkled little man wearing gold chains. Thor something. Of course, I told him it wasn't available. A pathetic attempt to divert me," she said to Bill.

Tracy made an exasperated sound and marched off with her French 75 punch in hand.

So Thor was out of custody and still trying to get into the shack!

"Just once, make the right decision," Bill said to Raquel before he followed his wife.

"Old fool," Raquel muttered, looping her arm in Enzo's and dragging him away with his Air Mail.

Enzo looked back at us and spoke in that French accent. "I like ze airplane."

"Well, that wasn't tense at all," Barclay remarked, and we laughed, a little nervously, until shouts interrupted us.

"You couldn't just leave it alone, could you?" came a female voice. I peered into the shadows and light projections and spotted Tracy Boyle over by the dessert table, facing her husband, her glass in one hand and a tart in the other. "You had to go at her again."

"I was just doing what I thought was right," Bill answered her.

"Were you? Or were you trying to make things nice for *Alice?*" Traci threw her tart at him.

He ducked, and the tart hit Mr. Mixy in the head as he helped himself to the chocolate truffles.

"Tracy!" Bill called.

But his wife had already stalked off into the night. Bill didn't run after her. Instead, he stared at her retreating form for a moment, then wandered off toward the gazebo near the low cliff overlooking the lagoon.

Poor Bill. Or poor Tracy. Or maybe both, having to deal with Raquel.

Mr. Mixy ambled over. "Hey, Pepper. Can you help me with this? Something hit me."

Why me? But I supposed the celebrity guest couldn't walk around with Key lime pie goo in his hair. I grabbed a bar towel and stepped out. "Turn around."

"Thanks, Pepper," he said as I used the towel to wipe the gunk off the back of his head. I got most of it. Maybe he could get the parrot to peck out the rest.

"Best I can do."

He gave me a cheesy smile. "I miss your hands in my hair."

I cringed, and Neil emitted a low grumble.

Mr. Mixy smoothed his head as I returned to my post. "Hey, I'm supposed to lead the midnight toast. They're going to set off a few fireworks."

I flinched, then put a certain sparky memory behind me. "Congratulations."

"So I get the champagne from you, right?"

I looked over at Neil, who looked at his vintage watch. "In thirty minutes, we'll pour. They have volunteers who will bring trays around, or you can get it here."

"Great." Mr. Mixy moseyed off. Wow, it was getting late.

I heard buzzes and pings, and Barclay looked at his smart watch and chuckled. "Luke says Cray and your grandfather are getting drunk at your bar," he told Neil.

"Kids today," Neil joked.

Fifteen minutes later, we got another update from Luke, which Barclay relayed. "Luke says that guy Bill Boyle just gave him his credit card. He's drinking there too."

"I guess he abandoned the party," I said. "Ask Luke if Bill has a woman with him."

Barclay used his phone to text Luke. "Nope. By himself. He apparently knows your grandfather and they're drinking together now," he informed Neil, who just chuckled. "Oh, and Ez and the Emeralds are rocking the joint."

Ez was a friend of mine, and her band played The Junction Box often.

Royce, Aunt Celestine, Mark and Diana walked back to us as we began to fill the event's commemorative champagne flutes, loading them on trays that zoo volunteers took out to deliver to the crowd. Other guests crowded around us, grabbing glasses outright, including Mr. Mixy.

Our friends took glasses, too, and watched Mr. Mixy give a toast. He said something about reaching for the stars, though he groaned for a moment when he lifted his glass, obviously still sore from yesterday.

"This concludes our obligations," Neil said. "Let's clean up and maybe we can get out of here before the fireworks."

Melody huffed. "Oh, you're no fun."

"Pepper doesn't like fireworks," he answered, then gave me a kind look. *Aw.* He was looking out for me.

"Now that you're done, I need to fill you in." Diana raised her voice a little to be heard over the chatter of the people milling around, waiting for the fireworks. "My university contact gave me the results from those plant samples. And they're incredible."

Chapter Twenty-Seven

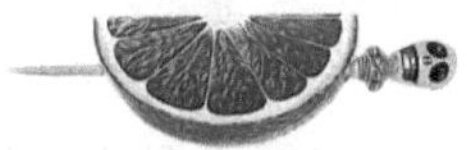

The analysis of the plant samples must be impressive if Diana was bringing it up here, now.

"What's the story?" I asked.

"It's something completely new. Or should I say undiscovered?" Her eyes sparkled like her barrette. "It's a native, I think, though it's related to one of the invasive plants I told you about, the Barbados nut, *Jatropha curcas.*"

"The one that lets you blow bubbles?"

"Yes." Diana smiled. "Only Alice thought the qualities of this plant were truly extraordinary, above and beyond the medicinal and biofuel possibilities of *curcas*. She alluded to extensive research and analysis that must be on her computer, as well as a lab space she was renting at the university."

"That's probably where some of that grant money was going," I said.

"Indeed," Diana agreed. "Now a lot of what she said in her journal makes sense. We just didn't have the missing piece, identification of the plant."

"She talked about emeralds and the Fountain of Youth," Mark said. "We thought she was referring to treasure being buried somewhere out there in the mire."

Emeralds. Like Ez and the Emeralds. Who were not gemstones at all.

"The emeralds are the plants?" I asked.

Diana grinned. "I think so. There was gibberish in the journal I thought was poetry. A metaphor. Stuff about a treasure with healing properties. Rejuvenating properties. I think she was talking about these plants. She'd found something extremely rare and most likely very valuable with potential to heal all kinds of illnesses. Some cultures already use *curcas* to treat viruses, infections, diabetes, even cancer. What if this is even more effective?"

"Something pharmaceutical companies would love to have?" Neil asked.

"Quite possibly," Aunt Celestine said. "Many drugs use natural plants as chemical templates, though the plants themselves are often more potent than synthesized medicine—though they can be toxic if used incorrectly."

Diana nodded. "The rarity of this plant makes it even more valuable if the research is as good as Alice hinted at in the journal."

"And now we have the DNA results to prove what she was looking for." Mark patted his chest, where his jacket didn't lay quite right. He must have the envelope in there. "We need her laptop, but the journal was the key. These plants are so hard to find, she wrote down every time and place she found them."

I nodded in excitement. "The GPS coordinates!"

"Exactly," he said.

Royce added, "But now it's all in peril of being plowed over."

"We have to rescue the rest of the samples," Diana said. "She was actually cultivating them. We can go out in the morning."

"You'd better tell Detective Keene," Neil suggested.

Mark nodded in resignation. "We'll have to. But I think she'll be reasonable once she understands."

I was about to ask them if they thought the plants were a motive for murder when the first explosion rang out over the lagoon. I ducked, then straightened up, embarrassed, as the glittering blossoms of fireworks lit up the sky over Bohemia.

The others looked at me in sympathy, and we all focused on cleaning as quickly as we could. I didn't hate fireworks, but I preferred being as far from them as possible after what happened in New Orleans.

Several minutes later, we finished boxing our supplies and loading them on a cart. The last fireworks rocked the air in a grand finale. As the last spark fizzled, Mark pulled his phone from his pocket and looked at it with concern. Then he answered it.

"Otter?" he said in the newfound, relative quiet. The crowd that had gathered at the riverbank started to move toward the parking area. "What on earth?"

We all turned to stare at him.

"Are you quite sure? Hang on a minute." Mark held the phone to his chest and looked back at us. "Otter says someone with a funny accent just tried to hire him to go out to the Swamp Shack."

"*You* have a funny accent," Barclay noted.

"Ha ha," Mark said.

I looked around. No Raquel. No Enzo.

"Enzo?" Neil asked. Great minds and all that.

"Was the accent French?" Mark said into the phone, then listened for a minute and spoke to us. "Yes. A Frenchman. Otter turned him down. But if it's Enzo, he might be going out there to clean out the shack."

"He must have heard us!" Now that I thought about it, he and Raquel had been lurking nearby, schmoozing with friends.

"Heard me, you mean." Diana looked rueful. "We must go out there at once. We can't let him have the plants."

"He must have killed Alice!" I pressed a hand to my head, trying to draw out a theory that made sense. "But why didn't he take them then?"

"It was supposed to look like an accident, and he was obviously biding his time," Mark said with confidence. "He must have figured no one wanted them."

"And he and Raquel are working together on the development," I added. "She owns the Swamp Shack, probably owns most or all of the locations where you two found the plants in the marsh. He could walk in there and take everything."

"But now that we know about it, he wants to get them before we have a chance to save them," Diana said. "Maybe he thought if he rented the airboat, he could beat us there."

"You have a handful of samples, though, right?" I asked her.

She looked worried. "Most of them were destroyed in the analysis. And if they don't let us onto the property anymore, we won't be able to collect more. One person can't control this discovery."

Mark barked into his phone. "Can you take us? Yes, now! How much?" Mark visibly swallowed. "All right. We'll meet you at the ramp in twenty minutes." He ended the call, looking satisfied. A man of action.

"Are you mad? I can't go in these clothes," Diana said.

"We don't have time to change," Mark said. "Enzo called Otter several minutes ago. He's gone. He'll find another way."

"He has another way," I said. "He told us Raquel had lent him a truck with a boat trailer. He'll just go out to the old Boyle place and get in that way."

"I thought I heard a boat that morning!" Diana exclaimed.

"But we can beat him if Otter takes us," Neil said. "I have room for six in my vehicle if Barclay and Melody take our supplies."

"No problem," Barclay said.

"You mean I'm not allowed to go out to the mosquito-infested swamp in the middle of the night?" Melody said dryly. "Oh, darn."

We laughed, but the humor was halfhearted. How were we going to do this?

Mark seemed ready to jump. "Obviously, Diana and I will go. Pepper? Neil?"

"Of course," Neil said, and I nodded, holding my belly.

"And me," Royce said. "Aunt Celestine?"

She smiled, I think because she liked him calling her "aunt." "I'd rather not. For one thing, I don't want to leave the dogs alone that long." Oh, yeah! Victoria and Astra were having a playdate. "I can take Mark's car back to our place, if that works for you. And I'll give the detective a heads-up. I don't think you should face this murderer without backup."

"Fine," Mark said. "Let's go." Keys were exchanged, cargo hauled, and our airboat crew headed for Neil's car.

"Pepper!" came a voice from the parking area out near the gate. Mr. Mixy!

"We're in a hurry, Stephan," I told him as we reached Neil's SUV. Everyone got in but me as I tried to get rid of Mr. Mixy.

"Let me come with you!" he whined. "I need to wind down."

"We're going to the swamp," I said. "Remember the swamp? The alligator?"

He froze, then assumed a look of noble bravery. "You'll need protection."

I looked around at the three very capable men around me and Diana. Not that we women needed them. Well, Diana probably didn't need them. I wasn't so sure about me.

"Come on, Pepper," Neil called.

"I'm going," I told Mr. Mixy.

"So am I! I told you I'm a changed man. I need to spread happiness with my talent. And, you know, I need to do good things." And before I could stop him, he'd yanked open the back door, climbed past a protesting Mark and Diana and settled in the back with Royce.

"Christ," Neil said as I got in the front. At least I had shotgun. Though I kind of wished I had an *actual* shotgun.

Speaking of men, none of them had the balls to kick out Mr. Mixy, either. What was that line from *Thelma & Louise?* You get what you settle for. And we were about to get a night ride with furry face into the swamp in a race against a killer.

OTTER just about fell over laughing when he saw us in our New Year's Eve finery rolling up to the dock, where clouds of mosquitoes, in spite of the cool weather, swarmed around the light pole there.

"You're kidding, right?" he gasped between guffaws.

"Shut it, little man," Diana said. "We need to go now."

"Hey! OK. No problem!" Otter, in his usual khaki getup, was still snuffling as we climbed aboard. "Wait. I said I didn't want to see this one again." He pointed at Mr. Mixy.

"I'd like to apologize for my behavior last time," Mr. Mixy told him. "I promise, I won't dig any holes. And I won't molest the wildlife."

Otter gave him a stern look as he started up the engine. "Just remember, I have a gun."

"Yes, sir," Mr. Mixy said.

Otter scowled at him, looked around at us and burst into laughter again. I mean, he was right. We looked ridiculous. The guys did OK; Neil left his tie in the car, Mark seemed at home in his, and Mr. Mixy, rather resourcefully, kept his scarf and tied it around his face. Diana and I had shed our bling and bags as well.

Since Diana and I wore dresses with bare shoulders, Mark had given her his jacket, and Neil had found his black hoodie for me, which I took gratefully. At least our shoes were somewhat functional. But our legs were exposed, and we both slapped at mosquitoes as everyone settled in and donned those painful hearing protectors.

"Here." Otter handed us a can of spray bug repellent, and we each used it liberally as he eased the boat away from the dock. No one else was around.

Neil pulled out his phone and looked at it as Otter cranked up the engine and we took off at speed into the moonless darkness.

I looked at Neil questioningly, and he showed me his phone. It was a message from Lissa. "Looking for Raquel. Is she with you?"

"No," was all he wrote back.

I realized I'd left my phone in the car, so I lifted one side of his headset and yelled in his ear. "Maybe she's with Enzo."

He winced as I dropped the hard earmuff back in place against his head. "Maybe!"

This was getting weirder. But I supposed if Raquel saw an opportunity to make a lot of money, she'd take it. Still, was a

New Year's Eve date in the swamp with a killer the way to go about it?

Or maybe she didn't realize what Enzo was? Or ... were they working together?

Neil tapped his phone, then showed me what he'd typed in his notes app since he couldn't text me. "We can't sneak up on him in this airboat."

I took his phone and typed, "We might beat him there. Scare him off."

"I guess we'll find out. We might need Otter and his gun."

"Enzo won't try to kill all of us," I typed.

Though I wasn't sure I believed it.

Chapter Twenty-Eight

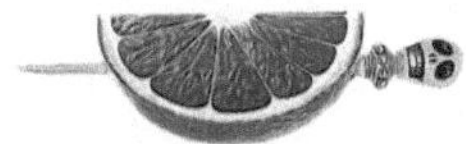

The swamp smelled different at night. The daytime sweetness of water hyacinths and other flora had given way to what I could only describe as wet earth, but the air was still fresh and pure.

I didn't need my glasses to see. Mostly, they kept juice out of my eyes. Tonight, they kept out the bugs, but I still twitched every time one struck me in the face as the boat hurtled across the water. I got the sensation Otter touched light speed at times, and I hung onto Neil's arm for stability and warmth. He placed a hand over mine. If it weren't for all the noise and the bugs and our race against a murderer, this might have been romantic. In the deep darkness of the swamp, the stars shone brightly overhead, maybe more than I'd ever seen. There was no moon to disrupt their dance, only the sweep of Otter's headlamp as he picked out his route among the grasses and riverbanks. Sometimes his light picked up pairs of red eyes staring back at us. I had a feeling I knew what those were.

Would Phantom be waiting for us, too?

"Argh!" I snorted and slapped at my face, trying to dislodge the bug that had flown up my nose.

"You OK?" I barely heard Neil through the earmuffs.

I just waved him off. I didn't think he needed to know I

was blowing insects out of my nostrils. Kind of takes away the mystery, you know?

Otter slowed down. We'd entered the winding avenue of trees, and in a moment, we glided into the clearing that held the Swamp Shack.

The windows glowed with a soft, warm light. As we approached, a new shape emerged from the gloom: another small boat tethered to the dock, opposite the kayak.

Otter slowed the engine down to idle, but there was no way whoever was inside couldn't hear our approach. I took off my earmuffs and dropped them on the floor.

A few feet from the dock, Otter cut the motor altogether, and we eased up alongside it to the tune of singing frogs. Mark jumped out and grabbed the rope to tie it off. He looked so out of place in his black dress pants, white shirt and sharp black bow tie. For a second I felt like I was watching James Bond. Especially when he had a quiet word with Otter, took our captain's pistol and stuffed it in his waistband.

Whoa.

"Ready?" Neil whispered.

I nodded and let him guide me out of the boat. Boy, I liked this dress a lot better at the New Year's Eve party. Now the chilly wind blew up my skirt, but at least it made it harder for the mosquitoes to land. Thank goodness for pettipants.

Diana and Mr. Mixy stepped onto the dock. Mr. Mixy was a problem. We didn't know what awaited us, but he could only make it worse.

"Stephan, we need you to stay on the dock and keep watch," I told him quietly. "If you see anything weird—" I didn't want him screaming, as he was wont to do. "Tell Otter or text Neil. You have Neil's number, right?"

"Um, no. But I can do that." He looked around nervously.

For once, I was sure we had the same thought: Where is Phantom?

He and Neil quickly exchanged numbers, and Mark, Diana, Neil and I headed for the steps.

Diana halted us at the bottom. "What's the plan?" she whispered.

We mused for a second. "We talk to him," I whispered back. "He's not going to initiate a bloodbath out here. It would ruin all his plans for world domination. We talk to him and play it by ear."

"A man who may have killed four people?" Neil pointed out.

"We don't know that for sure." Enzo's parents. His wife. Alice. "Look, we can't go in there guns blazing."

"Gun. Singular," Mark noted.

I snorted. And I led the way up the steps. We came out here for the plants. We had to try to get the plants. Then at least if Raquel and Enzo bulldozed the whole place, we might be able to save them.

The door was slightly ajar. No Cheesy Does It card necessary.

I pushed it open. "Enzo?" I called softly, peering inside. The kitchen light dimly lit the space. Neil's hand was on my shoulder, as if he might yank me back and out of trouble. But I didn't sense a threat. Not yet. "Enzo?" I said a little more loudly.

A strange noise of distress greeted me, and I stepped inside.

Enzo, still in his tux, tie gone, slumped in one of the dilapidated soft chairs in the living area. We all moved in. He appeared to be alone, and the group let me take the lead. I walked to him. He seemed kind of out of it. "Enzo? Are you OK?"

He blinked as if he'd just grown aware of my voice, then groaned as he straightened a little. "I need those plants."

"You heard us, didn't you?" Diana asked. "Back at the party?"

He nodded and sat up straight, then clutched his stomach. "I need them. They're mine. We own the property now. Raquel owns it, but I have an investment. They're mine."

"So you killed Alice for them," I said.

"No! You are wrong. I would never have killed her. She was going to help me."

I glanced toward the porch. The remaining plants seemed to be intact, still in their trays. As my gaze traveled back toward him, it snagged on a small, square plastic container on the coffee table. The lid was off, and inside were oval-shaped things, each maybe half an inch long, brown and flecked with amber.

"What are those?" I asked Enzo.

"Oh my God," Diana said, rushing over in her red dress. "They're seeds." She examined the handwritten label on the lid, then looked sharply at Enzo.

He lifted a trembling hand as if to stop her from taking the box, then groaned and grabbed his belly again.

Diana leaned closer and looked into his eyes. "You didn't eat these, did you?"

"I need them. I told you."

"Whatever you think you need, you do not need them in this form. If they're anything like their cousin, they're exceedingly toxic." She looked around. "Mark, grab that basin, will you?"

Mark spotted the shower tub and dragged it over. "Now what?"

Diana looked at Enzo. "I need you to vomit."

He looked up at her with a flash of his old charm in his eyes. "Enzo Desjardins does not vomit unless he has drunk a great deal of champagne. Not mine, of course."

Diana quirked her mouth in amusement. "These are poisonous. You have to vomit, or you'll be much worse off." She looked around. "He needs medical attention."

Neil nodded and pulled out his phone as Enzo protested. "You cannot have them!"

I stepped up and slapped him on the back. "Puke now. Argue later. Do it!"

He looked at me helplessly as Mark snorted a laugh. Then Enzo leaned over the basin and, with a couple of false starts, erupted in a series of ugly barfs.

"Dear lord, that's nasty," Mark said.

"Take it outside, would you?" Diana asked him. "And tell Otter to hang on and look for help."

Mark raised an eyebrow. "I'm only doing this for you."

Neil got off the phone. "They're sending an ambulance, but it might take some doing. They said it would help if we can get him to the mainland. I said we'd try."

"We can try to get him to the old Boyle place. Is that where you parked?" I asked Enzo.

Neil appeared with a cup of water and handed it to Enzo, who took a meager sip and nodded.

"So we have a few minutes?" I said to Neil, then to Enzo, "We don't get it. You'd better explain it to us. And if you heard us, you know you can't have these plants. Even if you could sell them, you won't get what you want for them."

"I don't want to sell them. I need them. The miracle plant. The Fountain of Youth. Alice told me all about it. We were —close."

He must have slept with her. But all that aside ... "What are you talking about?"

Enzo took a deeper draft of water and leaned back in the chair. "I am not well. And it will take a miracle cure to save me. I've pursued every cure you could imagine. Some were frauds. I thought, perhaps there is truth in myth. There often is. I studied the Fountain of Youth. Did you know there are several legends, several places? Even in France. I looked. I explored the Forest of Brocéliande, looking for the fountain associated with the wizard Merlin." He smiled at my skeptical expression. "I know. I was desperate. Then I read about Florida. It was, what do you say, a long shot. But I found out about this place and thought, if I could own a piece of this land, perhaps I could drink of the waters myself. And I got involved with Raquel."

He coughed, then eyed the box of seeds again.

"No." Diana pulled them away and popped the lid on them.

"Perhaps the leaves, then?" He looked up at her hopefully.

"No. We don't know enough."

I interrupted. "What is wrong with you, Enzo?"

One of his eyelids flickered. "Huntington's Disease. Do you know it?"

I shook my head. But then I remembered him spilling his drink, his odd eye movements.

"It is a disease of the brain, but it manifests physically. First it is subtle. Then it takes everything from you, and then you die. My mother had it. And so do I. She died of it. My father could not take the strain. A stroke killed him."

Oh, no. Poor Enzo. "Your wife?" I asked softly.

"When I married, my wife agreed with me that we would not have children. I didn't tell her all the reasons. Not the main reason. But she got pregnant anyway, and then I had to tell her. There was a chance the child would be all right, but a test showed our child would have it too. Marie threw herself off a balcony on a ship." A sob escaped Enzo, and he wiped away a tear. "I couldn't tell the world why. It was too painful. And I didn't want them to know about me. People don't want to touch a business led by a dying man. Drink a champagne made by a dying man. Champagne is about life. Joy. And it is all I have left."

"We should get him to the mainland," Neil interrupted.

"I didn't kill Alice. But I would like to kill the one who did." Enzo sounded stronger, angry now. "We had long talks about the Fountain of Youth, and she said, maybe it's not the water but what is in the water, near the water. The plants. She knew she'd found something astounding when she met me. She confided in me."

"Can you take him?" Diana asked, then nodded at Mark as he reentered the room. "Mark and I will stay here and collect the plants. All right, Enzo?"

He sighed, all his fight gone. "Yes. Do it. Perhaps you will find an answer for me. With Alice gone, I had lost all hope. But maybe."

"What about Raquel?" I asked. "Does she know about all of this?"

"Non," Enzo said as Neil helped him get up. "She just wants to make money. But I thought, once I learned about the plants, Alice would stay long enough to make her research count. And then she died. Now I am thinking, perhaps I could buy up some of the land. Preserve it. I don't know anymore."

"But where is Raquel?" I asked him. "You were with her."

"I don't know. She got a phone call and disappeared, and I heard you talking, and I sent her a message and I left. This was more important."

I looked at Neil. "Text Lissa, would you?"

He let go of Enzo and got out his phone. A moment later, he looked up at me. "No Raquel. She's not responding to texts, and she didn't show up for a small after-party she was supposed to host. Lissa found her bodyguard passed out behind Milk-weed Manor."

"That's weird," I said.

"Let me try." Enzo also pulled out a phone and attempted a call, then left a message. "Raquel, darling. Call me if you get this."

"There's still a killer out there," I said as Enzo put away his phone. Who hated Alice enough to kill her? Tracy Boyle was so angry tonight. So jealous. I wondered ... "Text Luke. See if Bill Boyle is still at The Junction Box. See if Bill has heard from his wife."

"He shouldn't be there. It's closed," Neil said, but instead of texting Luke, he called and put it on speaker.

"Hey, Neil! Where are you guys?" came Luke's voice. There was music and happy voices in the background.

"Long story," Neil said. "Is Bill Boyle still there?"

"Oh, no. He left a while back."

"Where'd he go?" I asked.

"I don't know," Luke said, "but I told him to get a cab. He's an angry drunk, man. He kind of got into this rage monologue about how he was going to make it right. About how the circus couldn't go on without the ringleader or something like that."

"That Bill Boyle. He hates Raquel, and she hates him," Enzo said. "I overheard Bill arguing with Alice once when I came to see her. Accused her of treasure hunting like all the others, throwing away the opportunity he had given her. Of course, he wanted Alice to stay and block the development. He had no idea what kind of treasure she really had, that she might have very well done that. I think she did not trust him enough to tell him. She seemed nervous about him. Maybe she did not think the plant would be enough to save this place."

Maybe Tracy Boyle was jealous enough to kill Alice. But then again, Bill was angry with the botanist too.

Bill had argued with Alice. He wasn't as cozy with her as his wife seemed to think. And he hated Raquel.

"Suppose Bill Boyle has Raquel?" I asked Neil. I walked over to the window that faced the old house. "I see a light over there. Were there any lights when you arrived?" I asked Enzo.

"Non."

Raquel was a nightmare, but if Bill was the killer and he had her, we couldn't just let her die. "We have to check."

"We have to go over there anyway," Neil said. "But we have to call the cops. This is getting way too dangerous."

I hated to admit it, but Neil was right. And we had to go now.

Chapter Twenty-Nine

Neil and I descended the steps with Enzo. Tendrils of low fog now swirled around the shack and the boats. I shivered.

Mr. Mixy came rushing over to us. "We didn't see anything. What's going on?"

"Everything's fine," I lied. "But we have to get Enzo over to the mainland to meet an ambulance. He's not feeling well."

"Need a ride?" Otter asked.

"Please stay here and help Mark and Diana get back," Neil said. He looked around. "We'll take Enzo's boat."

"You can stay with Otter," I told Mr. Mixy.

He shook his head. "I'm going to stay with you, Pepper. Maybe I can help." Then, without helping, Mr. Mixy ran over and climbed into Enzo's boat.

Even in the starlight, I saw Neil clench his jaw.

"Can I borrow your phone?" I asked Neil, then dialed Aunt Celestine and put it on speaker.

"Where are you?" my aunt asked right away. "I couldn't get ahold of Detective Keene. I had to leave a message. And Pepper isn't responding."

"This is Pepper. I have Neil's phone. We're OK. But we think Bill Boyle might have Raquel at his old house. And he might've killed Alice."

Neil looked at me in alarm. Maybe he hadn't taken that extra leap, but it was starting to make sense. Bill knew how to work an electrofishing contraption. He knew all about fishing and boating. He was angry with Alice for foiling his plot against Raquel, or at least that was what he thought.

"You be careful," my aunt warned.

"I will. Love you." I hung up.

"Let me call Ernie," Otter said, whipping out his phone and dialing. He told him in a few words that we thought Bill might have Raquel at the old Boyle place, then ended the call. "He's going to call Detective Keene, and they'll get out here as soon as they can. But even if they dispatch a patrol car before she and Ernie arrive, it might be a while."

"It might be forever," I said. "We can't wait."

We helped Enzo into the boat, and Neil figured out how to get it started. The motor whirred, quieter than the airboat. I waved at Otter, and we started the cruise over to the house at a low idle, the wisps of fog seeming to part before us. It wouldn't take long. And then what?

Neil's phone buzzed, and he pulled it out of his pocket as he steered. "Yes? Yes, Detective. ... No, we haven't seen anyone yet." There was a long pause. "Even after you found it in the river?" Another long pause. "We'll wait for you." Then he hung up.

"'We'll wait for you'? What if Bill has Raquel at gunpoint or something?" I asked.

"We're not equipped to handle that," Neil said.

"But Pepper's right," Mr. Mixy interrupted. "We can't do nothing."

Oh, great. The beardmeister was on my side.

"The detective was driving as she talked to me," Neil said. "She'll be here before you know it. She said they found

Alice's DNA on the kayak paddle, along with alligator blood."

"That's weird." Someone hit an alligator and Alice, too? "I thought the paddle was in the water a long time?"

"When it's cool like it is now, she said, DNA can survive a week or two. Said Ernie had a hunch and they sent the blood to the University of Florida to get a rush analysis, since no blood was found on Diana. Though they did find evidence of a blow to the head."

"That day we saw Phantom, he had a fresh wound," I recalled.

"That's right," Neil said. Then he made a gesture to indicate we should be quiet as the boat purred up to the shore at the old Boyle place.

I spotted a shape near the road, probably Enzo's truck, barely visible in the darkness and thickening fog. Closer to the house was another car that looked familiar.

Mud had overtaken the remains of a concrete boat ramp. Which I found out when I got out, slipped, fell and ended up covered in it. My fetching black dress was now a sheath of muck. I bit down the curse I badly wanted to say, mostly in the interest of being quiet.

Neil somehow stepped out without mishap, getting only slightly damp shoes. He pulled the boat up higher and led Enzo out and over to a fallen tree trunk where he could sit down. Mr. Mixy sat next to Enzo, who was shivering.

"Now we wait for the ambulance," Neil whispered.

"What if Bill hears the siren?" I replied. "He might do something desperate. He might think it's the cops."

"They're coming, too," Neil said.

"We can't wait, Neil. We can't. I need to at least look and see what's happening. Maybe we can help."

Mr. Mixy hopped up. "She's right. And I need to help Pepper!"

Then he stomped off toward the house.

Enzo groaned and slumped over. "Damn it," Neil said, rushing to set him upright on the log. The Frenchman appeared to be unconscious. Neil sat next to him to support him. "Oh, go on and stop Mixy before he makes things worse. And don't get involved. Please, Pepper."

I blew him a kiss. "No more than necessary."

I dashed off after Mr. Mixy, hating the cold, slimy feel of my ruined velvet dress clinging to my legs. Not to mention the prick and buzz of mosquitoes. This place was a freaking blood-sucker farm.

Where was he? As I got closer, I spotted the leopard-print suit against the white clapboard siding of the old two-story house, near the back. Even amid the fog and overgrown vegetation, his form was distinct. So much for camouflage.

Mr. Mixy crouched under a dirty window aglow with a soft yellow light. One of the panes of glass was broken, and as I scurried up to him, staying low, the sound of a voice floated out to me. I took a chance, put my finger over my lips so Mr. Mixy would stay quiet, and stood tall enough to peek through the smudged glass.

Raquel was tied to a wooden chair in what looked like a dining room. The old dining room table and chairs were still there. A dusty sideboard sat against the wall. But the floral wallpaper was stained and peeling, and bare wires stuck out of the ceiling where a fixture once was. Raquel's sparkling white gown picked up the light from an old-fashioned oil lantern on the table.

Seated at the other end of the table was Bill Boyle, still in his suit, sans tie. In front of him on the table lay a shotgun.

Yikes. I ducked back down and listened.

"I don't know how it happened. How you turned out so little like my sister," Bill said. "She was such a good person. She never would have destroyed the land like you have."

"Look at yourself," came Raquel's voice. "You're a developer, too. And your sister, my mother? She married a mobster, Uncle Bill. A mobster masquerading as a real estate guy. And she knew exactly what she was doing. You know why she kept that beach pristine? Back in the eighties, they used it for drug drops. I remember the boats coming in, the planes sweeping over the house at night."

"You're lying."

"I was a little girl. I didn't know until later that's what they were doing. But she knew."

"Even if it's true, you didn't have to sell off that lot before the body was cold."

"Oh, Uncle Bill." Raquel's voice was dry, but I could hear the stress in it. "I had nothing. Don't you understand? My father's business associates abandoned my mother to her fate. Whatever she had left went to medical bills. And you and my other uncles weren't around much, as I recall."

"And now you're going to destroy the marsh out here," Bill went on, as if he hadn't heard her at all. He sounded drunk still. Drunk and angry.

"Why don't we talk," Raquel purred as I tried to think. "Tying me to a chair? Really? We're family. Let's work it out. We'll sit right here at the table."

"As if that ever worked before. We're done talking. If I kill you, who will have the heart to go through with Boyle Lakes?"

There was silence for a moment, and I risked another look. Raquel stared Bill down, but he hadn't moved, and I didn't think either of them could see me.

Then she spoke. "Did you think I didn't know what you were doing? You can delay me, but did you think that Englishwoman would be there forever, doing God knows what with her little projects?"

"I thought she would find something that would stop you. She said she thought she saw an endangered bird. Plus she was researching plants. But she was looking for treasure just like the rest of the idiots who came out here."

"My goodness. You killed her, didn't you?"

Bill shuffled in his chair, and his voice sounded rough. "She betrayed me. And I figured the cops would blame you, who had the best motive of all."

"I should have guessed. That bit with the electrofishing equipment."

Bill laughed an ugly laugh. "Once I decided to do it, I told her it was something she could use to fend off the gator. I was going to show her how to use it. She didn't know any better. I was able to get right up to her, set it next to her in the water before I turned it on. But I wanted to make sure she wouldn't fight me, so I hit her with my kayak paddle first. The electrical shock finished her off. Unfortunately, Phantom took an interest in me, and I had to beat him back. Lost my paddle in the process."

"Your moral high ground isn't any higher than the swamp out there," Raquel said, glancing toward the window. She froze for an instant, then looked back at Bill.

She saw me!

"Listen to who's talking." Bill stood, the gun in his hand. "I think we need to go for a walk."

"Crap," I said under my breath.

I looked at Stephan, whose hazel eyes were wide as Frisbees. "I'm going to try to sneak up on him from inside the house. If you see them come out, don't do anything unless you feel like you have to."

"No problem." His voice was less than reassuring, but Mr. Mixy doing nothing was infinitely better than him doing anything else.

I scuttled around to the front porch and crept up the steps. The door was ajar, only the faintest light glimmering from inside, since the dining room was at the back of the house.

As soon as I stepped inside the foyer, I spotted a bright green kayak paddle leaning up against the wall.

After he killed Alice and scuffled with Phantom, Bill must have taken one of Alice's paddles to make his escape back here. That's why there'd been only one in the box.

I looked at it for a second, then grabbed it. It was lightweight, as the best paddles are. But I could get a lot of momentum if I had to swing it at him.

I carried it pointed forward and scurried as quickly as I dared down the hall, which went straight ahead off the foyer, past the staircase. There were mostly empty rooms on either side of the corridor, a typical layout of a traditional old house. It was probably really nice once, but now it reeked of decay, and the cobwebs everywhere weren't exactly comforting.

The light made it obvious which room they were in. "Stay still," I heard Bill say. "And don't try to run. I don't have to have very good aim with a shotgun."

"You're not giving me much incentive to cooperate, Uncle Bill." Raquel had softened her voice, but I didn't think anything would get through Bill's insanity at this point. I poked my head in. His back was to me, and he worked to untie just enough of Raquel's bonds so he could move her. The gun was on the table next to him.

She saw me, then looked away so he wouldn't notice.

I took a step inside. And the long paddle hit the doorframe as I did.

I froze. Raquel froze. Bill turned around.

He calmly stopped messing with Raquel's ropes and picked up the shotgun. "I should have killed you the other night. But I thought scaring you would be enough. I won't make that mistake again."

Chapter Thirty

He lifted the gun, and I dropped the kayak paddle and ran.

I ducked as the gun blast splintered the wooden doorframe behind me and boomed through the house like an explosion.

So much for Bill taking it easy on the old family homestead. I did a quick sensory check as I ran. It was a Christmas, er, New Year's miracle. He'd missed me!

I kept running right out the front door and down the front steps. He pounded down the hallway behind me. At least he wasn't about to kill Raquel. But did I really want to be her substitute?

I peeled off around the house, the side Mr. Mixy wasn't on, and away from where I knew Neil waited with Enzo. Now I heard sirens in the distance. Would they be quick enough?

"Where are you, Pepper?" Bill called as I dashed into the undergrowth that surrounded the house and tried not to be loud. The choir of insects and frogs might not be enough to conceal my clumsy efforts to hide, but the sirens were getting closer, too. And the fog was on my side. Except I couldn't see a damn thing.

"Let's make this easy," he called. "You can't go anywhere. What are you gonna do, swim with the gators?"

Oh, hell no. But I wasn't going to jump in front of his shotgun, either.

I crouched and tried to ease deeper into the brush. It was really dark out here, though the fog almost seemed to glow. Did it reflect the starlight? As my eyes adjusted, I started to make out grass and palm trees. Certainly he could see the same, and I was a lot thicker than grass and palm trees. And now I was up against the water. That meant I had fewer avenues of escape.

I almost fell over something low and curvy, but I caught myself and hoped it wasn't alive.

It didn't move. I let out a breath of relief. I realized it was a kayak, hidden in the scrub. Probably the one Bill used to access the shack. I kept low and eased around it, trying not to give myself away.

Bill didn't have to be careful. He stomped through the grasses, making systematic passes, getting closer. He knew this land better than anybody. Certainly better than me.

I froze as he made another pass, even closer to me. Then I backed up at a crouch. Almost instantly, I tripped over something and fell backward onto my butt. I held my breath, trying not to slap away the mosquitoes that swarmed me. Had I made a sound?

Bill's low laugh suggested I had. "Oh, Pepper. You know I'm gonna get you, right? Man, I haven't gone hunting in a long time. I've kinda missed it."

I felt around for whatever I'd tripped on. A log? At least it wasn't a critter. The short log was just narrow enough for me to pick it up. I eased off my behind and into a crouching position, the log in my hand. I'd never get close enough to hit him. But maybe I could distract him.

With as much force as I could manage, I wound up from

my crouch and hurled the log toward the water and away from me.

Splash!

I could make out Bill's diffuse silhouette as he wheeled with a cry and let out a blast toward the sound. He took a step toward where he'd fired.

And then another shape rose up out of the darkness behind him, wielding something long, swinging it in Bill's direction, hitting him square on the head.

This time Bill went down like a felled tree.

"Pepper?" It was Neil!

I awkwardly got to my feet. "Did you get him?"

There was a pause and some rustling. "I have his gun now. He's hurt. Help me."

I scrambled over and took the paddle, and Neil held the gun on Bill, who groaned and stilled.

The sky had changed. It throbbed now, flashing blue and red, an eerie light show in the fog, accompanying howling sirens that split the night as an ambulance and two police cars pulled up in front of the house.

"You OK?" Neil visibly relaxed when he saw I was intact.

"Well enough. Where's Raquel?"

"Mr. Mixy got her out of the house. They're with Enzo."

"Neil?" a female voice called. "Pepper?"

We turned to see Detective Cleo Keene walking toward us out of the murk, a bright flashlight in her hand, blinding me. "Raquel Tocks said her uncle tried to kill her and killed Alice, too."

"It looks that way," I said. "I heard him confess."

We all turned to look down at Bill.

Only Bill wasn't there. Detective Keene scanned the scrub

with her flashlight beam and lit him up several feet away, crawling toward the water.

She pulled her own gun and aimed it. "Back away," she barked at us. "Bill Boyle, stop this instant. You're under arrest for the murder of Alice Dalworth."

But Bill Boyle kept crawling, almost to the water, oblivious.

And then the water changed.

A massive, reptilian shape emerged from the misty marsh, accompanied by a deep, reverberating growl. The gator's open mouth gleamed with dripping teeth. His scarred face glistened and his eyes glowed bright in the beam of the flashlight as he rose. I sucked in a breath.

With dizzying speed, Phantom leaped forward and clamped onto Bill's arm. Bill cried out as Phantom dragged him into the water with seemingly no effort at all. And then there was thrashing and splashing and ... nothing.

I gaped in shock. Neil shook his head in disbelief.

Detective Keene just stared. "I've never seen that happen before."

Neither Neil nor I mentioned that she hadn't fired her gun, hadn't tried to stop the gator. And frankly, I was glad. Bill Boyle was not a good man. Maybe he had been once, but his principles had been mangled by a lust for revenge. And Phantom was due for a little revenge of his own.

Another shape emerged from the darkness behind us, making me jump: Ernie Alder, not in his uniform but in a nice dress shirt. "That wasn't pretty."

The detective holstered her weapon. "You wanna handle that?"

"We'll search tomorrow," the wildlife officer said. "Doesn't seem much point now, does it?"

"Agreed." Detective Keene eyeballed Neil and me.

"Makes sense to me," Neil said.

"Absolutely," I agreed.

"All right. They're loading up the Frenchman and checking out Raquel," the detective said. "Are you OK? Besides your dress, I mean." The corner of her mouth twitched. I had a feeling Cleo Keene was enjoying this moment a little too much.

"I'm fine," I said. "But we could use a ride."

She just looked at me, and Ernie smiled.

"I'll get an Uber," Neil said after a pause.

"Out here? On New Year's Eve?" The detective laughed, took the shotgun and kayak paddle and marched away with Ernie into the fog, toward all the flashing lights. "Come over here so we can get your statement," she called over her shoulder.

"Maybe Mark can pick us up," I said after she walked off. "Oh—but we took your car. And he doesn't have a key."

"You're brilliant," he said, making a call. "Mark? Where are you guys? What? I can't hear you. I'll text."

He ended the call and tapped out a text while telling me, "I think they're on the airboat. I'm telling him where to find my spare key."

"You have a spare key?"

"It's in a magnetic box up under the car. I don't usually use it when I'm traveling, but I almost always carry it locally."

Neil. Always prepared. I walked over to him, wrapped my arms around his neck and gave him a big kiss. And got mud all over him.

He looked down at himself, then up at me. "That's the dirtiest kiss I've ever had." And he kissed me back.

And that, to my delight, was the dirtiest kiss *I'd* ever had.

Chapter Thirty-One

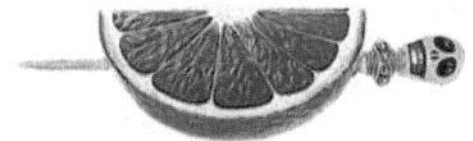

I stumbled out to the back patio late the next morning, coffee in hand, to find Aunt Celestine and Diana deep in conversation over a pot of herbal tea at the table.

Aunt Celestine, who had Astra on her lap, looked me over. "At least you aren't as bedraggled as you were last night."

"Gee, thanks." I looked down at myself. Clean, at least. Jeans. A Nola T-shirt. And surprisingly few mosquito bites, given my experience.

I'd been so tired, I barely remembered Neil dropping off me and Diana, and Mark and Royce and Victoria leaving. I'd given Aunt Celestine a quick summary of events while marveling at the wreckage Astra and Victoria had created in her living room. Her pillows were strewn everywhere, dog toys were scattered like tornado debris, and her favorite straw gardening hat, which Astra had never touched before, had been shredded into tiny pieces that were scattered like snow all over the floor.

After a hot shower, I'd fallen into bed and a fathomless sleep.

"It's a good thing you're awake, because Mark is having us over this afternoon for a party," Diana said, her eyes twinkling.

"A party?" I flopped into a chair at the table. "Where does he get the energy?"

"That's Mark for you." Diana sipped her tea.

Oh, yeah. Mark. And Diana.

"So," I asked her, "how was your date? Before we had to go to the swamp, I mean."

Her cheeks pinked. "I don't know that I'd call it a date."

"Oh, I would," Aunt Celestine said, and she and I laughed.

Diana, back in khakis and a nice white blouse, sighed. "He's so not my type."

I snorted. "Strong? Smart? Rich? Handsome? Totally lickable?"

Now Celestine and Diana burst into laughter.

"No," Diana said. "I mean, yes, he's all those things, but he can be so silly."

Then she grinned.

I just nodded and grinned back. All those two needed was a little time.

"What happened to the plants?" I asked her.

"I've secured them and will transfer them to Alice's lab space at the university. My friend here will oversee them and help me get her work into the right hands. Though I'm leaving a couple of seedlings with Celestine. I trust her green thumb."

I raised my eyebrows at my aunt, who gave me a knowing smile. "Happy birthday, by the way," she said.

Oh, yeah! It *was* my birthday. "Thanks. I'd kind of forgotten. And I really feel like I need to make this year count before I turn into a pumpkin."

"Ha!" Aunt Celestine said. "Twenty-nine was great, but in some ways, it only gets better."

"Agreed." Diana's eyes twinkled. Oh, yeah, her life was getting better all the time.

A couple of hours later, we arrived with Astra at Mark's

condo building by the ocean in my Angry Orange. I'd changed into a better shirt, black with a sexy V-neck.

Mark's holiday flat, as he called it, was in posh south Bohemia Beach, not that far from Neil's grandfather's house. Mark's home-away-from-home was on the tenth floor—the top. Of course. Modern and lined with windows that offered dazzling views of the blue ocean and beautiful beach, as did its wide balcony, this place was an absolute dream. Maybe it wasn't on the scale of his London mansion, but it worked for me.

The condo was already filled with the sounds of chatter and jazz when we arrived. We walked right in, and I set down Astra. Victoria skidded around a corner and ran up to her, barking, and then they sniffed each other and ran off together, tongues flapping. Apparently destroying my aunt's hat had been a bonding experience.

I followed my nose to the spread of food: Asian treats and lots of sushi. I grabbed a yellowtail handroll and gobbled it down, followed by a handful of gyoza. I loved those little pork dumplings. I hadn't really had breakfast, and this stuff was excellent.

When I came up for air, I said hello to Cray and Reginald Rockaway, then headed for the bar between the open living and dining areas. Barclay was doing the honors behind the curved bar, as modern as the rest of the place, constructed of blond wood with a thick glass top. Melody and Luke hung out on one side. Neil, Royce, Aunt Celestine, Mark and Diana stood on the other.

I walked up to Neil and kissed him on the cheek.

"Happy New Year, Pepper," he said.

"You too." I smiled.

"What'll you have?" Barclay asked me.

"I think I'm over champagne right now. Can you do a G&T?"

"Excellent choice, with my gin, of course," Mark said. "How are you feeling today?"

"Me? I'm fine. The question is, how is Enzo feeling?"

"I actually spoke with him," Diana said. "He's feeling much better. Vomiting helped."

"Lovely," Mark quipped.

"And he had some news. He's talked to Raquel, who's not inclined to go ahead with Boyle Lakes right now. Apparently she thinks the deaths associated with the place would be poison to house buyers. He's asked her about buying the entire property so that he might allow someone to continue Alice's research, and she was amenable."

"Of course, it's a business decision for her," I noted. "But that's really cool of him. And who knows, maybe he'll get what he wants."

"Perhaps," she said. "And the plant's ecosystem won't be destroyed."

"Are you going to be the one to continue her research?" Royce asked her.

"Oh, no. I have a job." She glanced at Mark, then back at Royce. "But I'm in touch with colleagues who I'm sure will be interested in her discoveries."

"I'm almost afraid to ask where Mr. Mixy is." Chuckles greeted my comment as Barclay handed me my drink.

"Then you haven't read the *Bohemia Bugle?*" Luke pulled out his phone, tapped the screen and handed it to me. "It's all online."

"'Cocktail TV Show Host Hailed for Saving Bohemia Benefactor,'" I read aloud. "Oh, you have got to be kidding me. The hero and the benefactor. Perfect."

Mark added, "I saw him being interviewed this morning on some TV news show. He talked about his near miss with Phantom and how it made him want to help people."

I rolled my eyes. "He's such a saint."

"And TV shows like any story that ends with the bad guy being eaten by an alligator," Barclay said.

"Is that official?" I asked him.

"They're reporting that Bill's body was found," Neil said. "Though identification was, uh, tricky."

I took a fortifying sip of my cocktail. "Let's not talk about this anymore. It's too depressing."

There was a pause where Barclay and Melody and Neil exchanged glances.

"Well, I have some happy news," Melody said. "Barclay and I do."

Luke froze, looking pale. But Neil was smiling. What was going on?

"We're opening a cocktail bar together in Bohemia Beach," Barclay said. "Neil and Alex Alwend are our investors, and we've both quit our other jobs except for maybe a fill-in shift now and then until we get up and running."

"At last, we're going to have decent craft cocktails beachside." Melody looked ecstatic. Finally, she would get out of that mediocre hotel bar.

"But—why didn't you tell us?" Luke asked. "Tell me?"

Or me, I wondered.

Neil raised a hand. "That's on me. I wanted to be sure we had our ducks in a row, and these guys didn't want to count their cocktails before they were hatched. They came up with the idea themselves and brought it to me for advice. I liked their plan so much, I helped them put together the financials."

"Wow." Luke still seemed stunned, like he felt left out. Plus his crush on Melody had to have him questioning this plan. In fact, I kind of wondered how Gina felt about this.

But Melody, still oblivious to Luke's yen, spoke in her usual unfiltered manner. "We're perfect business partners. We have zero sexual interest in each other. It's all about the cocktails."

Luke seemed relieved and smiled.

I laughed along with everyone else. "Congratulations. I feel a little out of the loop, but I understand why you didn't tell me."

"We kind of wanted to present it as a *fait accompli*," Barclay said. "But we still have a ton of work to do."

"A *ton*," Melody agreed.

A scary thought struck me. "Will you still work with the Bohemia Bartenders?"

"Of course," they said in tandem.

Relieved and happy, I lifted my drink in tribute. "Then we have a lot to celebrate."

"You're right," Aunt Celestine said. "After all, *it's your birthday!*" She said this extra loud, and a moment later, Gina entered the room carrying a round, elaborately iced chocolate cake with a sparkler sizzling on top. Jorge, Reginald, Cray and Millie followed her, and everyone launched into a raucous rendering of "Happy Birthday."

"Aw, you guys. Thanks." I got a little misty-eyed at their kindness as I watched the sparkler burn out. Sparklers I could handle.

As Gina cut the cake, Aunt Celestine gave me a funny card with a bookstore gift certificate. "Oh, and something came in the mail for you yesterday. I figured it was another present."

She produced a small box from behind the bar, and I froze.

Neil moved closer to me and put an arm around my shoulders. "That came in the mail?"

"Yes." Aunt Celestine's brow furrowed. "What is it?"

I set down my drink and took the box. "I didn't want to tell you—come over here," I said as folks lined up to get cake. But Mark and Diana and Royce had seen the box, too, and they followed me and Neil and my aunt over to the living area, where we sat around a glass coffee table. Neil, next to me on the couch, gave off an unsettled vibe that wasn't like him at all.

"What is it?" my aunt demanded again.

I looked at the label, just like the other one. "I'll have to open it to be sure, but it might be another threatening note from Beau."

"*Another* one?" she asked.

I explained about the egg and its vague threats, and finally, at everyone's encouragement, I carefully opened the box.

It contained another plastic egg, yellow this time, wrapped in the same purple tissue paper.

"Anything inside?" Royce asked, looking at least as worried as my aunt.

I shook it gently, then popped it open. Nestled inside was another piece of paper, folded up tight. I unfolded it slowly, worried about some kind of booby trap, but it appeared to be another poem.

I read it aloud.

Did you like my little song,
the Ballad of Beau Reed?
If you think I'll do no wrong,
consider this a seed.
Your fear will grow as you realize
I have them in my sights.
In spite of you, I'll win my prize
as Easter turns to night.

I looked at my aunt to get her reaction first. I thought she'd be scared or at least annoyed with me. But she huffed and said, "That little weasel. How dare he?"

A corner of my mouth lifted. "I think he's daring me to come stop him, whatever he's aiming to do."

"He's threatening my sister?" my aunt asked. "That's what you said the first poem suggested, right?"

"I think so," I said. "Now this one says 'them,' so I expect he's targeting both my parents."

"Or this is a trap." Neil's eyes found mine. "I said it before, and I'll say it again: His only goal might be to get to you, Pepper. We should go to the police."

"Do you really think the New Orleans police are going to do anything about bad poetry in an Easter egg?" I shook my head. "OK, if you want, I'll tell them or the FBI or whoever's looking for Beau. But I think I'm going to have to deal with this myself."

"I'll go with you," Royce said. "I need to go to New Orleans anyway and talk to your mother. Well, my mother—and my parents."

"Easter? Is that what he's referring to?" Mark cut in. "I'd like to see New Orleans on Easter."

"Might be fun," Diana agreed, then realized what she'd said and bit her lip as Mark turned to her with a huge smile. "I mean, not fun if you're dealing with that con artist."

"Who tried to kill you," Neil reminded me.

"I know! I know. But I have to do something about him. I can't have him hunting me my entire life." Just the thought of Beau gave me the creeps, but his gall also infuriated me.

"I'm going, too," my aunt said.

I looked at Neil with his worried expression, and after a moment of silence, Mark declared, "Well, I'm getting cake.

Who wants cake?" And everyone but Neil followed his cue and left us there on the couch.

Neil turned to me. "Is this how you want to cash in your Christmas present? A trip to New Orleans?"

I nodded. "Yes, please."

"I have a birthday present for you, too."

"You do? What is it?"

"A new suitcase for your trip to New Orleans. Or wherever, but now I guess it's New Orleans."

A slow smile took over my face. "You make me happy."

"That's what I want to do. I just don't want to get you killed."

I reached up and held his face in my hands and gave him a solid kiss. "You won't. But I can't let him run amok and hurt my parents, even if they're kind of clueless."

He grabbed my hands in his. "All right. You win. But I'll be there. Your friends, it looks like, will be there. Maybe we can even get the other Bartenders there."

"It'll be fun."

He sighed. "I hope so. I'll book the room."

The room? *One* room!

"Happy birthday to me!" I said and kissed him again. "You're better than cake."

Neil finally smiled. "But you want some cake, don't you?"

"Well, yeah, of course. Who do you think I am?"

WHAT'S NEXT

Don't miss *Why Oh Rye?* —Book 7 in the Bohemia Bartenders Mysteries—as Pepper and friends return to New Orleans for a Big Easy adventure filled with perils, parades and Sazeracs!

Want to get notified when the next book comes out? Subscribe to my fun, occasional newsletter—and get a free Bohemia Bartenders story—or follow me on BookBub or Goodreads.

I also have a Facebook group where we hang out and chat about life and books — please join us in Lucy's Lounge (answer the questions to get in). And you can always find me at LucyLakestone.com.

Read on for a look behind the scenes in the acknowledgments and a cocktail recipe!

Acknowledgments

I happen to live near the beautiful wetlands that inspired the settings in this book, and they go by many names if you ask a scientist, not just swamp or marsh. The St. Johns River connects these lakes and waterways as it wends north more than three hundred miles until it hits Jacksonville and the Atlantic Ocean on Florida's northeast coast.

I've taken a few liberties inspired by my own airboat expeditions out of fish camps and other spots on the river—as a tourist and as a reporter. Thanks to Captain Chance at Camp Holly for giving me and my friends an opportunity to experience the river at night, with all of its magic and glowing eyes. And thanks to Darren and Katrina for joining us on our little adventure. Hope it was worth all the bugs smacking us in the face.

The 1715 Spanish treasure fleet story is real. The Casanova story, I just made up, so don't go digging up any islands in the St. Johns. That said, there are lots of stories of lost treasure in Florida if you look.

I read a lot of books before I wrote this one to get a sense of the history of champagne; the most interesting was *Bursting Bubbles: A Secret History of Champagne and the Rise of the Great Growers* by Robert Walters. There's a lot more to the bubbly than the handful of labels you see in the grocery store on New

Year's Eve. While we colloquially use "champagne" to describe any sparkling wine, the denizens of the Champagne region of France, whose growers survived one war after another, will tell you that only their wines are entitled to the name.

I was also fascinated by books on plants and the river life as I researched this story. *Florida's Wetlands* by Ellie Whitney, D. Bruce Means and Anne Rudloe is full of facts and illustrations that show just how diverse—and threatened—this watery world is.

If you want to know more about monkey-fishing and other river shenanigans, I highly recommend Bob H. Lee's entertaining *Backcountry Lawman: True Stories From a Florida Game Warden.*

And just a word about alligators: They usually won't bother you unless you bother them. But if they are habituated to people and food, or see an easy target (like a small dog walking by a pond), bad things can happen. I find them interesting, and I treat them with respect. And living in Florida, I assume *any* body of water, right down to a drainage ditch, has an alligator in it.

As always, the pandemic does not play a role in this series, even though, were you to be fussy about math and moon phases and major events in Pepper's life, you might see the timeline suggests the bartenders are living in an alternate history. But if I have to live in an alternate world, I'd like it to be this one, please.

Thanks to the cool cats in Lucy's Lounge (our Facebook group) for playing "name the assistant" with their inspirations for Lissa's humiliations at the hands of Raquel—Cecelia Morgan, Christina Donalson, Kathryn Pease, Micki Kremenak Jordan, Karen Temme and Holly Martin. Cecelia's funny idea about the Louboutins earned her the prize of naming the long-suffering Lissa in this book. I also loved Christina's notion about Raquel's salads. I so appreciate y'all's good humor and encouragement. Cheers.

I also appreciate my chiropractor Joshua Flinn for not only helping me stay in the writing chair but for an inspiring anecdote and answering my silly questions.

I want to give a shout-out to my neighbor Dianne, whose dog Buddy is the acknowledged mayor of our 'hood. She tells him "Good dogs get treats" whenever she's trying to convince him to do something, and Pepper has adopted her strategy.

I'm hugely grateful to Maria Geraci for her brilliant story insights, encouragement and friendship. Other writers in our local group also offer invaluable support and kindness, as do the writers in The Office online and my dear friends in the Harbaugh Literary Salon. Thank you.

Massive thanks to my friend and editor Holly Martin for taking on this book and shooting me messages whenever she runs across something that makes her laugh. In a good way. You rock.

Finally, thank you to George for everything. He's been talked into many a research trip, but as long as there's a bar involved, he doesn't seem to mind.

 Cocktail Recipe

BERRY FESTIVE

Let's face it: Champagne is easy to drink on its own and pleasant when accompanied by even one other ingredient, whether it be juice or a liqueur. A full-blown cocktail almost seems like gilding the lily, but mixologists like to have fun. In this case, delicious fun.

This original cocktail owes a nod to the French 75 and the Kir Imperial, as it takes inspiration from both. It's simple, refreshing, festive and a little sneaky in that it does not shy away from alcohol.

I chose not Champagne with a capital *C* but a nice prosecco we happened to have on hand; any good sparkling wine and gin will do. I used Hendrick's floral Flora Adora gin in addition to the Chambord, a black raspberry liqueur from France that gives the Berry Festive a hint of pleasurable depth. Fresh lemon juice is a must.

Pour the following into a cocktail shaker with ice:

1 ounce gin
3/4 ounce Chambord
1/2 ounce fresh squeezed lemon juice

Shake well with ice and strain into a champagne flute. Top with chilled champagne. With a cocktail spoon, gently draw up the cocktail from the bottom if you prefer it more thoroughly mixed, though the subtle layering is quite pretty.

Add three fresh raspberries for garnish. If you want a more red-and-green look for the holidays, you could also add a sprig of mint.

The **BOHEMIA BEACH** Series

Award-winning hot contemporary romance

In a beautiful small city on Florida's east coast, artists meet, create, laugh and love. Where restless hearts are fueled by secrets and imagination, romance is impossible to resist. Welcome to the seductive tropical escape that's home to drama, humor and lots of heat – Bohemia Beach.

BOHEMIA BEACH

BOHEMIA LIGHT

BOHEMIA BLUES

BOHEMIA HEAT

BOHEMIA NIGHTS

BACK TO BOHEMIA - *story free to subscribers*

BOHEMIA BELLS

BOHEMIA CHILLS

Bohemia Beach Series Boxed Sets:

Books 1-3 | Books 4-7

The **STORM SEEKERS** Series

Writing as Chris Kridler

FUNNEL VISION

TORNADO PINBALL

ZAP BANG

Storm Seekers Series Boxed Set: Books 1-3

About the Author

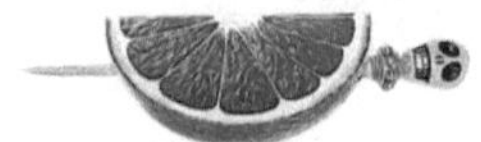

Lucy Lakestone is an award-winning author who lives on Florida's east central coast, among the towns that serve as an inspiration for the hot romances of her Bohemia Beach Series and the jumping-off point for the Bohemia Bartenders Mysteries. She's been a journalist, photographer, editor and video producer but prefers living in her imagination, where the moon is full and the cocktails are divine.

She also writes storm-chasing adventures as Chris Kridler, and in her spare time, she chases tornadoes.

Learn more at LucyLakestone.com

facebook.com/lucylakestone

instagram.com/mslucylakestone

amazon.com/Lucy-Lakestone

bookbub.com/authors/lucy-lakestone

goodreads.com/lucylakestone

pinterest.com/lucylakestone

youtube.com/@lucylakestone